RESCUING AIR

International Bestselling Author
ELIZABETH KNIGHT

Knight, Elizabeth
Rescuing Air

Editing: Ms. K Editing & Leavens Editing
Cover artist: Ryn Katryn Book Covers
Formatting: Creative Wonder Publishing

Here is to the beginning that is now coming to an end—
This series has changed my life forever.

CHAPTER 1
LAILAH

"Say that again," Jay demanded.

"Lilith sent demons to get your mother to try and keep you from bonding with me. She sent her to wherever they had their base set up in a remote location. This camp is a military base for them to train all the new demons that are using human hosts, those who've taken the serum. Lilith said it was in a part of the world that there weren't many people around because the demons that the Dark Lord rules over are too vicious and kill people," I shared, trying to remember everything that crazy-ass bitch had said.

Jay's face turned to stone as he escorted me into the house, where the others, still covered in blood and dirt, were sprawled out on the couch. My mother was in a tizzy, rushing to the kitchen, mumbling the need to grab supplies. Cami was on the phone, with whom I have no idea, but my guess was an Elementi of some sort. We needed to get them to a hospital was what we needed to do, with Micah and his broken leg. Not to mention having someone check on Hudson and his wound that had an extremely angry red welt over it from where Micah said he cauterized it.

Hell, even Jay was battered, with blood all over his face from the cuts and possible scalp wound. None of us were in any shape to deal with what was coming our way, and this battle was reaching the tipping point. What do you do when the people who were supposed to end this war were too beaten up to do the job?

"Alright, guys, the local team is sending over a doctor and a healer. We're lucky they have one in this state," Cami said, hanging up the phone. "What the fuck happened?"

All the guys looked at me, then over at my dad, who was pale and hadn't moved a muscle from the armchair he was sitting in. The TV played in the background. No parent ever wanted to see their kid looking like they were on the losing end of the fight, especially when you didn't know it could be a possibility. I'd told my parents who and what I was, but even if mentally they knew, it didn't really mean they accepted what also came with that knowledge. I made them stay in my home while Lilith was on the loose because of the shield. But now that Lilith was back in Hell, I felt better about them going back out into the world. We would leave when we could to deal with Jay's mom, drawing the attention away from them.

Heading over to my dad, I squatted down beside his chair and grasped his hand. "Dad…"

"What happened to you?" Dad demanded. "You told us it was going to be a fight. I just didn't think… oh, my baby girl." He reached out and cupped my face, his eyes filled with sadness.

I gave him a watery smile as my eyes started to tear up, covering his hand with my own. "I know it looks bad, but we did it. We accomplished what we needed to do for you and everyone else around here to be safe. There is still more to be done, but it's a victory, nonetheless."

"Like I give a damn about that when my little girl is looking like she survived hell. All of you look like you got put through a meat grinder," Dad grumbled, looking at the guys. "How do they expect you to keep fighting when you can hardly keep your eyes open?"

Mom came back into the living room with a first aid kit, dishcloths, and a bowl of soapy water. "You didn't have anything else for me to use, but I figured it would be just as easy to buy new ones."

"It's fine, Mom. Use whatever you like." I sighed, pushing up to find a spot on the end of the couch to sit.

My head still pounded and after using so much power, I was drained, feeling like an empty husk. All I wanted was to take a nap and wake up when this was all over, but that wasn't an option. Cracking open an eye, I watched Jay as he paced the living room, ignoring every-thing around him as he processed what I'd told him. Honestly, I was amazed he was still here and not calling his father for a chopper or something to use in a search for his mother.

Brayden tapped me with his toe, grabbing my attention. "What's up with him?" he whispered.

My answer was to shake my head and flick my gaze over to my mom trying to help clean up Hudson and Micah, who were both trying to tell her they could do it.

"Really, it's fine," Hudson assured my mom as he took the wet dishrag from her. "Micah's the one who can't really move around, but I can manage this on my own."

Micah glared at his friend but wiped it from his face as my mom started to cut off his pant leg. "Whoa!"

"We need to get a look at how bad the damage really is.

Having two boys, I've seen my fair share of broken bones." Mom tutted as she continued her work.

When I looked back at Brayden, he nodded, understanding that it wasn't good news and my parents could only handle so much.

"Quit your bitching, flame boy, the doctor will be here in twenty minutes, then you'll be begging for Bonnie to be the one looking after you," Cami pointed out with a grin.

Once Mom was done with Micah, she moved on to me, knowing I wouldn't argue with her. I knew she needed to do what she could to prove she wasn't a terrible mother by letting me put myself in danger to keep them safe. My mom had a big heart and hated when any of us would hurt ourselves when we were kids. Out of all of us, I might be in the best shape, probably with a concussion, but that was minor and could be dealt with easily enough. Mom wiped my face as silent tears trailed down her cheeks, but she didn't make a sound or say anything other than to get me to move so she could get a better angle on something.

"Were you in a car accident?" she finally whispered. I tensed, unsure of how honest to be with my parents about what happened. "We saw it on the news and the vehicle looked just like yours. Your dad told me not to worry, that it couldn't have been you guys, but now I think it really was—"

"Yeah, Mom, it was us," I told her truthfully. "The people we were after purposely hit us so they could bring us to their base of operations. Thankfully, they didn't want us dead, but they knew we were too dangerous to face head-on, so they had to resort to dirty tricks." Not completely true, but it was the best I could come up with for now.

She nodded and kept on cleaning my arm that was

covered in minor cuts from the glass and who knows what else. "It's not over yet, is it?"

"No, it's not, but I have a feeling we're getting close to all this being over," I answered, pulling her into a hug. "I know it's crazy to say, but this is what I was born to do, Mom. I have to do my best even if it puts me in situations where I might get hurt. Think of it like I'm in the military, special forces. I can't really tell you what I'm doing or where I'm going but know that it's to save a whole lot of people."

There was a knock at the door, startling all of us, but Jay was already on the move to find out who it could be. We all heard the door open and then Jay returned with three men I'd never met but who carried bags full of medical supplies. They must be the doctor and the healer. Why we needed both didn't make any sense to me, but I just didn't have the energy to argue.

"Hello, I'm Doctor Tager, this is my assistant Nurse Kaden, and this is Professor Zale. We heard you guys got a little banged up in the last encounter you had," Doctor Tager greeted, setting his bag down. "Thoughts on who I should start with?"

We all pointed to Micah.

"That was easy." Doctor Tager chuckled as he walked over, then kneeled where Micah was laid out on the couch.

"On our way down to the Chicago Elementi headquarters, we got hit by a truck and I broke my leg," Micah explained, pointing to his bare leg. "At least, I think it's broken. I can't use it and the pain is some of the worst I've ever felt."

Doctor Tager started to feel Micah's leg, poking and prodding at things, muttering to himself as he worked. "I want to take an x-ray to confirm, but I don't think you broke your leg. I think it's just a dislocated patella or kneecap. It absolutely hurts like a bitch, but on the bright side, it means you will heal much faster."

"So we have to go to the hospital after all?" I asked.

He turned to look at me with a gentle smile on his face. "No, thankfully the Elementi has funded us well and I have a portable machine to use for situations like this. Give me a moment to set it up and we'll take a look."

Doctor Tager and Nurse Kaden left the room and the front door opened again. Professor Zale headed over to Hudson, who was trying to scrub the blood off his side but was having trouble twisting the right way.

"Would you mind if I took a look at your wound?" Professor Zale asked.

Hudson looked up at him and shrugged. "I don't know how I got sliced in the accident, but when I woke up, I'd lost a lot of blood. We didn't have time or the chance to seek any medical help, so Micah used his fire to seal the wound. I've been keeping track of things and making sure I don't have any internal bleeding, but I feel as though it was just a surface-level injury to the skin and muscle."

Professor Zale raised a brow. "Medical student?"

"Biomedical, looking to go into research but had to take some pre-med classes."

Professor Zale nodded as he slipped on a pair of gloves and urged Hudson to sit back so he could get a clear view of the area. He, too, felt and prodded the area, humming as if making mental notes about whatever he was seeing. "I believe I have some remedies that will help soothe the burn, bring down the inflammation, and prevent infection. Would you mind if I applied it to you?"

"Ah, I see, you're a naturopath, aren't you?" I blurted out, feeling like an idiot for not figuring it out sooner.

I got a smile from the professor at my outburst. "Yes, but I'm also trained in the best remedies to heal wounds made from demons. Seeing that many of those need to be made from natural and holy items, the two practices often coincide. Speaking of, did any of you acquire a wound from a demon or get possessed?"

Mom let out a gasp at the question, clutching tightly to my dad. We'd talked about how dangerous demons were in the world to get them to agree to stay in this house, but I'd purposefully left out that side of things. "Dad, why don't you take Mom to lie down? I know this has been a lot the past few days. I'm sure she didn't sleep well."

Dad nodded jerkily and led my mother away to the room they were using.

"Forgive me, I assumed, being here, that they were aware of the world we live in and you are a part of," Professor Zale apologized.

"No, it's not your fault. I should have expected this, coming back home in the state we're in. My parents had no idea about any of this or who I even was. Truthfully, *I* didn't even know anything about this and got fast tracked when I was discovered to be Synergy," I shared, rubbing my head as the ache just got worse with all the stress of balancing both parts of my life.

"I didn't grow up in this world either, but when I married my wife, who was an Elementi soldier, I was read into the hidden side of our world, if you will. When she died of a wound from a greater demon, I knew I had to do something to keep that from happening. Thankfully, the Elementi are always looking for people to train, so it didn't take me long since I was already a naturopath," Professor Zale said as he worked on attending to Hudson's wound. "This world you protect needs you, but it doesn't make it easier for those of us left behind at home to wait for your return."

My heart broke for him and his history with demons taking the woman he loved from him. I knew firsthand how painful that type of wound was and not to have the help I'd received was unimaginable. Doctor Tager returned, and between him and his assistant, got it all set up rather quickly. Soon, we were all looking at Micah's knee on a laptop, showing us clear as day that his knee was indeed dislocated.

"This is good news. It means you won't be down for the count too long. I'll get this bone back into place, do another x-ray to make sure there is no other damage, then we can get you taped up and in a brace. It will take six weeks to fully heal, but you'll be able to walk with crutches and start putting weight on it again in a week or so. Seeing as you're an Elementi Warrior, I've learned you lot heal faster, so it could be less time than that. Trust your body to tell you what's going to work best."

A weight I didn't know I'd been carrying fell away from me, hearing these words. Micah wasn't broken and he would recover with no problems at all. All I had to do now was make sure he didn't push himself too hard once I told him about Jay's mom. The three men worked quickly and efficiently, checking over the rest of us and giving Brayden a sling to let his arm rest for at least a week. They guessed I did have a concussion but only a mild one since I didn't throw up. Jay also had one and needed a few stitches in his scalp for the head wound. We were all given the okay to take showers as long as we were careful and avoided certain wounds. It was a group effort, but we all managed to get clean and tumbled into bed where we passed out in one big puppy pile on my bed, feeling the need to be close to each other.

CHAPTER 2
JAY

The sun wasn't even up when I left the others sleeping surrounding Lailah. I, too, would have stayed to watch over her, worried that her nightmares might be worse after having Lilith invade her mind, but the need to find out what was going on with my mother drove me to start researching. Pulling my cell out of my sweats, I hit the speed dial for my father. He might not love my mother the way that normal people love their spouse, but he wouldn't want her in the hands of demons either.

Father's sole focus the past year was finding the location of the demon headquarters, once we figured out they were massing together. Every time we found something, it had been abandoned, having gotten there too late. We suspected they might have someone on the inside and now I knew it had to be true with everything we've uncovered so far. Since Lailah came into her power, I haven't been working with my father at all, seeing as we had our own messes to deal with that were more important and ones only we could deal with.

"Jalen," Father answered tersely in Japanese.

"Mother has been taken by the demons and brought to their base," I stated, using the same language, knowing better than to bother with greetings.

The phone was silent for a moment, telling me I'd surprised my father. "Are you sure?"

"The Mother of Demons told us herself. The plan was to use her as leverage to keep me from bonding with Lailah, but it wasn't needed in the end," I explained. "Do you have any confirmation of the demons location yet?"

"No, not for lack of trying. Every time we get close, they slip through our fingers. I can tell you that it's massive, which makes it even more impossible for them to move so fast."

"Lailah shared with me that Lilith said they have to be in a place with no people around them, since the Dark Lords' demons are too violent and kill everything on sight that isn't also a demon," I shared.

Father let out a huff. "That does nothing to help us narrow down an area."

"Father, they're training everyone who has been given the serum, so it would have to be a place they can keep the human host alive," I pointed out. "That cuts out all places that are too cold to easily keep a human alive. They wouldn't want to put that much effort into it. My theory is Africa, Greenland, Iceland, or the Amazon. Lots of space and easy enough to keep away from people."

"You don't think I haven't also thought of those places? It's too much ground for us to cover and with how easily they've been avoiding us, I'm not looking to send my people out blind. Besides, who's to say your mother hasn't been turned into one of them already, since they don't need her any longer? This is not a fight we can rush into. We need to be wise in the next moves we make. If they are gearing up for war like you say, then that changes everything," Father said.

My anger at the fact he was just going to brush Mother off as a lost cause had me clenching my phone so hard it started to creak. "Fine, you do what you think is best and I'll look for Mother with Lailah and my brothers, who actually give a shit about human life."

Before Father could give a response, I hung up the phone and chucked it across the room. I watched it shatter on the stone of the living room fireplace. *Fucking bastard.*

"Jay..."

I stiffened as Lailah ran a hand along my back before wrapping her arms around my waist and resting her head on the middle of my back. "Did I wake you?"

"No, I had a nightmare and knew I wasn't going to be able to fall asleep again. I noticed you were gone, so I figured you were up," she answered softly.

Grabbing her arm, I pulled her around so she was hugging my chest and I could hold her close to me, resting my head on hers. Neither of us spoke, just taking comfort in each other before we needed to face the world and all its problems.

"He doesn't care about her at all," I whispered. "What kind of man could just let his wife be taken by demons and not feel the need to try and save her?"

Lailah lifted her head to look me in the eye with her crystal-blue gaze. "Your father is an idiot who only thinks of power and personal gain. We don't need him to do this, Jay. We have you and you know everything he does, if not more. Use the resources we have and take from him what we need to get your mother back. So what if she's lost to us? Doesn't she deserve to be returned to her family? Of course I pray we'll find her alive and well, but demons don't know what mercy is, and that is a reality we need to face. But I promise you, Jay, we will find her."

Raising a hand, I smoothed back her wild blond curls from her face, then cupped her cheek. This woman, who had crawled so deep into my heart, knew what I'd needed to hear. It wasn't false hope, or the assurance that everything would be alright, not that she told me the truth of the situation. Many would be angry with her for such a callous way of saying things, but I would always take the truth over a lie or wishful thinking. Bending down, I pressed a kiss to her lips, trying to convey my feeling for her through it. She was right. My mother deserved to be brought home no matter if she was alive, possessed, or dead. Japanese people had incredibly strong feelings about laying their loved ones to rest, ensuring they were looked after and could join their ancestors. This I would do for my mother, as her son, since her husband wouldn't.

"Thank you, Beautiful," I murmured, my lips brushing hers as I spoke. "I love you."

"I love you too, and we will always take care of each other, no matter what happens," she answered. The strength behind those words made my heart swell with pride.

It wasn't all that long ago that the woman I held in my arms was timid and quiet. Now, she was facing down the Queen of Hell and the Dark Lord, who were trying to turn Earth into another version of Hell. Scars littered her body and mind from those encounters, but it only made her stand taller. Yeah, the PTSD and nightmares were still something we were working on, but even those were getting better. What I worried most about was the fact we were down a brother, a fellow knight—Parker, the literal heart of our group. He'd been set up by Lilith to make the wrong choice when it came down to helping his ex-girlfriend or Lailah. Parker had chosen wrong and broke the Oath that he'd given Lailah, along with her heart.

Matters of the heart were much harder to heal than the physical. I was mad at him for hurting her, for letting someone come between them—Lilith especially. He needed to atone for his sin. I knew Lailah was going to make him work for it, but I did hope they could make it through this. Not just because we were going to need him to defeat the Dark Lord, but because I knew they loved each other. They were meant for each other. Each one of the five of us Elementi Knights had pieces of our soul missing, and Lailah filled that hole. A feat I never, in all my life, thought would happen.

"How do we get started? Where do we look first?" Lailah asked, resting her head against me once more.

"We put together all the information that we do know, things we've picked up from all the situations we've experienced. I think we know more than we think we do and we'll see it once we put it all together on paper. Micah needs to heal before we can even think of attacking them head on. It kills me to delay, but if we aren't at our best, we will fail when it comes to taking on a demon army."

She nodded and pulled out of my arms. "Sounds like you need a coffee and I definitely am going to need some chai if we're going to do a research project this early in the morning. You get things set up. I'll bring back caffeine and food."

With a nod and a smile pulling at my lips, I watched her

head into the kitchen, tilting my head just a little to get a better look at her ass in those sleep shorts. God, I wanted to turn it bright red and watch it jiggle as I thrust into her from behind. I'd been holding back my darker desires, knowing it might trigger her, but when the time was right, I'd help her understand the beauty of pain and pleasure.

CHAPTER 3
LAILAH

Two cups of caffeine and a sunrise later, the rest of the guys started to drift downstairs, helping Micah manage his crutches. Jay was hunched over his computer and I was looking over some information from their previous missions on a tablet, trying to catch up on what he already knew about the Dark Lord's army. This wasn't going to be a quick mission, but we needed to sift through things with fresh eyes to make sure nothing was missed or any assumptions were made. Now we had the knowledge of what their plan for the future was, using the serum to make conduits and hosts for the demons. Taking in the information with this in mind made some things make more sense, like how they needed to get someone in at the labs and with Brayden's family. The person in the labs could be like Tabitha, the nanny, who was a human that was gifted demonic power, or possibly promised to gain some with the creation of the serum. It had been a long con, taking years in the making. The Dark Lord hadn't planned on me showing up when I did—right at the tipping point of them getting away with it.

Now I was here, bonded to four out of the five Elementi Knights, getting stronger every passing day as we strengthened our connection. Losing Parker was going to be a blow we couldn't afford, but I refused to let the fate of the world dictate who I gave part of my heart and soul to. There was no way we could do this mission without him, but that didn't mean he was forgiven or all was forgotten. I had promised Jay we would get his mom back in whatever way possible and I planned on keeping that promise, no matter how uncomfortable it made me though.

"How long have you guys been up?" Brayden asked, getting Micah settled in one of the armchairs. "And what are you working on so intently?"

I glanced at the time, surprised to find it had been three hours. "Ah, since four—"

"Don't avoid the harder question, Lailah," Micah muttered, scowling at me. "What are you guys working on?"

Jay closed the lid to his laptop and looked at the others for a moment before answering. "The demons took my mother to their camp. It was a backup plan to stop me from bonding with Lailah, but they broke Parker first."

"Why didn't you wake us up to help, damn it? Also, why the fuck would you hold this back from us? We have every right to know, not be left in the dark to think things were fine," Micah shouted, his body rigid with anger. I could feel it beating against my own shields, letting me know just how pissed my fiery lover was.

"Really?" I shot back, my own irritation flaring up. "I don't know, maybe because you needed sleep and time to let your bodies heal. You three had it the worst, and there's nothing more to be done other than let your body do what it needs to. Jay and I couldn't sleep, so instead of twiddling our thumbs, we decided to be useful and get a head start. There is so much I needed to get caught up on that it made sense. We were going to tell you. It's not like we planned to hide it, but you needed sleep."

"Guys, please let's not argue," Hudson cut in, handing out coffee to the others. "Lailah is right. We needed sleep before we could handle this news. Nothing has been done without us, so there's no sense in getting all upset."

Micah glared at him, letting out a scoff as he took a sip of his coffee. "Of course you would be on her side. Can't risk losing the only pussy you've ever gotten."

My brows shot up at this. Micah had been a lot of things, but never this kind of cruel. "That was a low blow, Micah, and you know it. I don't know what crawled up your ass and died, but you better get your shit figured out before I figure it out for you. Apologize."

"You can't order me around like I'm a dog, Lailah," Micah snapped.

This had me out of my seat and up in his face, refusing to let this stand. "What the actual fuck, Micah? Hudson didn't deserve any of that from you. He simply stated his opinion, and you went right for the kill. Don't think I won't lock you in your bedroom and take away your crutches, so you can't leave, while you think about your life choices. I lost one of you already and I'll be damned if I let this group shatter when we need each other the most. So, apologize for being a prick—please."

Micah blinked at me a few times and his anger seemed to dim as a different type of fire started to build. Heat simmered just under the skin as he refused to break from my gaze, letting me know how turned on he was that I'd just verbally spanked him in front of the others. The man might like to be in control, but it was clear he didn't want a submissive partner all the time.

"You're right," he said finally and blinked, ending the standoff. I tried to back away, but he grabbed my arm and pulled me onto his lap, wrapping his arms tightly around me. "Hudson, I'm sorry, man. That was a dick move that you didn't deserve. I'm angry at this whole thing and at being wounded, knowing I would slow the team down if we needed to move fast with this."

Hudson nodded and waved off his apology. "I get it. There are times that I feel useless to this team and it can get under my skin rather easily. Thank you for your apology, but I have a feeling each of us will need to apologize to the others by the end of this battle. Demons feed off turmoil of all kinds and are very good at stirring it up."

Micah kissed my neck and whispered in my ear, "Thank you, Cookie Monster."

"Did you really think I was just going to let you be an ass?" I murmured back.

He shifted me so my ass was pressed right up against his rock-hard dick. "Promise you won't hit me for saying this, but you pissed off and getting in my face like that was hot as hell."

"Seriously, you're going to pull that right after I scolded you?" I spluttered, trying to get up, but he only held me tighter, moaning as I wriggled in his grasp.

"You keep that up and I'm going to come right here in front of all of them," he said against my neck, his lips brushing my skin. This got me to sit still instantly, causing him to chuckle as he pulled me against his chest. "That's better. Now you have to sit here until my boner goes away in case your parents come out."

"You're evil, you know that?" I grumbled.

"Yeah, but you love me anyway," he countered.

The others were trying not to stare at us, but it didn't really bother me. It was inevitable that they would all catch one of us fooling around together at some point and I didn't want them to ever feel like they couldn't be free to act comfortably around me.

"Now that we have that settled," Hudson spoke, bringing us back to the matter at hand. "What can you tell us about the situation?"

"Unfortunately, there isn't a lot for us to go on and we're on our own. My father doesn't see the need to put in the energy to go after Mother, since he believes she's most likely dead or possessed and beyond our help," Jay informed the others.

"I'm sure you'll all agree with me that I told him no matter what, we will bring her home. We owe her that and it's what any of us would do for our families in the same predicament," I added.

They all nodded in agreement with my sentiment.

"Jay and I spent the morning going over everything we learned from all our encounters and the knowledge that we have now to track their past movements. Jay's father has been searching for this camp for months but is always a few steps behind, missing them. Lilith made it clear that the Dark Lord needs to keep them in places away from people stumbling upon them because his demons tend to kill them and draw attention. There is more that I learned as well from spending time with her in my head..." I ventured, unsure how they would all react to this next bit of information.

Brayden leaned forward and grabbed my hand, giving it a squeeze. "We'll handle whatever comes our way, Angel."

"The Dark Lord is a Prince of Hell. Not one of the top

four princes, but one of the sub-princes, Beelzebub. He's just under Lucifer in the ranking of the four main princes, which is why he has so much power and control. This means he's also a child of Lilith, since she gave birth to all the Princes of Hell. Beelzebub also worked in conjunction with his brother Astaroth, making them two out of the three Evil Trinity," I explained, pausing as I watched all of them look at me in fear and shock.

"Holy fucking shit, we are so screwed," Micah swore, dropping his hands from holding me to run through his hair.

I took the moment to stand and face all of them. "This is a gift, guys. If I hadn't shared her mind, there is no way that we would have understood how bad this is and we would've walked into the fight unprepared. Their goal is to make literal hell on earth but *their* hell, not the one ruled by the four princes, but by the Evil Trinity. Lilith will be their queen and be free to roam the world once again, not to be locked away like she is now. When I returned her to Hell, I drew the attention of the four princes, hoping they would notice she wasn't in her cell any longer. I have no idea if it worked, since Lucifer is sure to be involved in this as well. Guys, Hell is waking up to a war among the princes, if we let it happen, I don't know that anyone will survive it."

"That is a heavy realization for this early in the morning." Brayden sighed, rubbing his chin, deep in thought. "How did we miss this? Do you think the Elementi knew and didn't tell us?"

"It does seem odd that they would miss something so massive, doesn't it?" Hudson mused. "We did lose Mr. Creed. Who knows what information they got out of him or if they have others on the inside, steering us in the wrong direction?"

"I think we need to call Beth," Cami announced, causing us all to snap our heads up. There she was, sitting on the railing, looking down at us from the second floor like it wasn't at all odd for her to do so. "There might be double agents in the Elementi, but it won't be my sisters. They drank all the Kool-Aid and believe in their souls they are doing the right thing."

"How long have you been listening, midget?" Micah asked, crossing his arms.

She just grinned at him as she jumped down, landing on the couch in a heap. "Let's see, when did Lala flip you over and beat your ass for being such an ass?"

"Fuck, Cami, why didn't you just come down and join in the conversation instead of being such a creeper?"

"Are you kidding, flame boy? It was far too much fun watching the five of you interact like no one was watching. Shows me just who wears the pants in this relationship, and that person doesn't have a dick, in case you were wondering," Cami stated with a wink at me. "So, am I calling the den mother, or are one of you?"

Hearing her call Beth that made me think of Parker and I knew I was going to need to broach that subject at some point. None of the guys were going to be happy that we needed to include him on this, but I wasn't going to hunt the Evil Triad without the full team of Elementi Warriors.

"I think it's better if you call her," Micah suggested.

Cami just rolled her eyes as she held the phone to her ear. "Chicken shit, that's what you are. Scared of my big sister when she finds out what all went down yesterday."

"Not scared, just a healthy respect for her is all," Micah explained, trying to redeem himself.

When Beth picked up, Cami switched it to speaker phone so we could all hear. "Cami, I thought I would be hearing from you sooner. They never made it to the Chicago HQ and now I'm hearing a doctor along with a healer were needed? What the hell happened?"

"You're on speaker phone with everyone, Sis," Cami warned her. "I'll let them explain what's going on."

The five of us all looked at each other, unsure who should take the lead. They all motioned for me to do the honors. "How much time do you have, Beth? This is going to be a long story."

"You guys are always my priority. I have all the time you need," Beth assured me.

"So, where did we leave things with you? I know Cami has been keeping you in the loop and helping us with things on your end," I asked, not wanting to waste time rehashing something that was already known.

"Phoebe had been taken, you managed to find the power plant they were holed up in, events happened between you and Parker, then you were going to Chicago to figure out where the other base of operations was that the demons were using," Beth rattled off, surprising me how well informed she'd been kept.

"Turns out we didn't need to go looking for the demons. They found us."

Micah scoffed. "She means they rammed into us with a truck to incapacitate us and make getting us back to their hideout easier."

"Oh my God, are you all right?" Beth gasped.

"Beaten and bruised, for the most part. Micah has a dislocated knee that will take some time to heal, but it's better than being broken. That's not the worst of it though..." I said, trailing off as I readied myself to go through all this again.

It took about an hour to cover everything with Beth,

getting her up to speed and answering her questions along the way.

"Makoto, the old fool," Beth growled after hearing his feelings on the matter. "Jay, I'm sorry to hear about your mother. You have the full weight of the Elementi at your disposal. Tell me what you need and I will make sure that it happens. You have my word on that."

"Thanks," Jay answered in true Jay fashion. I was beginning to think I was the only one he talked to in full, complete sentences.

"That goes for the rest of you as well. In my personal opinion, it seems that we're coming to a head in this fight and even though you have the power of the angels, having backup isn't a bad idea either," Beth pointed out. "Keep me informed and I'll work on things this side of the world, tracking down any suspicious movement or money being moved around."

"There's one more thing," I said, cutting in. "Keep this to only the people we know we can trust. It doesn't matter if they're loyal. The more people who know, the more that can get out."

"Wise advice, Lailah. I'll keep it in mind. Until we talk next, stay safe." Beth hung up, leaving us to figure out the next step.

CHAPTER 4

LAILAH

After we hung up with Beth, I didn't really know what our next move should be. This was out of my depth and I thanked God we had Jay, because he was the only man I would trust to lead us through this. I looked over the possible locations that they could be hiding and my gut told me it had to either be Africa or the Amazon. The other two countries just wouldn't hide them as easily as a rainforest would.

I didn't have any time to check in with the guys as my parents joined us, their bags packed. "You guys are leaving already? What about staying for breakfast?"

"Lady Bug, I would love that, but we've been away from the restaurant for three days. Your dad is going to have a fit if we miss another day, and it's shipment day as well," Mom answered, pulling me into a hug. "If you need us, we're just a call away. I get the feeling we'll be more of a hinderance than help with all that you're dealing with."

When she explained it, I knew she was right. There was nothing they could do except feel overwhelmed by what we had to do. They had a hard enough time seeing me and the guys yesterday. I could only imagine how they would react to us charging off halfway across the world to take on an entire army of demons.

"I love you guys," I murmured as I kissed Mom on the cheek and did the same for Dad. "We might need to take off to deal with settling things, but I'll make sure to let you know before we leave."

"Sounds good." Dad nodded, giving me one more hug before they left.

Unable to move, I just stood there, staring at the front door, feeling like it might be the last time I saw them. If we went into battle, there was no telling what could happen. We'd made it out of each of these altercations by the skin of our teeth. This next move was going to be the final battle and with the small amount of information we did have, I knew it was going to be the battle of the ages.

Arms wrapped around me. "Sunshine, talk to me. I can feel your pain, but I don't understand where it's coming from."

I glanced at Hudson over my shoulder, knowing he was right. I needed to voice my thoughts or they would swallow me whole. My therapist kept telling me that talking about my fears kept them from having power and ruling in the dark corners of my brain. Grabbing one of his hands, I pulled out of his hold and led him to the couch to sit next to me, so I was safe between Jay and him. Taking a deep breath, I let it all out, not holding any of my many concerns back.

"This is it. When we hunt them down, we'll fly out there and confront them. Parker and I are broken, but we need him. There is no other option. It will take the full power of the Elementi Knights to end this war between Heaven and Hell here on earth. I don't know how I feel about that, knowing how much he hurt me and knowing I have to trust him to keep me alive, along with you guys. What if Parker and I can never mend things between us? Do I want to? Does it even matter if we all might die in this fight? We thought it was one source of evil we were fighting —The Dark Lord. Now we know it's Lilith and the Evil Trinity that we're up against, and they don't give a shit about anything but taking over our world so they can rule it for themselves. Let's say we live through this. What happens to the people who have been dosed with the serum? Will this ever be over? Is there a chance for us to really build a life together outside of this ordeal or are we just slaves to fighting and surviving for the Elementi?"

The room was so quiet you could hear a pin drop as they absorbed what I'd just dropped on them.

"Lailah, how long have you been holding all this in?" Brayden asked, something in his voice making me look up at him. His face was tight with anger and I didn't know if it was directed at me or something else, but that wasn't what I was expecting from him.

Shrugging, I looked down at my hands picking at my t-shirt. "Some things for a while, others after I thought I was going to lose to Lilith. I had no idea if I was going to make it out of that insanity or not. It was a gamble, a stupid risky one, to see if I could trap her in my own body. If that failed, I could have killed us all and ended the world, because that's what Synergy can do. In the right hands, it can save the world. Otherwise, it can bring the world to ruin. What nobody tells us is if saving it will ruin me... or you guys. I will fight, but I'm not fighting for the world. I'm fighting for *us,* otherwise it's not worth it to me."

"Are you saying you don't want to do this?" Hudson asked, confused.

"What is this?" I countered.

This made Hudson pause to think as if he wasn't sure either.

"Just to be clear, you're not talking about leaving us," Micah cut in, his voice all but a growl.

My head snapped in his direction at the absurd question. "Absolutely not. The only good thing out of this whole situation is getting you guys. I'm not with any of you because we're bonded by some magical power or have Heaven's blessing. I fell in love with each and every one of you without any of that, unable to ever choose between you all. What I'm getting tired of is having to be the people on the front lines sacrificing everything, including our lives, for a fight that might never be over."

"It's not just you guys," Cami whispered. "All of us in the Elementi have given everything to this fight." She looked up at me, giving me a watery smile as tears fell down her cheeks. "I don't blame you for questioning their motives though. I do, every goddamn day. It cost me my first love. One of the reasons I didn't want to come back to Ryevick when they asked. Why would I want to help protect the one person who could put an end to this, when she was already too late to save the woman I loved?"

Over the time that I had been friends with Cami, I knew there was something in her past. Brayden's parents even hinted at it when we were out there visiting them. The pain I could see in her face told me everything I needed to know —how this story would go and how she still mourned the loss of this person.

"I hope you don't take what I said as belittling the pain you've gone through, or that even you guys have, having lost family and friends. Coming from the outside and looking in, it just seems like no one pushes back or questions things, only pushing forward to keep the promise made to the angels," I said, feeling the sadness and pain coming from all my men.

"No, Lala, I didn't think that at all. I've been where you are. Hell, who am I kidding? I'm still there if I'm being honest with myself. Of course, my opinion changed when I met you and realized you had no idea that any of this was going on and you just got chucked right into the fire without a chance to question if this is what you should be doing. No one asked any of you if you wanted to be the Elementi Knights and put your life on the line to save the world. It was just assumed and expected, because you're the only people who can do it." Cami sighed.

Each of us took a moment to just sit there and think, knowing that I'd called attention to something that seemed taboo to even talk about. For generations, the Elementi had been training the next generation of knights when the others pass away, without question. Now here I was, the element that was supposed to save the world, questioning what we needed to do and the reason I was brought into this world. What I wouldn't give to have an angel appear and explain to us what the hell was going on.

"Then we change the story," Jay stated, breaking the silence.

I looked at him, brows creased, not sure where he was going with this.

"A mad man on his deathbed was visited by an angel who told him that Synergy was coming when we needed you the most. I agree that now is that time, but what they said is it was the weapon that would turn the tide for whoever was bonded to them. Lailah, you chose us, and we chose you. So, I say we choose each other again and we don't fight for the Elementi or the world around us that has no idea the sacrifices that happen every day. This fight—this fight is *for us.* You want a future where we can settle down and make a life for ourselves, really get married, maybe have kids, watch them grow up ignorant to this darkness. If that is what we want, then we need to make that world for them. Take down the evil once and for all. Let them know if they dare to come back, we will smite them once again, because we have something precious to protect. Fuck the Elementi. Let's do this for us and the future we deserve," Jay proclaimed, surprising the shit out of all of us.

Micah shot to his feet, forgetting about his leg and came crashing back down, missing the chair, swearing. "Fucking hell, goddamn leg!" Once back in his chair, he glared at us, daring us to comment on his actions. "Jay's right. Fuck everyone else. We do this last battle and *when* we live through it, we're done. That's it. No more Elementi, no more fighting or dealing with demons. We will live our own lives."

"I agree. This last battle will take everything we have and once it's finished, so are we. They can't ask us for more than that," Hudson commented, nodding in agreement.

Cami snorted. "I mean, they can and will, but I think you have the right idea to do what you have to for your future and I'll do the same. Once this is over, I'm out as well. Maggs has been wanting to branch out and see the world, not be trapped at the school, working underground her whole life. I know she'll come with me. You guys are my family too, and whatever kids you end up having need a crazy aunt that will help them get into the best kind of trouble."

"There is one glitch, guys," Brayden cut in. "What do we do about Parker?"

All eyes turned to me. Rubbing my face with both

hands, I buried my fingers in my hair, knowing I had to make a tough call. "We need him for this fight. I don't know about anything past that, but he needs to be a part of this. I'm sure there will be fights and moments where I'll need to walk away, but that isn't an option if we want a future. One thing I don't question is needing all six of us fighting together to make it through this. They have worked so hard to keep us from completing our bonds, it has to be important. They wouldn't waste the effort otherwise. Lilith was extremely worried when it looked like I'd bond with all of you before she could get to one of you."

"Fine, he can come to help with shit but I refuse to let him stay in the house," Micah bit out. "I also can't promise I won't beat the shit out of him again."

"Works for me, but when we head out to wherever we're going, we can't risk him being separated. He's not bonded to me. They can kill him and then we're fucked on a whole other level," I reminded them.

They all grumbled an agreement before I looked at Cami. "Would you mind being our go-between? Personally, I don't want to talk to him just yet, even though I need to."

"Of course, Lala. I'm not happy with the bastard either, and I get not wanting to be cornered into talking to him on the phone," Cami assured me. "I do think it would be better for me to head back, though. I'll be more help working with Beth since I know everything and I'm not as blinded by the organization as she is about who to trust or. How about I stay for a week, see where we are with things and then I head back and have information to share firsthand instead of over the phone or email?"

She was right, this wasn't her fight and she couldn't come with us when we went after the camp. "Sounds like our best option right now. We can always reevaluate later. Nothing is set in stone."

"Now, can I suggest taking the afternoon off to just relax, watch movies and let your bodies recover? We've done a lot today. Jay, I don't want you to think finding your mom isn't urgent but things will go better if you're not burning the candle at both ends," Cami reasoned, making a good point which I never thought I would see happening.

Jay wilted a little next to me. "No, you're right, Cami. We're all stressed, bruised, and tired. We'll think more clearly after having a day to rest."

So, that's what we did. We rested, knowing it might be the last bit of peace we would get for a while once we got into the thick of things. We needed just a moment to heal and remind ourselves even with powers, we were still only human, despite what the world told us.

CHAPTER 5
LAILAH

Two days passed in a routine of sleeping late into the day then waking up and getting right into research, tracking down any leads they could think of. I wasn't that much help but Jay handed out tasks for us which made it easier, but when we hit a wall, we knew we needed to bring Parker into this. For all that he was a big child and didn't take much in life all that serious, he was one talented computer whiz. We all kept running into roadblocks being unable to get the information we needed. Parker would easily be able to hack into what we needed with the right technology and know-how. Cami made the call and filled him in on what was going on. It appeared that he'd been staying with my parents of all people, but from what Cami gathered, he'd been holed up, working on his own angle dealing with the demon problem.

I was curled up on the couch, leaning on Brayden with Micah sprawled out next to us when the knock came at the door. Immediately, my stomach started to churn with worry, having no idea how this was going to go. It was such an odd place to be, missing him, knowing that even though

I wasn't sure how I felt about him, he still held a part of my heart. My trust in him was shattered, but I missed Parker's lightheartedness, the pranks he would play on the others. He could always find a way to lighten a tense situation in the right way to make us all laugh, or at least smile. The past few days had been so quiet and brooding as we processed all that we'd been through and survived. Parker completed us and added to the group in a way that only he could, but I didn't know how to even start to work on things when we had all this other stuff going on. On the other hand, it seemed so stupid to be this upset with him. Lilith set him up to fail, using everything they could to ruin him. But ultimately, he made the choice to abandon me to save Phoebe, and that was what broke us.

"Hey, Cami, thanks for reaching out and giving me a chance." Parker's voice echoed down the hall into the living room.

His deep tone rumbled across my skin, bringing tears to my eyes that I brushed away quickly as he entered the room. There he stood, looking as haggard, if not slightly worse, than the rest of us. Dark circles rimmed his eyes, his hair was a mess, and he had the starting of a beard, like he couldn't be bothered to shave. "How can I help?" was all he asked, taking a moment to look at each of us.

"How much did Cami tell you?" Jay asked, taking point on this.

"That the demons took your mom to use against you if they failed with me, and your father isn't interested in helping to find her," Parker answered.

Jay nodded and turned the laptop around so Parker could see the screen. "I need your help hacking into these companies where we traced some money movement. They match to the previous camps but we can't get to the other end of things. There has to be people helping them in the normal world, funneling funds to keep them hidden. If we can get our hands on one of those people, then we can figure out where they are now. From what we gathered, their camp is too big for them to keep moving it the same way they did before, so it has to be hidden well."

Parker cracked his knuckles and sat right on the floor, in front of the coffee table the laptop was on and got to work. That was it. There wasn't any other discussion or pushback like he normally would give if he didn't feel included in the master plan. The tension in the room, just having him here, was suffocating, so I slipped off the couch and headed into the kitchen to make myself a cup of tea.

"You okay, Lala?" Cami asked as she hopped up on the counter next to where I was working.

"I don't know," I answered honestly. "How do you even begin to learn to trust someone again? There isn't a magic formula to fix something like what we've been through. Most people might think I'm silly and not see the big deal, but when that Oath connection between us crumbled away, it was as if a part of me died. These aren't normal relationships that I have with these men, and I can understand why losing one of them would cripple or even kill me. We are bound to each other through love, magic, and spirit. That isn't something you can move on from."

"When I lost Kim, I wasn't sure that my heart would ever mend," Cami whispered, her voice tight with emotion. "I know it isn't the same but I understand that kind of heartbreak. It's been three years now, and I didn't truly believe that I would find a love like that again. It took the right person to come alongside me, willing to be patient as I figured things out and let me take my time as I got to know them. Maggs understands that Kim will always have a place in my heart and isn't threatened by that. She even asked me to tell her stories about Kim, so I can share that part of my life with her, since we were together all through high school."

"Cami, I'm so happy that you have Maggs and she is everything you need, but I don't understand what you're trying to tell me." I sighed, leaning on the counter and dropping my head into my hands.

She ran a gentle hand over my head in comfort. "I know I give the big idiot a hard time, but give him the chance to prove to you that he can be trusted again. Don't push him away. I'm not saying forgive him, he hasn't earned that, but instead, keep an open mind to the possibility that he can be willing to be what you need right now. Parker is part of your soul. Losing the Oath didn't change that. He got lost and fell off track. Does he deserve to grovel and pay his penance? Absolutely! Just as Maggs kept letting me know she was there for me and cared, waiting for me to be ready. Let Parker have that chance."

"You make that sound so simple."

"It's not. I hated Maggs for a long time because she didn't take the hint I wasn't interested in anything other than a fling. Attachments and falling in love again were the furthest thing from my mind but she refused to let me ignore her. Then we became friendly, and I went to her parties, found out she worked for the Elementi and knew our dangers, which Kim never did. When I saw her again after the summer, I decided she'd stuck around after all the shitty things I put her through, so she must really like me. So, I gave her the date she'd been asking for. Now, I couldn't ever picture my life without her. I'll always love Kim, but Maggs is my forever person. She took the time to prove to me she wasn't going to walk away from my woundedness."

Cami paused then shifted. "You hear all that, dipshit? I just laid out everything you needed to do if you really want to make this work."

My head snapped up as I realized she wasn't talking to me anymore and found Parker lingering in the doorway of the kitchen. I gulped, wondering how long he'd stood there and what all he heard of our conversation. Not that I said anything I wouldn't say to his face, but I didn't know if I was ready for him to know exactly how I was feeling. Cami hopped off the counter, gave me a peck on the cheek, and left the kitchen, knocking Parker with her shoulder as she went.

"I have no right to ask for a second chance, Lailah, but I'm not strong enough to walk away from you," Parker murmured as he took a few steps closer, still leaving plenty of room between us. "What I did to you, and the pain I've caused you, make me worse than the demons we're fighting. I will be whatever you need me to be, without question. Just say the word and I'll do it. Just allow me the chance to still be in your life. I'm never going to ask for more than that, since I don't deserve that kindness from you as it is."

Hearing his plea and the vulnerability in his voice, my heart ached as it echoed the pain I could sense from him. The kettle whistled on the stove, breaking me out of my paralyzed state and gave me something to do as I figured out how I wanted to respond to his request. Parker didn't speak, move, or try to push for an answer as I finished making my tea. I turned to face him.

"Help us find Jay's mom and survive this battle with the Dark Lord, then we can figure out where we stand," I answered. This wasn't a yes or a no, but it would give him the chance to be useful and see if there was something left to save between us.

Parker sagged as if relieved, which confused me. "Thank you for letting me stay to help and not tossing me out for good. I know I said this before but I won't fail you or the others again."

"There are rules though," I warned. "I can't have you move back in or stay here overnight if it's not necessary. After things happened with Lilith, my nightmares are back and I need to know that everyone in the house is a safe person. The other part is, I'm not the only person you need to repair relationships with. You and the others need to work your shit out on your own time. I'll give them the same speech but I can't handle you guys fighting among yourself in front of me."

"I can deal with all of that," Parker answered, a determined look on his face.

"Alright then," I said moving past him with my mug, returning to the others where I paused as they all looked at me. "I just explained my expectations to Parker with him being here and helping but one of those expectations is the same for all of you. All of us have issues to work on if there is any hope to fix things but I won't tolerate you fighting in front of me. We need to deal with the big picture, so whatever beef you have gets dealt with elsewhere and on your own time." They all nodded as their eyes shifted from me to Parker who was standing behind me. "Anyone else have concerns they need to voice?"

When no one spoke up I let the issue drop and returned to my spot between Brayden and Micah. I only had so much emotion to give to things and for this matter, I reached my max.

The rest of the day fell into a peaceful atmosphere as we worked on our sections of things, allowing Parker time to look through what we'd found and see what he could come up with. The sun faded and stomachs rumbled, making me smile.

"I'll get dinner started," I announced, getting up as Brayden grabbed my hand, making me pause.

"Do you want any help, Angel?" he asked.

Leaning down, I kissed him and shook my head. "No, I need a break from dead ends and cooking helps me think. I'll call you guys when it's ready."

I sent up a prayer as I left them alone for the first time since the whole thing went down that they wouldn't kill each other.

CHAPTER 6
PARKER

Watching Brayden kiss her so casually was like a knife in my heart. The man whose whole purpose was to feel feelings and influence them was the one who'd fucked up in the worst way possible. I wasn't surprised when she kicked me out of the house. I wouldn't want to share space with someone who shattered my heart and saved an ex-girlfriend who was inhabited by Lilith the Mother of Demons, leaving her to fend for herself. I meant every word I'd said to her in the kitchen. I didn't deserve the easy way out of this, or to still be part of her life at all. I'd once again been the fuckup and acted without thinking, like I always seem to do.

The moment she left the room, the atmosphere changed as Micah locked his gaze on me from his spot on the couch. I'd noticed the knee brace, and I was genuinely glad to see that he wasn't in a cast, knowing how much that would piss him off even more.

I knew Lailah was the one person none of us couldn't live without, and over the past seven months that she'd been in our lives she had brought us all closer. We were far from being perfect and we still got into fights because they didn't trust me not to hurt her, and what had I done? Just what they expected.

"I don't know what other rules she gave you in order to feel comfortable letting you be here but know that if you step out of line, I will end you," Micah growled.

I wasn't surprised in the least that Micah was reacting this way. Lailah was his everything. They all knew it before Micah admitted it to himself. "If I hurt her again, I'll let you kill me, Micah."

This response seemed to surprise him but it really shouldn't. If I fucked up my second chance, I didn't deserve another. Putting me out of my misery was a more fitting fate.

"The only reason we called you and allowed you back into this home is because we can't do this without you. It requires all of the Elementi Knights to defeat the Dark Lord and the Evil Trinity, not to mention the added difficulties if Lilith joins in," Hudson informed me. His tone was cool and detached like it used to be before he met Lailah, closing himself off from me.

"Look, guys, I'm not going to fight whatever hoops you make me jump through to be here, alright? My only request was to be allowed to be part of her life in some way, and if it's helping hunt down the bastards that have been haunting her dreams, then I'm all over it. I realize that means we'll also have to come to some agreement for you to accept me being around her as well, so do what you must. I'll take my hits," I shared, laying everything out there so they could decide what to do next.

Micah scoffed. "Don't act like such a martyr. You deserve all that you're getting and then some for what you're putting her through. We're the ones who've had to pick up the pieces after you destroyed her and I'm not letting you do any more damage."

"I get it. I would do the same thing if the roles were any different, but I'm the asshole that hurt her. I won't deny it."

"Good, because there's no other way to look at it," Brayden muttered. "I just don't get how you could have let something like this happen. Phoebe was your ex, and she was dating Lailah's brother. Why would you ever think to put her before our girl? Is it because you still loved her and thought you could rekindle things with Phoebe?"

The question smacked me right in the face, because this is probably what all of them were thinking. Why else would a man who says he's in love with someone to the point of giving an Oath turn his back on them? Every time I close my eyes, I think over that moment again and again, trying to understand it myself. It was so simple looking at it now that Phoebe, while an innocent, wasn't in the same danger that Lailah was. In the end, Phoebe was lost to us, having been a conduit for Lilith. There was no way to remove a demon without killing the host.

"I was blinded by the need to protect someone that I felt wasn't able to defend themselves. I knew Lailah was strong and could hold on until you guys got there, but Phoebe was an innocent, even if she was trying to make a move on me. I'd shut her down more than once already. She shouldn't have been my priority because Lailah is everything to me. I just didn't see it until I lost her," I answered as honestly as I could. "Nothing I do or say can ever right that wrong but I will grovel and pay my penance to keep even a sliver of hope she won't cut me out of her life for good."

This answer seemed to appease Brayden and Hudson, but from the look of doubt on Jay and Micah's faces, I knew they didn't believe me. That's fine, I didn't need them to, if Lailah did. Her opinion was the only one that mattered. If I could mend things with her, then the guys would fall in line with her decision, but I would always have them watching out for the next time I might fuck up.

They dropped the matter for now as I dove back into the work they'd given me. All the banks were offshore and only used account numbers with no names or locations tied to the transactions. I needed to come at it from a different angle and see if they used the same account for something else that wasn't as secure. Losing myself to my work, peeling back layer after layer of the web they wove to keep things hidden, I finally got the breadcrumb I needed.

"Dinner's ready," Lailah called, snapping me out of my computer-code fog.

Turning, I looked at her standing there wearing an apron that Cami got for her and flour smudging her face. The need to brush it off her cheek and kiss those lips was overpowering, but I knew that wasn't an option, and I might get stabbed for even thinking I could try. So instead, I cleared my throat and asked a simple request. "Would you mind if I kept working? I just caught on to a lead and I don't want to lose the momentum I have or risk them figuring out someone is digging for the information."

"Of course, I'll bring you a plate to eat in here, unless you want me to set it aside for later?" she inquired, removing her apron.

"I'll come grab some later if that works," I hedged, not wanting her to feel like I didn't want to eat her cooking since everyone knew how much I loved it.

She nodded and turned back to the kitchen as the others followed to eat at the table together. I didn't really think I would be welcome at the table as it was and it would probably make everything super awkward. Brushing that aside, I dove back into the trail I found, leading me on a merry chase through shell company to shell company until I found the end of the line. Frowning, I started digging into the corporation, trying to figure out just what it was that they did or how they made their money. It didn't seem like a normal business where it had a corporate office or any kind of brick-and-mortar building. Everything was run on the internet, hidden in the background of all the shell companies that were fronts in all different industries.

Could this even be an actual business or is this just another front that's better constructed? What really threw me was the fact it had been around for fifty years, doing what I didn't know. Their taxes were legit, even if it did seem to be too clean, too perfect, for it to be true. Every business had a little dirt, using the write-offs to cover something personal, or even using the company card for dinner out. No one followed all the rules unless they really didn't want someone to be looking into them. This had to be what I was looking for. I was just missing the obvious part of it.

Now that I had a company name, maybe I could ask Jay to look into it using his contacts and see if the Elementi had any information. They were always good at keeping an eye on businesses and people who seemed to be hiding things. It was always in these situations they found a demon trying to go unnoticed in the background. They knew what would draw out attention, riding the line of doing what they needed and keeping off our radar. Looking up from the computer, I found it was dark outside, and the TV was on with the guys relaxing, watching some show while I worked.

I'd been so absorbed in what I was doing that I didn't even notice they'd come back to relax. Clearly dinner was over and done with and had been for a while. Lailah was curled up, sleeping with her head on Jay's lap as he massaged her head, doing his best to keep her asleep. If the nightmares were back, constant contact seemed to be the best thing to remind her that they were there even when she was passed out. Her face was utterly relaxed and peaceful, something I hadn't seen in days, since every time she looked at me, sadness filled her crystal-blue gaze.

"Jay," I whispered, drawing his steel gaze. "I have a company name but there's something really odd about it. There aren't any records of employees, leases, how they make their money, or even who the founder is. I'm gonna send this off to Beth and see if she can use the Elementi contacts to dive into it. My thought was you might have a different perspective on it from the military side of things. They cover their tracks differently than the standard money laundering types do."

"Leave up the information you need me to look at and I'll see what I can find. Wait on sending it to Beth. It would be best to keep things close to the chest while we can, if you think you have them backed into a corner," Jay directed. "It's late. If you can't do any more, then I think it's best if you head out for the night. We'll talk tomorrow. Make sure you check in with me before you come over."

The cool tone Jay was using, as if I was one of his soldiers to order about stung, but I'd promised to do what was needed to help.

"I need some different things if this is the type of work I'm going to be doing so we don't get caught in a trap. The last thing we need is for them to catch onto us and walk in the backdoor, looking at everything we have on them," I said, getting up and stretching after being hunched over the coffee table for hours.

"There's a plate she made for you in the oven," Brayden commented. "It would upset her if you didn't eat."

Nodding, I wandered off to see what she'd made and found personal chicken pot pies along with mashed potatoes. My stomach grumbled, smelling the amazing aroma as I pulled the tray out to one set aside for me. Leaning on the counter, I wolfed the meal down and heard someone enter.

"I'm leaving to head back to Ryevick at the end of the week," Cami warned. "Until then, I'll buffer for you where I can with the guys but you have to fix this, Parker. I know how much you love her, even if it took you fucking it up to realize just how much."

Setting the fork down, I met her fierce gaze. "They all want answers I don't really have, Cami. This element has been a curse to me my whole life. It puts me into situations that set me up for failure. The first time I felt like I was getting a handle on things was with her around but now I'm just a joke of a knight."

Cami marched up to me and kneed me right in the dick. The sudden attack and the pain stole the air from my lungs as I crouched over, moaning in pain. "What the actual fuck, Cami?"

"Oh, you just seemed to like punishing yourself so much I thought I would help," she quipped. "Grow the fuck up, man. We get it. You're a wounded puppy that's whining about losing his favorite person, rolling on his back, baring his throat, waiting for the killing blow. Instead of just waiting to be kicked, prove to those assholes you learned your lesson. Show the woman you love just how much she means to you in every way you can, instead of tiptoeing around. Lailah has four other men in her life that remind her every day that she is their world. Fight for her, fight for your place back, or get the fuck out of this house and don't ever come back. You'll get them all killed if you keep this up."

"There wasn't another way you could have explained that without ruining my chance at having children someday?" I grunted as I finally managed to stand upright. "I'm pretty sure my dick just became an innie in the hope to protect itself from that ever happening again."

"So did I make my point? I was hoping the extra blood to your thinking brain might be helpful," Cami commented with a grin. "You're lucky that's all I did and that I'm willing to even give you advice on how to fix this."

"Could your advice come with less pain next time?" I begged. Her glare had me holding up my hands in defense. "Okay, okay, I hear you. No more wounded puppy. I'll work on it. First, I'm going back to Lailah's parents and icing my dick, so take comfort in the knowledge I'll still be in pain you crazy ankle-biter."

"Good enough for me," Cami chirped, spinning on her heel and leaving so I could finish my dinner before I left.

CHAPTER 7

LAILAH

"Sunshine, we should get you back up to bed," Hudson whispered, running a hand down my arm. "You fell asleep at the table again."

Blinking, I sat up and found he was right. I'd had a nightmare at three and couldn't fall back asleep, so I came down to go through the records of the mystery company.

"This is the third time this week we've found you here," Hudson chided. "I don't think it's healthy to have you so involved in this. Maybe we need to send you back to Ryevick where Cami can keep an eye on you and give you some space from us and all of this."

My heart slammed in my chest at his words. "Are you trying to get rid of me?"

"What? No, Sunshine, that isn't what I want at all," he spluttered, pulling me onto his lap. "I'm just worried about you. Things are regressing, not getting better, the harder we push to find Jay's mother. My first and only purpose is to make sure you're healthy and happy, which I should point out, you are neither of those things."

I looked up at him, seeing the truth in his words as he leaned in and kissed me softly. "I'm sorry. I didn't mean to freak out. My brain just went into panic mode hearing you say that."

"Talk to me. Tell me where your head's at. You always used to come to me when you couldn't get out of your own thoughts, but this time, you're just internalizing it," Hudson pleaded, resting his forehead against mine.

"It's all the same things." I sighed. "Will we find his mom in time? Can we really do this? Parker, me, you guys, the Elementi—it might be easier to tell you what I'm *not* thinking about. The only time my brain turns off is when I'm cooking or working on things like this where I have to pay attention to the details."

He hummed in understanding as he pulled me close, resting his chin on the top of my head. "I'm going to ask you a question and you need to answer it honestly."

"What's the question?" I asked, feeling I knew what it was already.

"Not until you promise to at least think about the answer before you give it," he challenged.

I wrapped an arm around his neck to have him as close as I could get him. "I promise. Now ask your question."

"Is Parker being here every day making things worse?"

As I promised, I thought about his question, the one I had a feeling he was going to ask me. It was so hard to answer because it just wasn't that simple to put into words. Since the first day he came over to help, he's been invaluable to us, getting information from places none of us could access. Come to find out, no one knew about this mysterious company called Alpite but that was about all we knew about it for sure. Each time we uncovered something, it led to another wild goose chase. It just proved that once we figured it out, we would have exactly what we needed to find the demons' military base of operations.

Something else had changed in him as well, as if a switch had been flipped and he did everything he could think of to be an active person in this mission. He brought me flowers—my favorite kind, tulips—and I don't think I'd ever told any of my guys that they were my favorite. Gone was the wounded bleeding man who only wanted to beg for my forgiveness. Now I saw him fighting for me or us. We had a long way to go for me to ever think about opening my heart back up to him but I could see him trying.

"No… in the list of things making this whole situation hard, he isn't one of them. I think I'm just reaching the breaking point of how many times I can take a hit like I have in the past year. There needs to be an end to all this, Hudson. I might be Synergy, the weapon you've all been waiting for, but I'm still Lailah too. Not that any of you have forgotten that or made me feel like I have to keep pushing myself. A year ago, I had no idea what I wanted for myself. The rest of my family had plans, dreams, and aspirations— not me though. I drifted, getting lost at every turn, then I stumbled into this world and found I did have a purpose. It just wasn't one I chose for myself. God, I feel like a broken record when it comes to this, which might be why I'm not talking about it," I shared, burying my head into his neck and placing a kiss on his pulse that I could feel beating steadily against my cheek.

"Sounds to me like you need someone to remind you just how strong you are," Hudson murmured, his voice turning husky with desire. "Will you let me worship you, my sunshine? Help you to forget everything that's going on in the world around us, force you to just feel what's happening in this moment, right here, right now."

What woman in her right mind would say no to that?

"Yes," I whispered against his skin before I pulled back and stood in front of him. Grabbing his jaw, I tipped his face up to look at me, knowing what he wanted from me. He was the only man out of the four who wanted to be told what to do in the bedroom. "Are the others asleep?"

"No, but they're all in their rooms tonight," he answered, telling me what I really wanted to know.

Hudson knew that part of what I was struggling with was having no control over what was happening, so he was giving me this gift. "Get on your knees."

Confusion flashed over his face as he followed my order.

"Show me just how much you're willing to do to keep my mind off things," I directed, taking off his glasses then settling his hands on my hips.

I'd taken to wearing lounge clothes since I seemed to be falling asleep in odd places throughout the day. I was only sleeping three or four hours a night. Realization bloomed in his eyes as he started to smirk. He hooked his thumbs in the elastic band of my shorts and underwear, pulling them both down to my ankles. Lifting one foot then the other as he held me steady, he tossed them somewhere behind me then grabbed my left leg and threw it over his shoulder. I yelped and grabbed onto a handful of blond hair as he wasted no time devouring me, his tongue thrusting into me as if I was the most delicious thing he'd ever tasted.

Hot damn, I need to challenge him more often if this was the result.

"Holy shit, Hudson," I moaned as his hands slid to cup my ass and gave him the leverage he needed to get deeper.

He started to trace a finger around my back entrance that everyone had been threatening to convince me to try. I wasn't against it. I just didn't know if I would like it, and it seemed so dirty, even if they all were excited with the thought. His finger pressed against the opening but didn't try to go further, almost as if he was just getting me used to the idea. My attention was completely diverted when he pulled back enough to latch onto my clit and sucked on it hard, adding just enough teeth to add friction. I screamed as I came, unable to fight to keep my voice quiet. I shuddered as he lapped at me, keeping the orgasm going as long as he could. Giving one last kiss to my clit, he slowly set my leg back down, making sure I was steady enough for him to stand.

He cupped my cheeks and pulled me into a kiss that he put as much vigor in as he had my lady bits. I could taste myself on him, but I was too preoccupied with his tongue battling with mine to care. Picking me up, I gasped in surprise but he just set me on the table and pressed me back as he worked up my shirt to uncover my bra. He didn't bother to take it off, instead just shoving it out of his way, exposing me to him. Hudson gazed down at me, his clear blue eyes showing just how hungry he was for me and determined to make sure I couldn't think of anything but him. Slipping two fingers into me with his thumb rubbing my clit, I arched on the table. "Oh God, Hudson."

"That's right, tell the others that I'm the one down here making you moan. They like to tease me about being more submissive in bed, but all I want is to give my sunshine all the pleasure I can," Hudson whispered as he kissed down my chest before descending upon a nipple.

None of the guys were ever selfish but Hudson had a

love for foreplay that none of the others did, taking his time to drive me wild before he ever thought about relieving his own need. His fingers pumped in and out of me while he worked my breasts over with his mouth and his other hand kept my mind overloaded with sensations. Another climax came bursting forward, hitting me so hard I almost sat up from the table. He held me in place as my body shivered under his touch. Finally, he removed his fingers but still strummed my clit as he used one of his lubed fingers to press more urgently at my tight entrance.

"Just relax," he murmured into my ear. "I've been doing some research and there are some neat tricks we can do that are enhanced with anal stimulation. If you hate it, then I won't ever do it again. This is all about you and getting the last drop of pleasure I can out of you."

I trusted Hudson to take care of me so as the tip of his finger passed the tight barrier, I forced my body to relax. The sensation was odd but not unpleasant. He didn't move his finger in deep, just enough to give me a feel for the stimulation. Pairing that with his continued attention on my clit, I came faster than I thought possible, the feeling sparking through my body like a shock of electricity.

"Look how beautiful you are, my sunshine. Your eyes glazed with contentment as I pull yet another orgasm from your stunning body. When you fall apart, it's heavenly," Hudson said as he finally slid into me, pulling me up into a sitting position, wrapping me in a tight hug.

Clinging to him, he moved at a slow steady pace, just letting our bodies feel the movement. At this point, I was so sensitive, it wouldn't take much for me to come again, but he kept me on the edge. Kissing along my neck, he nibbled on my ear, making me lean to the side to give him better access to what he wanted. The feeling of our bodies wrapped up in each other was euphoric in a way I never knew possible. I felt loved, cherished, and the safest I had since we came to Wisconsin. My quiet observant knight knew what I needed, even when I didn't. Silent tears fell down my cheeks as I clung to him, letting this man I loved with my soul take care of me. Finally, we both reached our limit and came one after the other in a beautiful crescendo.

"I know this is hard, my sunshine, but we'll do this together and make it out the other side," Hudson whispered into my ear as he pulled me from his neck to look me in the eye. "Don't fear what we have to face because you won't be doing it alone. Each of your knights will be right behind you, ready to defend the future we all deserve." He kissed away the last of my tears before stripping me the rest of the way out of my clothes. Then he scooped me up and carried me upstairs into my bedroom where we wrapped ourselves in the sheets, and I drifted off in his arms, wrung out in the best way possible.

I didn't even have to open my eyes to know where I was and who was here with me. The darkness of the void the Dark Lord liked to bring me to was vast and terrifying, and a feeling of utter loneliness sank into my skin. It has been months since the last time we'd interacted this way, but I'd been expecting it ever since I banished Lilith back to Hell and the Princes who wanted to lock her up.

"Little Synergy," his evil voice purred, making the hairs on the back of my neck stand up. "Have you missed me? It's been awhile since our last conversation."

"Can't say that I've even noticed your absence with the joy of meeting your mother," I commented.

The funny thing about being tired of dealing with all this is that it made this whole interaction less intimidating. We'd done this song and dance before and I'd always made my way out of it unscathed.

The Dark Lord snarled at me. "Yes, she told me all about what happened between you two and how she succeeded in breaking one of your relationships, leaving you vulnerable to me entering your mind like this. How are you sleeping? Nightmares keeping you awake still? I decided to throw in some new ones to keep you tired, restless, and stupid. The carelessness of this inter-action is proving to me that it's working."

"What? You're the one giving me nightmares?" I gasped, my brain finally catching up to the reality of my situation.

I'd thought with four out of the five bound to me that I would be safer from the Dark Lord, but if he's been in my head this whole time, then I was dead wrong. Could it be that he'd given up on using me to gain what he wanted, seeing as I was too much effort to deal with in the real world?

"Ah, it seems you're finally catching on. Mother warned me you weren't as bright as I thought you were and you know moth-ers, they're never wrong." He chuckled, the sound like nails on a chalkboard.

I needed to get out of here, and quickly, but I'd never been able to do this on my own. The guys always came for me when I needed them. Closing my eyes, I focused inward, trying to grasp onto my bonds but there was nothing. It was a hollow space in my chest. How could I be cut off from them? It shouldn't have been possible for him to do that.

"Now, now, Little Synergy. You're in my world now and I've put a shield up just as you have back home, to keep them out as *we had this little chat. No one you are bound to has any idea that something is wrong, and I have you right where I want you," the Dark Lord sneered, his clawed hand wrapping around my throat. "My brothers know about my plans, which is forcing me to move them to happen faster than I wanted. If I take you out here and now, it might be less fulfilling, but then I'll have one less pest to deal with as I bring Earth into a new era ruled by me!"*

His grip tightened, and I thrashed, trying to pull at his hand, but he was too strong and his fingers were so long they wrapped all the way around my throat, his claws digging into my skin. Without my power to call on the others, I was left helpless and alone in the darkness, with pure evil trying to steal my life from me. In desperation, I called out to whoever might listen with the last ounce of air that I had in my lungs, unwilling to die like this.

"Get your hands off her, you creepy bastard!" Parker's voice rang out in the darkness.

A flickering purple light was making its way over to us, but with the lack of oxygen, my vision was starting to fade.

"You shouldn't be able to be here! How did you get through my barrier?" the Dark Lord roared, dropping me to the ground.

My eyes were still blurry, but I caught glimpses of Parker and his long-bladed staff going head-to-head with the Dark Lord. Parker had an evil smile on his face as he attacked, pushing the darkness back with him as his purple light grew, filling the space. "Did you forget I'm not attached to her at all now, or the fact that shattering the Oath left a blight on me much like the mark you left on Lailah? Yeah, asshole, I can enter the void now too, probably even follow you into Hell if I needed to. Sadly, we can't stay and play. Just know that we're coming for you and when we do, you're going to lose."

Parker released his weapon and scooped me up. "Sorry,

Trouble, but this is gonna be a bumpy ride," he warned as he ran, tucking me in close against his chest.

"How?" I croaked.

"I don't know, Trouble, but I'm so glad I didn't ignore the nagging feeling you needed me. Just be ready for them to be pissed and screaming when you wake up," Parker shared, as I felt myself starting to wake up and the brush of a kiss on my forehead.

CHAPTER 8
LAILAH

"What the fuck do you think you're doing here?" Micah demanded, his furious voice echoing in my ears, giving me the first sign to tell me that I was back.

Groaning, I shifted onto my back, bringing a hand up to my neck. The moment I touched it, I hissed in pain, making it clear that the Dark Lord had left his mark and proof that everything that just happened was real.

"Parker," I whispered, barely loud enough to be heard over the yelling.

"Guys, shut the fuck up. She's trying to say something," Brayden cut in as the bed dipped beside me. "Angel, what the hell happened to your neck?" He gasped and reached out as if he was going to touch it but stopped himself.

I licked my lips and swallowed but it was so painful. Rolling my head to the side, I found Parker pinned to the bedroom wall by Jay, with a pissed-off Micah standing in front of him as if he was blocking the sight of him from me. I locked eyes with Parker, begging him to answer the question so I didn't have to.

"The Dark Lord tried to kill her in her sleep," Parker

stated, fury blazing in his eyes. "The fucker put up a barrier to keep you guys out, making sure you didn't have a clue what was happening."

Jay dropped Parker and turned to me; his gray eyes wild with fear. "Is he telling the truth?"

I nodded my head before croaking out an answer. "Yes, he saved my life."

"Care to explain how the hell you knew what was happening? I'm going to need that house key from you before you leave as well if you're going to pull shit like this," Micah growled.

"Oh, I'm sorry, I thought saving the life of the woman we all love was a good enough excuse for my actions. Next time, when I can't get there in time, you'll be the reason she's dead in bed next to you. Hope that's okay with you," Parker snarled.

The whole situation was devolving, and I needed to put a stop to it. Sitting up, the sheet fell away from me, exposing my naked body, forgetting that Hudson and I didn't bother to put anything on before getting in bed. Although it wasn't what I had planned, it did the trick as all my guys froze, laser focused on my bare breasts. Rolling my eyes, I let out a huff, which got Hudson moving, flashing the guys all his goods as he went into the bathroom and appeared wearing a robe and offering me mine. Then he returned to the bathroom, only to return with a glass of water, which helped ever so slightly with speaking.

"Stop, please," I managed to say clearly enough. "Fighting is what he wants and we can't let him win."

"Cookie Monster, I know you believe we can't do this without this fucknugget but I know we can," Micah challenged.

Shaking my head, I continued, "What happened

tonight proves that's not true. If he hadn't come for me, I would have died. I was already on the verge of passing out as it was. No, we can't do this without him. I'm certain of it now." Exhausted from the encounter, I sagged against Hudson who was sitting beside me. "The Dark Lord is who's been sending me the nightmares. He wanted me tired and off my game and it worked."

"Sunshine, we're all under a massive amount of stress. Don't let the Dark Lord fill you with fear," Hudson cautioned.

Anger spiked through me at his cavalier take on this, causing me to shoot to my feet. "You don't get it! I almost died next to you in my sleep, with no one around to help me!" The shock and hurt on Hudson's face told me I'd gone too far but none of them besides Parker was understanding how screwed we were. "Parker has to stay at the house from now on. I don't give a shit what any of you think about this. It's my life that hangs in the balance if something goes wrong. He's the only one who can get to me if I ever need him again."

Brayden was the first of them to approach me, taking my hands in his and lifting them to his lips. "All we want is for you to be safe, Lailah. If that means Parker stays in the house then that's what will happen. You come first, no matter what. Seeing the marks on your neck has left us all a little shaken, knowing you got hurt under our watch. I'm sorry that we forgot to consider your feelings in our panic."

This was the magic of Brayden. He was my rock, the man who kept me grounded in reality. "I'm sorry too." I turned back to Hudson who was still sitting on the bed, trying to hide his feelings. "Hudson, I shouldn't have yelled at you like that. You didn't deserve that from me. Just...

when I didn't think this whole thing could get worse, it did, and I lashed out at all of you." I pulled away from Brayden and kissed Hudson tenderly, putting all my feelings for him into it. The one thing Hudson always struggled with was arguing. Any kind of yelling from me reminded him of his stepmother.

"Thank you for your apology. I shouldn't have brushed off your feelings either. None of us responded well in the heat of the moment." Hudson sighed, resting his head against mine. "But as Brayden said, if Parker needs to be back in the house then he can stay in the guestroom on the first floor."

"Wasn't there a loft over the garage?" Micah muttered.

"For tonight, let's just have him on the first floor. We'll figure out a more thought-out situation for all of us when we aren't all on high alert," Brayden suggested as he climbed into my bed. "Sorry, Angel, I know Hudson wanted a night with just you, but I won't be able to sleep if I can't hear you breathing."

I wasn't going to argue with him, feeling the need to have them all close. Before getting back into bed, I pulled on sleep shorts and a t-shirt that read *Nope. Not today.* I felt it was fitting and the need for any and all comforts was welcome right now. Parker left the room and I curled up with my four guys joining me in bed. It made me the center of the puppy pile, giving them a sense of purpose as they protected me from anything else that might show up in the night. The chances of the Dark Lord pulling the same trick twice seemed unlikely, but it took me a long time to fall back asleep.

The rest of the night was uneventful but as we all gathered around the kitchen, it was a tense atmosphere as the guys watched the coffee maker work. When the whistle of the kettle blew, it made everyone jump, and I almost dropped the mug I was holding, waiting for the water. Taking a shaky breath, I set the mug aside and turned off the burner, cutting off the sound and setting us all at ease.

"Looks like my PTSD is rubbing off on all of you," I muttered.

No one responded to my comment as the coffee maker beeped and they passed it around as if it had some magical power to cure all evil.

"I was thinking," Hudson said, breaking the silence first. "We should reach out to Nona and see if she has any thoughts on a way to protect you while you're sleeping. We can make barriers for places. Why can't we create one for the mind?"

"Man, that's a smart idea," Brayden agreed, perking up a bit then just as quickly it faded. "Wouldn't she have said something before about it?"

"No, we thought the dreams were part of her trauma. But now that we know they're being sent to her, it changes things," Hudson countered. "Yes, the Dark Lord has slipped into her mind before. We've all seen it, but that was before she was bound to most of us. That has to offer more protection, right?"

I hopped up on the counter, bobbing my tea bag as I thought over the idea. "It's worth asking. No one has had to deal with this, so it could be as simple as not having thought to look for a solution. I'll call her later today. Right now, I'm just not up for dealing with her analytical inquisition."

Jay walked up to me, settling his hands on my thighs

and pinning me to the counter. "Tell me the truth. How are you feeling right now?"

Giving Jay a sad smile, I set my mug down and wrapped my arms around his neck, just wanting to be held for a moment. He responded immediately, caging me in with his body as if he could stop the whole world from getting to me. "I'm alive, pissed off, and ready for all this to be over. It needs to stop, Jay. I can't keep gluing myself back together each time the Dark Lord decides to come and rip me apart. One of these times, I won't be able to do it and I'll be left a husk of what I once was."

"I will never let that happen, Beautiful. Even if I have to put you back together myself. It kills me to see you like this, knowing I can't find them and bring you their heads on a platter like you deserve. This is the first time I've failed everyone I love. It doesn't sit well with me," Jay shared, baring his heart to me. "If I can't fix you at the end of this, then we'll be broken together."

Fisting a hand in my hair, he pulled my head up and seared his lips to mine, trapping me in a kiss that was harsh. His emotions bled through to me as we kissed, showing me what he hid from everyone else—he was terrified of losing everything. While I was the one the Dark Lord was targeting, the others were dealing with pain of their own in all this. None of us would leave this battle unscathed by the demons we fought against. We would need each other to pick up the pieces along the way. Breaking the kiss, I gasped for air as we both just clung to each other, sharing the burden we both carried.

"Something needs to change. We've been on the defensive, reacting to whatever they throw at us," I whispered. "I think it's about time we take the battle to them, don't you?"

"Couldn't have said it better, Beautiful," Jay answered,

pressing a kiss to my forehead. "I think it's time my father and I had another chat as well. He is a member of the Elementi even if he runs his own military. We're going to need all the help we can get and he owes it to my mother to show up, no matter what we find."

"Lailah," Parker called out from somewhere in the house.

Pulling back from Jay, I saw him enter the kitchen with papers in his hands. When he looked up and saw the situation he froze and started to leave. "I'll come back—"

"What did you need?" I asked as Jay shifted to lean on the counter next to me.

Parker hesitated then decided to take me at my word. "These bank statements you went through last night for Aplite, why did you highlight these five? I can't see the connection to them or anything else we've been looking into."

"That's why I highlighted them," I answered with a shrug. "Everything else made sense, but why in the world would you need to order that much copy paper, or napkins for a business that we aren't even sure has a building? I ran the program you set up for me to input the account numbers too and they were all supply companies. When I looked up the websites, it was all office goods. When I matched the invoices to the vendor, they came up with, a company in South Africa. Clearly, paper goods weren't what they ordered, but I didn't know how to dig any deeper than that."

Parker's eyes went wide as he rushed forward to hug me, making Jay grunt as he got shoved into the counter. "You did it, Trouble! Holy shit, you found the breadcrumb we needed to bust this wide open!"

I patted him on the back, loving the fact I was getting a hug from him since he gave the best hugs ever, but flinching at the use of his nickname for me. I'd told him he couldn't use that anymore. It hurt too much to hear, knowing we didn't have that relationship at the moment.

"Care to share with the rest of the class what's happening?" Brayden asked, as Parker released me and took a few steps back.

He waved the sheets at them, barely able to keep still. "When I couldn't figure out the connection I looked up the vendor myself. This company is in South Africa and I would bet my left nut that it supplies their base of operations."

"I don't follow," Jay commented, frowning.

"This company doesn't ship anything outside the country or outside the southern half of the continent. It gives us a location to start with! Now we can fly to South Africa and get a meeting with someone in the company. We can get them to tell us what they really sent them and where. This is the break we needed, and we almost missed it because we were looking for something more obscure. Since no one has really looked into this company before, they wouldn't know they don't have a brick-and-mortar place of business, so even on taxes and things, they would assume to have office supplies accounted for. Lailah is a fucking genius and put it all together even if she didn't realize it!"

"So we're going to South Africa?" Micah asked as if he didn't really believe what Parker was saying.

"Cape Town to be exact," Parker answered with a grin.

Micah nodded and hobbled his way out of the kitchen. "I'll get the plane ready for us to leave tomorrow."

I couldn't help but smile to myself. Finally, we had

enough to make a move. Once we had whatever information we could get from this company, it was time to bring the fight right to the Dark Lord's doorstep. The Elementi have been waiting for this day for centuries and it was time to see what they were made of.

CHAPTER 9
LAILAH

Sitting on the plane looking out the window, I didn't quite believe we were heading off to Cape Town with a meeting scheduled with the head of one of the world's largest supplier companies, Pride Resources. Yesterday, we did as much research about the company as we could, so we knew what we were getting into and who to talk to. It helped to have the sons of some of the most well-known families in business as my partners, allowing us to get a meeting with whoever we requested. They had items that would be useful to all the different businesses their families owned so it was easy to pretend we were looking for a new supplier.

"How did your parents take the news?" Parker asked, sitting across from me.

I'd decided not to tell them where I was going or what we would be doing when we got there. I made sure that Cami and Beth knew what was going on so they could contact them if it was needed, but my parents needed to stay out of this whole thing. "They didn't like it but there isn't much they can do about it when I won't give them more information."

"Your mom just worries and your dad only sees you as his little girl. Once this is all over, I'm sure they'll understand why you chose to keep them out of the loop," he said, giving me a half-smile.

"How do your parents deal with all this? You all fly around the world, living a completely different life without fear that they'll get involved," I questioned, knowing they hadn't really checked in with their family much since coming out to Wisconsin.

Parker shrugged, looking out the window at the clouds below. "The moment they learned we were Elementi Knights, they no longer controlled our lives—the Elementi did. We went to training all summer long then back to school until we graduated. Instead of the split, it became a full-time gig to train while at school, giving us a slight break for the holidays and the summer. If you hadn't been struggling the way you were, we wouldn't have left for the summer. Instead, it would have been intensive training to get you closer to where we are in skills and knowledge. That's our life, to be the weapons against the demons, always ready to be sent on a mission someplace. Personally, I think they would have pulled us out of school completely if we didn't need to keep up appearances for the outside world."

"You know, the more we talk about the Elementi, the more it sounds like they're just as evil as the demons," I commented, trying to fight against my anger at the whole thing. "The moment they found out who I was, they started to control my life without my knowledge. How is that not considered something the angels would disapprove of?"

Parker let out a dark chuckle as he met my gaze. "That's

where the whole freewill thing comes into play. The angels can't control what we do, only judge the intentions of our heart, which is what they care about. To be honest, I'm surprised I wasn't stripped of my powers once the Oath was broken because now I'm tainted goods."

"Guess that means your heart is still in the right place," I whispered, dropping my eyes to the book I'd been staring at but not really reading.

"There is only one person who I want to believe that, but it won't be easy to convince them of that. In the meantime, I will do my damndest to prove that I'm worth the effort," Parker stated.

I knew he was talking about me. Even though having him around all the time again the past few days hadn't been as hard as I thought it would be, I wasn't willing to accept things could be fixed. We fell into a comfortable silence and soon he fell asleep, his snoring filling the air of the cabin, making the guys glare at him. Choosing not to be bothered by it, I slipped on my headphones and reclined my chair, letting my music pull me into that place between wakefulness and sleeping.

"*Synergy...*"

My eyes snapped open, terror flooding my body, but the moment I saw I wasn't in the darkness, I relaxed. Instead, I found myself lost in a vast world of bright white light with a being in front of me, wings unfurled behind them. I'd been here once before when I first accessed my powers and the angel told me who I was and what my mission was.

"*Synergy, it is time to complete your mission.*"

A sense of bone-deep weariness settled over me at their words, making me snarky. "Really, I wouldn't have guessed that with how well things are going. You sure it's time?"

The angel ignored my words and stepped closer to me.

"You and your knights must defeat the evil that is flooding the earth before all is lost. This was never what God intended for his people, but they chose to allow the demons to gain a stronghold in their world. You six are the only hope because we of the Heavens can't intercede. It's forbidden."

"So you want us to clean up your mess? The demons should never have been able to make this happen. Aren't you supposed to keep them banished to Hell? What if we say no?" I challenged.

A glowing hand reached out and pressed on my heart. *"You will not say no. The reason you were chosen as Synergy is the love you have for others. Who else could love five men the way you do? Even when one has broken your heart and betrayed your trust, you do not cast him aside as many would. Do not let the demons win by hardening your heart. You are stronger than you or the demons realize. Trust your heart and the men who each hold a piece of it."*

"How can you say that when you voided the Oath between me and Parker?" I snapped, shoving the hand away, but I never made contact. It just went right through the arm like it wasn't even there.

"We did remove the Oath between you. When he gave the Oath, he thought he understood what he was saying, but he didn't. We needed him to learn, to lose, to suffer, and to grow. It might seem cruel to you and him, but it is like when you prune a bush to help it grow bigger and stronger. It might hurt initially but the benefit outweighs the harm. All things will work out for the better... have faith in the knowledge that they were created for you and you were created for them. No one but the six of you can bring down this evil. We just needed to wait for the right time before bringing you into the world," the angel answered.

Everything about this was crazy. None of it made sense. If the angels were able to make this happen then why couldn't they clean up their own mess? Was God that cold that he would just abandon us to this fate because he wouldn't step in?

"No!" the angel barked. *"Do not let those thoughts dwell in your mind. They are from the devil and his minions. Everything about this is going according to God's perfect plan. You might not see it but have faith and trust. What else do you have if not faith?"*

The force that the angel said this made me take a step back in surprise. Who knew you could piss off an angel?

"When you return to wakefulness, all of you will be rejuvenated and healed. It is all we can do from this point forward. Heed my words, Synergy. Without faith and trust in each other, there is nothing else..."

A flash of white light blinded me and I gasped as I woke up, almost falling out of my seat as I got my bearings.

"Trouble, what's wrong?" Parker asked as he kneeled in front of me, resting a hand on my knee. "I didn't feel anything demonic."

Clutching my heart, I shook my head. "No demons this time. It was an angel."

Shoving out of my chair, I got up and looked back at the others who were all sprawled out, sleeping peacefully. Would it ever be safe for me to sleep anymore? If it wasn't demons coming to kill me, it was angels forcing their plans on me.

"Lailah..." Parker spoke tentatively, resting a hand on my shoulder. "Talk to me. What happened?"

"I need to wake the others up. This is something we all need to talk about." I sighed, letting my shoulder lean into his touch a moment before I stepped away.

I wanted to believe that Parker and I would be able to figure this out, but I just wasn't willing to allow myself to get hurt by anyone right now. I was too shattered and barely holding myself together as it was. My issues with him would just have to wait on the back burner longer.

"Guys," I called out as I shook Brayden's shoulder then Jay's. "Come on, guys, I need you to wake up. Something's happened."

It worried me slightly that it took so much effort to get them awake but once they were, I noticed something different about them. All of us had been working ourselves to the bone and still recovering from the car accident that was almost a week and a half ago. Now, any lingering bruises they had were gone, along with the shadows under their eyes from lack of sleep.

"What happened? Was it the Dark Lord?" Micah asked, getting to his feet without any sign of pain from his knee. He took a step toward me then paused as he seemed to register the change. "What the fuck! My knee doesn't hurt, like at all. As if it never happened."

"Ah yeah, that's what I wanted to talk to you guys about," I shared, causing all of them to snap to attention.

Hudson frowned at me. "Did you do something to us? I feel the most rested I have since before New Year's."

That broke my heart, knowing that was when my nightmares and PTSD started. "So I was just visited by an angel—"

Brayden's jaw dropped at this. "I'm sorry, what? Did you just say an angel came to you?"

"Unless I've completely lost my mind, which could totally be a thing at this point, they came to tell me it was time for us to end this fight with the Dark Lord," I explained. "At the end, they said something about healing all of us but I didn't think that was actually going to happen."

"Holy shit, I got healed by an angel," Micah muttered to himself as he hopped around, testing out his knee. "The things we experience in this life are just crazy, you know that, right?"

"What else?" Jay asked, crossing his arms as if expecting something bad.

I took a seat on the couch now that Micah didn't need to keep his leg elevated. "They just kept telling me that I needed to trust that we could do this, that everything was planned. We knew it was time for this fight to come to an end, but now it's as if that's the only hope humanity has to survive. If we fail, the rest of the world will go to shit. The demons will run the show and God will let it happen because we did it to ourselves. If I'm understanding the cryptic way the angel kept talking, we are God's way of saving the world... like, no pressure."

"Wow, that's kind of heavy," Parker grumbled. "Did they have any good news?"

"Not unless you count the fact that they took the Oath from you to teach you and help you grow into a better person. Do you feel better for them doing that to you?" I asked, pissed that they would fuck us both over like that just to prune the dead weight from us.

Parker's face turned dark as he processed what I said. "They did this to us?"

"Ha! Sorry, douchenozzle, you don't get to blame the angels for your fuckup. She just said they stripped the Oath from you for the stunt you pulled. That doesn't fix the fact you did what you did," Micah cut in, poking Parker in the chest as he spoke.

"I know what I did, Micah!" Parker roared. "The agony of having her look at me with pain and sadness kills me! Nothing I do will ever atone for how I hurt her, but I can learn to be better and never cause her that much pain ever again. Trust me when I tell you that your daily reminders of my fuckups are not needed. I'm very good at reminding myself."

This seemed to be enough to make Micah back off and take a seat next to me, pulling me to his side with his arm wrapped around my waist. It was like he wanted to prove to Parker that he was on the outside physically. I understood his feelings, but I believed that Parker agonized over his choices all the time. "Enough, please. This isn't helpful to anyone, especially since the angel made it clear that we need all six of us to pull this off. They said we were made for each other, that they were waiting for the right time for us to be brought into the world so we could end things with the Dark Lord and the demons. Somehow, we need to find a way to at least be able to fight alongside each other."

"I don't give a fuck what those angels or God himself says. I don't trust that fucker to watch my back," Micah spat.

Parker glared at him. "Then let's hope I'm a better man than you and I decide to keep you alive through this battle. It would certainly make my life easier to just have a demon kill you off."

"Stop! Parker, you sit over there and, Micah, shut the hell up," I growled. "None of this is helping us figure out how to even find the Dark Lord before the world goes to hell—literally."

CHAPTER 10

MICAH

If Lailah hadn't told us we couldn't win this fight without Parker, I would've thrown him out of the plane in a heartbeat. That fucking bastard didn't deserve to breathe the same air that the woman I loved more than life itself breathed. She'd already endured so much, without Parker having fucked up and broken a piece of her heart. The images of her sobbing in their arms when they got home and refused to let Parker back into the house is burned into my mind. It killed me to know I'd seen the writing on the wall but the others didn't agree with me about how to deal with the issue. They were at fault as much as I was but that didn't help things now that the fucker was weaseling his way back into her life. Over my dead body would I let Parker hurt her again, no matter how much Lailah wanted to keep him around.

"What's the plan for Cape Town?" I asked, turning to Jay. This was his operation. He knew the best way to handle getting the information they wanted.

"It will work best if Brayden or Hudson act as the person looking for a new supply holder since they have the largest companies that have a building. My father's company could work but I don't want them to know we have a private military at our beck and call. It'll put them on edge," Jay explained. "Micah, I know things are being worked out, now that you and Lailah are bonded, but your family business is more political and own property so it wouldn't make as much sense."

"So we're just going to ignore that my pop owns the largest tech company in the eastern hemisphere?" Parker grumbled, glaring at me like it was my fault.

Jay carried on like Parker hadn't spoken, making me fight to keep a smirk off my face. The idiot had no idea how pissed the rest of us were at him. Jay didn't let anyone fuck with people who were his to protect, and he was feeling a little raw right now with his mom missing. "At some point, someone will need to leave the meeting room and find a computer to put in a jump drive that holds a virus to feed us all their information. We use it on many of our jobs dealing with demons. They like to hide things in plain sight."

"Would it be best to have you do it, Jay, since you're familiar with it?" Lailah asked, worry written on her face.

All of us knew it should be Parker but not a single one of us trusted him to do the job right. It was too important, and it was too soon to give him a job that crucial.

"I need to be in the room to help direct the conversation to see if we can get them to slip up about Aplite. They're going to be our referral to this company so they'll assume we know what they really do," Jay answered.

I groaned when the others looked lost as to what to do. "I'll deal with hacking the computer. I'm the only other one who's comfortable with computers."

"Hey!" Brayden yelled, knowing that comment was directed at him. "I know what I need to know but technology causes so many other issues in our world that I choose not to interact with it."

"We know, you never let me forget it," I muttered.

"Besides, I think it's better that I act as the client since I'm more of a people person than Hudson," Brayden pointed out. "No offense, Hudson."

Hudson just shrugged. "I would have to agree with you. Out of all of us, the one who has the best chance at getting them to spill their secrets would be you. Even Lailah has commented on your silver tongue a time or two."

"Great, so Brayden will do the talking and Jay will look intimidating, while I deal with the computer part of this," I confirmed, going over the plan.

Lailah raised her hand like she was in class or something. I just snorted and snatched up her hand to hold, keeping it from doing anything else.

"What about me and Parker?" she asked.

Jay looked a little worried with what he was about to say. "I think it might be best to have you, Hudson, and Parker stay behind at a hotel. It'll keep you out of sight and throw off the enemy to have us split up since we typically do things together."

Now I knew why he was nervous. Lailah hated to be left out of the action if there was a chance anyone could get hurt. Too many times things went wrong when we didn't have everyone together.

"No, absolutely not!" Lailah snapped. "How can you even suggest that? You know what happens when we split up."

"Beautiful, I understand your worry, but this is going to be the safer option. The Dark Lord doesn't know we're on to him so the less we can draw attention, the better. The world is looking for all of us together, but if there are only a few of us with a legitimate reason to be there, it won't cause waves. No one else knows about what went down in Wisconsin other than the Elementi," Jay reasoned.

I could tell by the set of her jaw that she didn't like the idea but finally she nodded. "Fine, but you will keep in touch with us through the whole process. I refuse to let anything happen to you as we get closer to the lion's den."

"That's fair," Jay agreed, relaxing ever so slightly that she gave in.

Just when we thought we had the matter settled, Parker exploded. "This is a bunch of bullshit and you all know it!"

"Parker," Lailah chastised, frowning.

"No. I'm sorry, Lailah, but this is absolute utter horse-shit. The person who should be doing this is me. I should be going to that meeting, posing as the buyer because I can manipulate his emotions. With a simple suggestion, I can make him more relaxed and at ease with us talking. Getting him to spill his secrets will be as easy as taking candy from a baby. Hell, I might be able to convince him to put the jump drive into his own laptop and give us what we need. You're all ignoring how right I am because you're pissed at me. I get it, you don't trust me to do something this important."

Anger flashed across Lailah's face as she looked at the rest of us. *Fuck, the bastard was about to get us into trouble with her.*

"Is what he's saying true?" she demanded.

Jay didn't back down though he met her head-on. "Yes."

"This isn't about us or our personal issues, guys. How could you be okay with going ahead with a half-assed plan when you have a better option available?" Lailah challenged.

"It isn't wise to put an unknown factor into play on a

mission like this. Parker has proven he isn't reliable to watch our backs. To put him in such a position where we *need* to trust him isn't something I can do," Jay stated, ready to go toe-to-toe with our girl.

Lailah got to her feet and stood in front of Jay, hands on her hips. She wasn't going to back down. "That isn't going to work for me, Jay. I get what you are saying, but wouldn't it be better to have him go with you and Micah, who have no problem beating his ass into the ground if he fucks up, than to miss this chance?"

Welp, if I was worried about her getting soft on Parker, I wasn't now. That shit right there was cold and accurate.

Jay contemplated that a moment. "If we do this, will you stay back at the hotel with Brayden and Hudson without any fuss?"

My brows shot up at this. How could Jay be okay with Parker having such an important role?

"Yes, if you use the best that we have for the mission, I'll feel more comfortable staying back out of sight," Lailah answered, reaching out a hand to shake on the agreement.

That woman has learned how to play each and every one of us. She knew it was more important to keep her safe than to deal with Parker, so in an odd way, they both got what they wanted. After they shook on it, Jay grabbed her and pulled her onto his lap where he then bit down on her spot where her shoulder meets her neck, making her moan. "That was a dirty trick, Beautiful. Don't think I'm not aware of what you just did."

"Someone has to get you guys to pull your heads out of your asses," she quipped.

Jay's response to that was to start tickling her until she was crying and begging for mercy. Then they curled up together and napped the rest of the three hours to Cape Town.

It didn't take long for us to get settled in at the hotel and pull ourselves together for the meeting. Showered and dressed to impress, needing to act the part of Parker's assistant, which made me want to punch him all the more while Jay got to be security. The town car came to pick us up, and we hurried to duck inside, trying to stay out of the open as much as we could. If we could do this entire trip without being noticed, it would be the best-case scenario. Thankfully, none of us had many connections with people in Cape Town, making it easier to stay hidden. Parker sat facing us in the car since neither Jay nor I wanted to sit next to him—childish I know, but this wasn't our first choice to begin with.

"Parker, do you understand what we need to get out of the target?" Jay asked, handing him a tablet that had a picture of the man we were meeting with.

Parker took it and looked over the basics of the man's life so he knew how to manipulate him best. "Believe it or not, this isn't the first time I've done this. My pop liked to take me to meetings to help me gain control of my powers. I, of course, was a stupid shit, and turned it into a game. This time though, I know what's at stake and I won't fuck this up. I'll prove to all of you that I can add value to this mission."

I let out a huff of laughter. "Really, you think that if you prove you learned your lesson that we'll just forget everything else that happened?"

"Fuck you, Micah. You've had it out for me since the day

we met all those years ago. Now you just have the rest of the group behind you, supporting your hate, giving you free rein to fuck with me. Lailah wanted me to work on fixing things between all of us but I don't think that will ever happen for you and me. Once you've decided to write someone off from your life, there isn't a thing on this earth to change your mind," Parker said, his anger edging his words with a bite.

He was right about the fact I never liked him. Something about his attitude always rubbed me the wrong way. I don't know if there was ever going to be a time that we could say that we actually liked each other. Lately, we'd been tolerating each other just so it didn't upset Lailah. If she ended up forgiving him, I didn't know what I would do with that. I didn't think I'd ever be able to leave her in his care.

"Just a reminder, assistants are seen and not heard," Parker shot back as he tossed the tablet to me.

"Don't worry, I can be trusted to play my part. It's you we're all worried about," I rebutted.

Arno Botha, the CFO of the company, was meeting with us, so that proved they weren't messing around and knew Parker's family was a big account that they wanted to land. This meant they would do all they could to make us choose them and that played in our favor. The drive to their headquarters didn't take more than fifteen minutes and after our conversation ended, it was a quiet ride. We had no idea what kind of information we would get from this meeting but I prayed it would be enough to point us toward the next step in this never-ending battle.

We were greeted in the lobby upon our arrival, taken up to the third floor and shown into a conference room. They offered Parker tea or coffee, ignoring us as the help who didn't deserve the same attention as the man holding the money. I sat next to Parker and set the tablet on the table, pretending to take notes about something as we waited. Jay stood like the military man he was. It didn't take long before Arno joined us, shaking Parker's hand then extending it to me as well.

"Thank you for being able to make this meeting on such short notice. We were in the area on other business and it just made sense," Parker shared as we all got settled.

Arno bobbed his head in understanding as he slid over a folder of information and opened it. "I hope I gathered the information you needed. If not, then it should be easy enough to gather quickly. Now, you said that your company is expanding into the region and you wanted a more local source to stock things for your offices?"

"Exactly. Last year, we opened a branch in Dubai and it's been wildly successful. We felt it was time to push our reach even further. Our friends over at Aplite said they had a great experience with you and that we should look into your services," Parker said, slipping that hook into the conversation in a way no one would think twice about.

I watched as a soft glow of purple hung around Parker as he pulled on his power to relax Arno. His shoulders lowered and then his breathing seemed to become deeper, as if he was in a meditative state of mind, completely unconcerned with anything.

"Aplite... yes, they have become one of our biggest clients over the past year. Are you looking to venture into the side of business they are in? Seems odd for a tech company to need *those* types of supplies, or is tech just the front you use?" Arno asked, his words slurred ever so slightly like he was drunk.

"We partner with many companies, one of them being a

large private military group. You know how tech and military always seem to go hand in hand these days. What I want to know is how much can you offer us and if you can get the same things you did for Aplite," Parker pushed, leaning forward, his gaze never breaking from Arno's.

Arno frowned as something Parker said didn't match up with what should have been said. "What exactly did Lord Beelzebub tell you we procured for him?"

"He gave you his true name?" Parker demanded, a worried tone in his voice.

I could see that he was losing Arno with this line of questioning and something needed to be done. "How impressive to be given such a gift in the form of knowing his true name."

"Yes, after I gave up my first-born son to his army, Lord Beelzebub blessed me with the knowledge that my son would help rebuild this world into something greater," Arno shared with a smile. "He even said I was supporting them by getting the supplies they needed. Are you starting a second training camp for those injected with the serum? That would be the only reason he would send you to me and give you the proper code word to use."

All of us froze as Arno told us something more valuable than he could imagine. "Yes, he's moving the battle up and needs to get more followers prepared. I have a thumb drive here that he asked me to give you so you could put whatever information on there we needed, along with the list of items he's gotten from you. This way we don't need to bother our great Lord while he is dealing with the pesky Elementi Knights."

Arno gave us a lazy drunk smile, holding out his hand. "I am always happy to be of help to our Dark Lord. May his reign over this world be long and prosperous."

Catching Jay's eye, he gave a simple nod, telling me he thought this was far too easy. Something else was going on here and I just couldn't put my finger on it, but it was important to figure it out and fast. Just before Arno was going to connect the jump drive to his computer, he typed in a code and that's when it hit me.

Grabbing Parker and Jay, I dropped to the ground taking them with me. "Get under the table now!"

They didn't question me and scrambled to get under the large thick conference table, trying to get to the opposite end from Arno. The world seemed to stop as a small *beep* sounded and the world exploded around us. I took the flames and wrapped them around us, creating a shield of sorts, burning up anything that tried to land on us. What I couldn't stop was the floor underneath us from trembling and shattering apart, sending us careening down to the second floor. Dousing my flames since they would do more harm than good, I felt the wind whip around us. Jay used the air to thrust up at us, slowing our fall so when we landed it wasn't as rough. It also shoved all debris that we could have landed on out of the way, allowing us to survive the bomb with minimal damage.

"We need to get the fuck out of here. I don't know how it happened but someone leaked that we were coming here," Jay shouted over the fire alarm as he pulled me to my feet. "If they've taken Lailah, there is nothing in this world or the next that will stop me from burning hell to the ground."

The look of determination and rage on Jay's face made me thankful that I was on his side, because that man could be one scary motherfucker.

CHAPTER II
LAILAH

The guys had been gone all of ten minutes and I was a nervous wreck. "How will we know if something goes wrong? There is no way for us to reach out to them without causing problems."

"Angel, please come play cards with us. It'll take your mind off of things and help you settle," Brayden suggested, waving me over.

"Do you really think I can focus on playing a card game right now?" I grumbled as I sat down with a huff. "It better be something simple like Go Fish or I'm never going to have a chance."

Hudson chuckled. "If you want to play Go Fish, then we can play Go Fish."

"How are you both so calm?" I demanded, tossing my hair up in a messy bun, tired of dealing with it. "It's like you don't even care that this is crazy dangerous and we are sitting here playing kids games?"

Brayden grabbed my chin and forced me to look him in the face. "I understand you're worried but don't take your feelings out on us. Neither of us deserve it."

He was right. I was anxious and lashing out at them because they were here and safe. I knew they would forgive me if I snapped at them, but Brayden was right, they didn't deserve that from me. "I'm sorry. I just don't like us being apart."

Pulling me with his hold on my chin, Brayden brought me to his lips where he kissed me slowly and deeply. I moaned into his mouth, reaching out to him, needing this contact, to know that they were here with me. When he pulled back, he grinned at me, knowing he'd managed to settle my nerves somewhat. "Angel, trust in your men. We've been training for this all our lives and they will come back to you."

"You really believe that?" I asked, surprised at Brayden's confidence.

"Without a doubt. Those three will come back to you no matter what," Hudson assured me as he moved to stand behind me.

"Three of them... so you don't think all is lost with Parker?" I inquired, pulling out of Brayden's grip, and looking up at Hudson.

Out of all my men, Hudson had been the one to keep his thoughts on Parker to himself. I knew he had an opinion but Hudson wasn't one to share his thoughts until he clearly understood all the facts and could make a judgment.

"This is my humble opinion, but yes, I believe that things between you and Parker can be worked out. He did something that hurt you down to your very soul, but I don't think the connection between you both has been severed completely. The wound will take time to heal but the man I see Parker turning into is willing to wait and work for your forgiveness. The old Parker would do anything and everything to bribe you back to him, using his charms, money, or whatever means he could get ahold of. Now, I'm not you, my sunshine, but I do know how big your heart is," Hudson explained, kissing my temple. "The choice is yours, whatever you decide to do. We will follow your lead."

"Yeah, some more willing than others, but if you choose to give Parker another shot, we won't get in the way," Brayden agreed. "It's your relationship and no one else can tell you how it should work, not even the angels. So if you don't think things can be fixed, don't feel pressured either."

Both of them were presenting me with opposing sides of the same argument, but they were trying to support me either way. "I'll keep what you said in mind. Right now, I just need us to get through this next part so I can have them safe and sound where I can see them."

With that settled, they talked me into playing a few rounds of Speed with them, the fast-paced nature of the game forcing me to give it my full attention. My focus was so fixed that when a booming knock came at the door, I almost fell out of the chair that I was kneeling on.

"Police! Open the door!" a man shouted.

I gaped at the guys as I felt like my eyes would pop out of my head. I was so shocked. "What is going on?"

"I don't know but I don't like it one bit," Brayden said through clenched teeth. "Stay back. I'm going to take a look."

The man pounded on the door, repeating the same thing over again, his voice even louder, if that was possible. Brayden peeked through the peephole in the door and swore. "Shit, it is the police. Don't say anything and let me handle this."

Hudson wrapped an arm around me, holding me tight to his side as Brayden opened the door. No sooner had he turned the handle then a swarm of men dressed in blue uniforms with *police* written across their Kevlar vests entered. One grabbed Brayden, slamming him up against the wall, pulling cuffs out and slapping them on his wrists. "You're under arrest for the bombing of Pride Resourses."

"What?" I blurted, not understanding. "Was there a bomb there? Do you know if everyone's alright? Did everyone make it out?" I demanded as I was dragged away from Hudson and had my own hands cuffed behind my back.

"Shut the fuck up. We don't owe you any answers," the cop snarled, dragging me out of the room.

None of this made sense. Why would they think we were the ones to set a bomb off there? How did they even know we were here in this hotel? The guys had used fake names for the booking and we'd flown in on a private jet. Nothing we did should have been traced that fast... unless. There had to be someone in the Elementi spilling our secrets, and they had to be extremely high up in the system to do it. Beth and Cami were the only ones we'd talked to, but I refused to believe it was either of them. This had the Dark Lord written all over it. He was pissed that his plan didn't work to just kill me off. Now he had to get rid of me another way, and it seemed he found it.

"Where are you taking us? I'm an American citizen," I stated, hoping that would mean something here, but I didn't put much hope in it.

"I believe I already told you that I wasn't going to give you any answers. Now move it or be dragged the rest of the way, your choice," the officer barked, shoving me forward.

Knowing this was a losing battle, with so many of them against the three of us, I complied. They led the three of us out of the hotel and shoved us into the back of a van with *police* written on the outside. Two officers got in the back with us, making sure we didn't cause any trouble while two more got into the front seats. They put the sirens on and blasted out onto the streets as if the hounds of hell were coming after them whi,ch made no sense to me. If they were the police, there would be no need for them to make a mad dash from the scene like that... unless.

"Who do you *really* work for?" I demanded, glaring at one of the men sitting in front of me. "I know it's not the police, so my guess is the Dark Lord or one of his minions."

One of them just gave me an evil grin as he chuckled, but didn't answer. He didn't need to. That told me everything I needed to know. Instead, I turned to Hudson and Brayden who looked furious to be sitting there unable to do a damn thing. If these people were actual humans, then our spirit weapons wouldn't do anything to them, but if they were hosts for demons, it might give us the upper hand. First, we needed to create a distraction or throw them off their game.

"I'm really impressed that there aren't any major potholes in the road. One would think with the ocean so close the salt would eat away at the asphalt," I mused, looking out the front window, trying my best to catch Brayden's eye. "Wow, we're heading for the coastline. It's so pretty. You know, we didn't get much time to explore before you came to kidnap us." If Brayden couldn't catch on maybe Hudson would.

"Shut the hell up before we make you," the driver growled.

I just clicked my tongue in irritation. "Sorry, I'm just nervous. An enormous wave or a crack in the ground might open up, killing us all. It's the PTSD from the fun times I had with the Dark Lord."

For some reason, I was channeling my inner Cami right

now to keep from losing my shit as I tried to get us out of this mess. I'm not sure I could have made my point any clearer but neither of the guys seemed to show any sign of understanding. In fact, Hudson had his eyes closed and was relaxing as we flew down the coastal highway to God knows where.

Just when I thought all hope might be lost, the ground rumbled and rocks from the cliffs we were driving next to pelted the van, making the driver swerve to avoid crashing into a boulder that landed in the road. "Fuck! Someone, knock them out! They're trying to use their powers on us. The Dark Lord warned us they were tricky," the driver yelled back. He seemed to be the leader of the bunch.

Before the guards across from us could make their move, I lunged forward, crashing into both of them. It was a mess of limbs as I kicked out, clipping one of them in the jaw as the other tried to shove me off him. I'd managed to hook my hands on his utility belt, clinging on for dear life as the van jerked to the right, slamming me into the bogus cop who got smashed up against the wall of the vehicle.

"No, no, this can't be happening! There is no way they could do that!" the man in the passenger seat screamed. He tossed his door open and leaped out of the still moving van.

What had gotten him so freaked out? Then I saw it as the road curved—a massive wave was rushing toward us and there was no way to avoid it. Looking around the van, I tried to see something I could grab onto but with my hands behind my back it made it all that more challenging. There was a bar running along the length of the van for them to hook cuffs to. It wasn't the best idea, but it was the only one as I lay on my side and gripped the bar with both hands. This was going to hurt, but there was no way I was going to let them kill us to make way for the Dark Lord.

Hudson opened his eyes and when he saw what was coming, he gulped. "Brayden, you better hold on to something. It seems my powers are a lot stronger than I anticipated."

"Fucking hell," Brayden muttered as he turned to grip the honeycomb metal sheet keeping us separated from the front of the van.

The wave rocked the van to the left before the wave picked it up and slammed it into the cliffs. My arms ached as they got wrenched by the impact as I clung to the bar for dear life. The wave seemed to carry us as it swept back toward the ocean, taking us off the road and tumbling under the water's surface as we rolled. Unable to hold on any longer, I face-planted on the chest of one of the guards while the other landed on top of me, creating a cushion each time we slammed into the side of the van. Finally it stopped, and before I could even think about how glad I was to survive, water started to fill the van. I was trapped with a body on top of me but using every bit of strength and determination I had, I shoved him off.

My fingers brushed something metal on his belt, and I discovered it was a key for the cuffs secured to his belt by one of those retractable cords. Fumbling for what seemed like an eternity, I got one cuff undone so I could flip around and see what I was doing this time. Now free, I ripped the key off his belt and went for Brayden who was unconscious, blood dripping from a cut on his forehead. Getting his hands free, I shook him. "Brayden, you need to get up. Please, my love, I *need* you to wake up and save us one more time."

With a groan, his eyes fluttered open. "What the hell happened?"

"No time to explain. I need you to use your power to lift

us out of this water before the ocean becomes our permanent resting grounds. While I love the beach, I'm not planning on dying here," I said, speaking as fast as I could, feeling the water sloshing around my ankles.

"Is Hudson okay?" Brayden asked as if he didn't hear what I just said.

Grabbing his face I forced him to look at me. "Brayden, get us out of the water."

"Right, okay, give me a sec. My brain is pretty rattled," he muttered, bringing a hand to his forehead and hissed when he touched the wound.

I left him to pull himself together, and I freed Hudson and tried to wake him up. If Brayden couldn't get us out of this, then I hoped to God Hudson had some power leftover to use. This was the first time either of them had used so much. I didn't know how I knew but both of them were running low. As I checked over Hudson, I couldn't see anything wrong with him but he wasn't waking up no matter what I tried.

"Lailah, I don't think I've got it in me to do this. My head is killing me and I can't tell up from down, with how dark it is," Brayden whispered, anger tinging his words.

Reaching out to him, I could feel the self-loathing that he couldn't do this for me. He couldn't save us and we were counting on him to do just that. My white knight was convinced that he was going to fail us when we needed him the most.

Crawling over to him, I straddled his legs and pressed my body against his everywhere I could, then I wrapped my arms around his neck before sealing my lips to his. I poured my power into him. This was my purpose. I could give and take energy from any of them, doubling the strength of our combined powers. As I shoved as much power into him as I could, he clung to me, drinking it all in and sending it right back out into the earth below us. The water was around our waists now but it didn't matter, because together, Brayden and I were going to do this.

The van groaned as it started to be pushed up out of the water. It moved steadily, but I didn't stop our endless loop of power as I charged us both full of power. This was how we were going to beat the Dark Lord, together as a team supporting each other, making us that much stronger. If I could create this much power with one of my bonded men just thinking of what it would be like with four of them was crazy. The angel had been right. I'd been holding back, not trusting myself or these men of mine to push things to the limit.

When the sun flooded the van once more and the water receded, I opened my eyes and pulled back from Brayden just enough to see us once again above the water. "You can stop now. You saved us," I murmured against his lips.

"No, *we* did it. There was no way I could have done that on my own," Brayden corrected as he rested his forehead against mine. "Holy shit, I can't believe that just happened. Hudson created a tsunami."

"Yeah, he sure did, and it was awesome." I chuckled.

CHAPTER 12
LAILAH

Now wasn't the time to celebrate things, since we were still trapped in a van with men who wanted to kidnap us or possibly even kill us. Then there was the whole bit about Pride Resources getting blown up. I had to believe that those three were safe. Seeing as I was still alive, it had to be true, since everyone kept telling us if one of them died, I would know or it would kill us all at the same time. The van was lying on its side and the metal grating keeping us from the front was bent and hanging, giving me enough room to squeeze through.

"Brayden, keep an eye on Hudson and see if you can't handcuff the fake officers to the van. I'm going to see how far out from the shoreline we are," I said, already wiggling my way up front.

The driver and other guards were in a heap, since neither of them had put their seatbelts on. The windshield was splintered but remained intact. I remembered Jay telling me some special film held it together so it didn't shatter and hurt the person in the car. I could kick it out and get a clear view of what was going on. It was a lot harder than the movies made it seem but I managed and gasped at the destruction the rockslide and wave had caused to the shoreline.

An entire section of the road was washed away as if there'd never been a way to drive through. There were a few cars stopped with people milling about, looking at the disaster that happened, spanning the width of a mile. One of the guys groaned behind me and before he could even open his eyes, I kicked him right in the head. I'd had enough of playing nice through this whole nightmare. I was over it. It was time to put away Lailah, the lost girl who didn't know what she wanted for her life, and instead pull from my strength as Synergy to make her mark in the world.

Quickly, I cuffed the two men together and then cuffed one of them to the door they were lying on in case they wanted to come after us. Sending up a prayer, I hit the unlock button and the faint *snick* told me we were home free. The back of the van had two doors, making it easier for us to get out of this damn vehicle than trying to get the guys to fit past the grate to get up here. Making my way back, I kneeled next to Hudson who still wasn't waking up even as Brayden tried splashing water on his face.

"I wonder if it's because his powers are too low," I mused.

"At this point, anything would be worth a try so we can get out of here and back to shore," Brayden grumbled, wiping the blood from his face with the shirt he'd removed.

It was then I noticed that the cut was gone, and the swelling had also reduced. Reaching out, I grabbed his chin and moved his head around, looking him over as if I'd been mistaken about where the injury had been. No matter where I looked, he was fine. "How do you feel?"

"Pissed the fuck off, but surprisingly good for all we've just been through. My head aches but nothing I can't handle. I'm more impressed that the bleeding stopped. Scalp wounds are known to be bad bleeders," Brayden rambled, not realizing just how impressive that really was.

"It's gone," I said, pointing to his head. "The gash you had is gone, like it never happened."

He blinked at me. "What do you mean? How could it just be gone? Did an angel come and heal us again?"

"No, I think *I* did. When I was giving you power, what if I also healed you?" I whispered.

Quickly, I turned to Hudson and took his face in my hands, leaning down so my forehead touched his. This time I let my power slowly fill Hudson from his big toe all the way up to his head, completely replenishing his energy. When he started to overflow with my power, I pulled it back into myself, only to cycle it back to him, like a current of energy was flowing between us, giving and receiving. As I did this, I felt more of his own power entering the mix, his blue swirling with my gold until the blue overtook it. Then I seemed to have this sense to just filter out my own power, leaving the blue energy behind, refilling him until it was bursting out of him.

"Lailah..." Hudson groaned as his eyes started to blink open.

It was at that point I noticed his glasses were missing. "I'm right here. The world might be a little foggy since your glasses fell off so don't be surprised."

"I can see perfectly," he shared, sitting up slowly, rubbing his eyes with the palms of his hands as if he didn't believe it himself. "What happened to me? I feel like I could swim across the ocean."

"Funny you should say that because we're gonna need

to swim back to shore. I got us out of the water but I'm not sure I should mess with the earth more than I already have," Brayden said as he got up and kicked open the back doors, showing our situation. "That wave you created could have taken out a small city but thankfully the cliffs kept it from getting too out of control."

The men who'd kidnapped us stirred, and I wondered if they might be a little more forthcoming with their information now that they got beat to hell. I turned to the guy closest to me and patted him roughly on the cheek. "Hey, buddy, you in there?"

He moaned but managed to open his eyes. Peering down at him, I waited for the understanding of what happened to register in his brain. "How are we not dead?"

"That would be because I need something from you," I answered. "Who sent you to kidnap us and where were you going to take us?"

"Why the hell would I tell you anything when you're just going to kill me?"

"Oh, I'm not going to kill you. In fact, I'm not going to do anything to you at all," I responded, my eyes wide at his thought process.

He searched my face as if that would tell him if I was lying. Since I'm not very good at lying, it was a safe bet he would be able to spot one if I had. "I don't know who the guy is, but we were paid to falsely accuse you of the bombing and lock you away in jail. We couldn't kill you but we had to make sure you couldn't leave or get word out to anyone that you'd been taken. This was only supposed to be a simple grab-and-go job. We'd been warned about your powers but I didn't believe it was that big of a threat."

"Seems that was shortsighted of you," Hudson

commented. "Are you ready, Sunshine? I don't think they know anything all that helpful to us."

"Yeah, I think you're right. We need to find the others and see what they've learned." I sighed and headed for the back door of the van.

"Hey! You can't leave me here! You said you wouldn't kill me!" the cop begged.

Glancing over my shoulder, I shrugged. "I said I wasn't going to do *anything* to you, including help you get out of here. Let's hope for your sake that someone decides to check out this random floating van in the ocean in time to save you."

"I thought the Elementi were supposed to be the good guys who couldn't sin?" he called after us.

"Yeah, well that all changed once I showed up and the Dark Lord made it personal," I answered and dove into the ocean.

It didn't take us long to get to shore and find someone who was willing to take us back to the hotel. Since they were dirty cops, I had to hope that there wouldn't be any more issues with them showing up. The three of us needed clean clothes and cellphones to try and reach out to the others. Jay made us all switch out our phones for burners that couldn't be traced. This again made it clear that someone was spilling our secrets, and we needed to get to the bottom of that before we could make our next move.

I dialed Cami's number, and she picked it up right away. "Lala, tell me you're okay!"

"What? How did you know we'd been taken by dirty cops?" I asked, confused at how she knew already.

"I'm sorry, what? You got kidnapped?! I was talking about the bomb going off at Pride. How the hell did you manage to get kidnapped on top of that?" she demanded.

Okay, now that made more sense. If they were tracking the news or activity in Cape Town, they would know about the explosion. "We split up. The guys seemed to think it would draw less attention if all of us didn't go. They knew the Dark Lord was after me so they had Brayden and Hudson stay back with me while the others went to the meeting."

"They let Parker go on the mission?" Cami questioned, her tone surprised.

"Cami, we all know he was the best person to sweet talk information out of people and is the best at technology and hacking if we needed it. It would have been stupid not to have him go," I snapped.

There was a pause on the other end of the line telling me that I might have been a little too harsh to Cami. "Well, damn girl. Clearly getting kidnapped is not something that puts you in a chipper mood. For the record, I get why you picked Parker to go and I agree with you he was the best choice. I'm just surprised Super Trooper and Flame Boy went along with it, since they are team 'kill Parker' is all. Moving on—what do you need from me?"

"Someone has to be giving out information about us. There is no way that someone could know that we split up, or that we were even in Cape Town but you, Beth, and whoever else you guys told. Something's not adding up. However they're getting information is going to get us killed. The people who tried to kidnap us were dirty cops who were going to frame us for the bombing," I explained. "How can we be missing something that's right in front of our faces?"

"Fucking cunt-camels," Cami swore. "Alright, I'll see what I can do and get Maggs to help me since she can do the tech things I can't. You guys deal with things on your end and I promise I will figure out what the fuck is going on."

The simple promise took a weight off my shoulders that I didn't realize was slowly crushing me with worry. Hanging up with her, I noticed Brayden was on the phone so I turned to Hudson who was on the couch with his eyes closed. "Hey, who's Brayden talking to?"

"He's trying to find out where they took the people they rescued from the blast. Figured we could start at the hospitals since none of the guys are answering their phones," he answered, opening his blue eyes to meet mine.

Even though I'd restored his power, it seemed the energy high was short lived. His body was tired even if he had more than enough power to flood the whole city. "Should we leave someone here just in case they couldn't call us?"

"That's a smart thought but do we really want to split up even more than we already have? You were right when you said it was a bad idea," Hudson pointed out. "Nothing ever good happens when we're separated."

I curled up beside him, letting my head rest on his shoulder as my adrenaline came down, leaving me to feel every sore muscle. It would seem while I could heal the guys, I couldn't do it to myself. That was fine with me. I could deal with the bruises and soreness.

"No, no, I will not call back later. You can put me on hold but I'm not going to be ignored," Brayden growled into the phone. "Trust me when I tell you it will be safer for everyone if you don't make me come down there to look through every room myself." He paused as he listened to whoever was speaking. "Oh really, I see, then since that will be more convenient for you, we'll be down there ASAP." When he hung up the phone, he chucked it onto the bed where it harmlessly bounded to a stop. "They don't have any information to give us and if we want to look over the dead bodies, they're conducting viewings."

I could feel the blood run out of my face and my body turned to stone at the idea that they could be dead. "There's no way they can be dead! I'd know if they were dead. The Bond would tell me if they died."

Son of a bitch! Why hadn't I thought of that sooner?

Closing my eyes, I reached out to the glowing balls of silver and red energy that I held within me. Clinging to them, I sent my power down the line, calling out to them, begging for any kind of response to let me know they were alive. Jay's energy flared to life, and I got a pulse of emotions. It was love mixed with fear and anger. Jay was alive! Then I was hit next with Micah's fury telling me he was indeed alive but pissed the fuck off. I guess I would be too if I'd almost been blown up. The only other feeling I got from them is that they were not close by. I couldn't remember where the Pride building was.

Snapping my eyes open, I grabbed one of the tablets and pulled up the maps, trying to get a sense if they were still in the city or if something else happened. "I don't think they're in the hospitals. They reached out to me through our bond but they feel farther away than they should."

"I felt Micah's answer to your call," Brayden said as he flopped onto the couch next to me, dropping his head into his hands. "That much anger echoed through you into us."

"Do you get a lot of echoes?" I asked, curious since they'd never mentioned it.

Hudson blushed, telling me that there might be certain

situations where it happened. When neither of them answered, I let it drop.

"Alright, so here is where Pride's building is. It's only a short drive away. They felt much further inland but where would they be going?" I questioned as I searched the map, trying to put myself in their shoes.

Brayden's head popped up. "Can I look at that?"

Handing over the tablet, he typed something into the search bar and an odd-looking website appeared. He typed in a login and password before a list of locations and addresses were revealed.

"What is that?" I inquired, looking over his shoulder.

"These are the locations of different bases that Jay's father uses for his military. It would seem that there is a site on the outskirts of Paarl near the mountains. That has to be where they're going. It's the only thing that makes sense. They wouldn't trust any other location in the city, knowing they've been compromised and their mission was a bust. Jay probably had them ditch their phones, or they lost them. He would never let them use an unsecure line to reach out to us with the base's location," Brayden explained as he went back to the map to show me where they were going. "We need to grab our shit and join them. This place clearly isn't safe for us to stay and there's nowhere safer than with Makoto."

"Alright, how do we get there?" Hudson asked. "I'm guessing taking a cab isn't going to be the best idea."

"We can take a ride to Paarl and then we'll have to make our way on foot or see if they reach out to us at that point. According to the news reports, they have about an hour's head start on us," Brayden said.

Not needing any more encouragement, I packed every-one's things. It wasn't very much since we'd hardly spent any time in the room but I took all the mini soaps and things just in case, unsure of where we were going to end up. Brayden called us a ride and fifteen minutes later, we were on the road to Paarl. Fingers crossed this drive would be uneventful and we wouldn't have to cause any more natural disasters.

CHAPTER 13
JAY

It was pure chaos to get out of the building and there were already cops and firemen at the scene to deal with the aftermath of the bomb. It had been big enough to take an enormous chunk of the building out since it was on the top floor. What was odd though was the cops weren't really concerned about controlling the area. They were looking for something or someone. I paused, having a gut feeling that we were the ones they were looking for. Clearly, someone had leaked our location, that's the only reason Arno would have a bomb in his laptop. The Dark Lord knew we were here in Cape Town and he didn't like that we were getting close to his army. It wouldn't surprise me if he tried to do whatever he could to get rid of us.

"Over there!" one of the cops shouted, pointing at me.

Fuck! My hunch was right. They were looking for us. There was no way we could go back to the hotel with them searching for us. I had to hope Lailah and the others would be safe there, and the leak came from inside Pride.

"Guys, we gotta go," I snapped as the other two hadn't

registered the danger yet. "We aren't out of the trap yet but I know where we can go."

"What the hell do the cops want with us?" Parker growled as he took off after me.

I glanced at him over my shoulder. "Not sure I want to stay and find out but if you do, by all means, I won't stop you."

"Fuck you, Jay," Parker sneered.

In an effort to stay out of sight, we headed for the thick of the crowd who was rushing into the streets to get away from the burning building. We ducked down a side road and then ran full out until I veered off to a parking lot of cars behind a building. "If they're looking for us, we can't go back to the others."

"No, we can't leave them behind. What if they're going after them too?" Micah challenged as he pulled out his cell.

Lunging forward, I grabbed it out of his hand and chucked it to the ground, slamming my heel on it. "All we know right now is that they knew we were coming here to meet with Arno. If there is a chance that the others are safe in the hotel, I don't want to draw attention to them. There's a leak but we don't know where it's coming from, so it's better to keep contact to a minimum. I can get us some-where safe and then send people out to get Lailah and the others," I explained as I dismantled my phone and Parker did the same.

"How the fuck do you know someone in Cape Town?" Micah demanded.

I glanced up at him knowing his anger wasn't really meant for me, but if I could hold back the fury that I felt at how things went down, he could too. "My father has a base here. It's not well known, but we needed a foothold in Africa since there is so much corruption and smuggled goods in and out of the country. South Africa seemed like a safe bet to put a training base that wasn't really for training but intel gathering. It's in another town closer to the mountains."

"Well fuck, haveing that kind of equipment at our use makes things easier. For tracking down who the hell is selling us out I mean," Parker pointed out. "How do you plan on us getting there?"

Pulling a knife out of my boot, I slammed it into the back passenger window of a car, shattering the glass. Quickly, I unlocked the car and got to hot wiring it as the other two hopped in. The car rumbled to life easily enough, and we were off, heading in the opposite direction of the Pride building. Once there was enough distance, I headed inward toward the mountains. My heart ached knowing that Lailah would hear about the bombing and not know if we were alright or not, but I would do anything to keep her safe and alive. At the moment, whoever was hunting us was on our tail. I would draw them away from her and once it was safe, let her know we were fine.

"Did we get anything from that meeting?" Micah asked, rubbing his head. He'd used a lot of power to keep us safe from the bomb blast. It wouldn't surprise me if he was feeling drained.

Parker snorted. "Dude, do you really not realize that he told us a shit ton of information?"

Micah twisted in the front seat and glared at him. "Obviously not or I wouldn't have asked, you fucking moron."

"Nice to know you aren't as amazing as you think you are," Parker taunted with a smirk. "One good thing is that the Dark Lord doesn't know we caught onto him or that he is the owner of Aplite. It must be his shell company to fund everything he's doing to take over the world. Even demons need cold hard cash to make things happen. Arno also told us that he's the Dark Lord's supplier and sends him all the serum he needs. I thought it was guns, but that's when I started to lose my hold on Arno. Pride definitely supplies everything that the Dark Lord needs for his training camp, as Arno called it, but it seems they aren't relying on human weapons. This could be a good thing or a bad thing."

Glancing back at Parker through the rearview mirror, I frowned. "What do you mean by that?"

"That, I think cock nugget could explain better than I could," Parker said, nodding to Micah.

Micah slouched down in the seat, crossing his arms like a child pouting after they were told they couldn't have something. "Sorry, I thought I wasn't all that amazing. You sure you want to hear this from me?"

"Micah!" I growled. "This is bigger than the two of you and our personal issues—spit it out."

Letting out a sigh, he sat up straighter but kept his gaze fixed on the surrounding scenery. "If they aren't going to use human methods to bring us down, it means they've found a way to channel their demonic powers. It will be like fighting an army of Tabithas, only some of them will be far stronger than her. That also means we might not be able to bring in any backup to this battle. Humans wouldn't stand a chance against them and there aren't enough holy weapons to supply everyone."

"Fuck," I swore, slamming my hand onto the steering wheel.

"Yeah, that about sums it up," Micah muttered.

"How could they have found a way to do that? Everyone we've encountered so far has been unable to use their demonic nature, even Lilith. Yeah, she had some powers, but they weren't anything close to what I'm sure she could really do," I questioned.

"Those weren't fully possessed people. They were conduits where the demon was still trapped in Hell," Micah shared. "I'm thinking they found a way to get demons fully out of Hell and into the person's body, allowing them to have all their powers. Lilith and the Dark Lord are too powerful, which is why they needed Lailah for it to work, and she banished Lilith back to Hell. The Dark Lord would need to go for one of us if he wanted to really be on Earth. Unless they found a way to create enough dark energy for him to survive off of here on earth without a body."

"You mean like in spirit form or something?" Parker asked, leaning closer to the front to hear better now that we were on the highway. The wind was loud through the broken window.

"That could be one way, or if they created a sacred circle for him to use, trapping him in one spot. There might be another way but not one that I can think of. If only they hadn't killed off our demon expert!" Micah grumbled in frustration. "Mr. Creed would know the answers to all this shit."

"Guess we all should have paid better attention," Parker mused.

The car fell silent as we all thought over the years of training and how we didn't really appreciate it the way that we should have. Now, when we really needed it, there were holes in our education. At this point, we didn't know who to trust and ask. Brayden and Hudson's parents were working tirelessly to find a way to neutralize the serum, but we didn't know enough about demon venom to move things along as quickly as we'd like. So far, from what I heard, it was all dead ends with backtracking to learn more about demon venom itself. Was this how Lailah felt all the time? At a loss for what to do and not having the slightest clue where to even start looking for the information?

I knew she had to be worried about us and cursing the fact that we talked her into separating. After this whole ordeal, I knew we wouldn't hear the end of it, but after this was over, I wouldn't mind being attached to her hip. Glancing back at Parker, my mind couldn't seem to wrap itself around the fact he left Lailah to protect someone else when she needed him. I would let the world burn if it meant I could save the woman I loved and who held my heart in her hands. Pulling my thoughts out of that downward spiral that just made me mad, I took in the road signs noting we were over halfway to Paarl. The traffic was light since it was the middle of the day, which I was thankful for.

Reaching over, Micah turned on the radio and flipped through the stations until we found one that was speaking English. *"This just in... a rogue tsunami level wave has hit the east side of the peninsula, wiping out a large section of scenic road R44. This wave then resulted in a landslide but thankfully,as far as we know, no one has been injured in this random catastrophe. It will take some time for the road to be repaired so we suggest avoiding that area for the time being. More reports on the bombing that happened at Pride Resources. The police believe they know the people who are behind this and are actively searching for them. No terrorist groups have claimed reasonability for the bombing so we will just have to wait and see what the police have come up with. Now, on to traffic..."*

"Did they just say a tsunami type wave happened out of nowhere?" Parker asked.

Micah and I looked at each other, knowing that the only person who could make that happen was Hudson. We'd heard in history books how the past Water Elementi could do such things but Hudson had never been that strong. Although, there hadn't been much chance for him to try his powers out to that extent since he bonded with Lailah.

"Should we find a way to contact them?" Micah asked.

"If they were taken and needed to fight back, I don't think they'll be able to take a call from us," I responded, sarcasm thick in my voice. "Now it's even more important to get to the base so we have backup. We don't need to worry about the police coming after us to pin the bombing on."

"No need to be an asshole about it, Jay," Micah muttered.

Opening my mouth to respond to him, I felt my powers explode inside me to the point I couldn't see; the light was so blinding.

"Pull over, now!" Parker yelled, lunging forward and grabbing the wheel. "Take your foot off the gas, Jay. You're going to get us killed if you don't slow down!"

I could feel when we moved off the smooth asphalt of the road and hit the rocky terrain. Using the last part of my willpower, I let off the gas and pressed on the brakes, trying not to bring us to an abrupt halt. When the car finally stopped, Parker shifted it into park and I could lose myself to whatever the hell was going on with my powers. It was like I got pulled under in a sea of white light only to have bursts of green and gold popping off like fireworks around me.

What the fuck was happening?

I caught images of Brayden and Lailah but they happened so fast I couldn't figure out what was happening. While I might not be able to see with my eyes, I could feel what was happening. Lailah was terrified and feeling trapped. Sensing she needed my help, I sent my power to her, letting her take what she needed. Just when I didn't think I had more to give, I was slammed with a return of power. It was intermixed with all our powers, as if she'd pulled from all of us and was giving us back the extra. Soon, the moment ended, and I was able to see the world around me once again. My heart was hammering in my chest like I'd been given a shot of adrenaline.

"What in the holy hell just happened?" Micah rasped, looking as bewildered as I did.

"I don't know, but I'm betting it had something to do with why Hudson needed to create a wave that big," I answered. "Parker, I think it's better that you drive since you don't have to worry about anything happening to you."

Parker grimaced at the reminder that he wasn't attached to Lailah in any way. "Yeah, fine, it's better we live to find out what's going on than to die a sudden and horrible death, crashing into a mountain."

"You acted fast and kept us alive," I pointed out as I slid into the back seat. "Good work."

"Wow, your gratitude is so touching. What will I ever do with all these warm fuzzy feelings?" Parker muttered as he got the car back on the road. "How much farther do I take this road?"

"Take this all the way until you hit a town. That will be Paarl. Then we'll have to ditch the car somewhere and make our way to the base on foot. Can't have the cops finding a stolen car on their property," I said, resting my head against the window, still feeling unsettled by what just happened.

Lailah, what had happened to you three?

Lost in thought, trying to come up with our next move, I was once again blindsided by my powers rioting in my body. Thankfully, with Parker driving, there was no danger to anyone as Micah and I got lost in a whirlwind of energy. This time, flashes of Hudson and Lailah kept appearing, and I got the sense that Hudson wasn't doing well. Lailah was worried but this time things seemed slightly more controlled as she took from us, giving me the chance to focus on what she was doing. She was collecting from us and then pouring it into Hudson until he couldn't hold anymore, which was when she sent the energy back to us. It took a bit for her to pull out her own, giving us back what she took and then some.

"The fuck is going on? Now you guys are glowing," Parker called out.

Whatever Lailah was doing to us wasn't over yet, trapping us until she cut the connection, allowing us to return to what was happening around us. Parker was still driving but he looked between Micah and me with wide worried eyes. Lifting my hand, I could see that he was right. I was glowing with a faint silver light, matching my energy. This time, instead of feeling panicked and on the bad side of an adrenaline spike, I felt healed, well rested. Even the old injury in my knee wasn't aching. *What the hell had Lailah done?*

"Jay, I get you don't want to reach out but we need to contact them sooner rather than later. I don't like that we have no clue what's going on with them," Micah stated, turning to look at me. "How much longer until we get to the base?"

"Fuck the plan of leaving the car, we need to get back faster," I said, rubbing my hands over my shaved head. "Once we hit the town, it'll be another fifteen or twenty minutes to get where we need to go."

"Why the hell can't anything about this go right?" Parker grumbled.

Following my directions, we finally pulled up to the gates of the base. Parker pulled up to the guard stand and one of my father's men stepped out. "This is a private facility. You're going to need to turn around and leave."

Not wanting to slide into the seat with all the glass, I got out of the car and walked up to the guard. "I'm Jalen Minh, Makoto's son, and team leader of the Alpha-Seven."

"Sir." The guard straightened and saluted. "I apologize, I wasn't informed you would be coming to the base."

"At ease, this is an unannounced visit," I assured him. "We were on a different mission in Cape Town and ran into some trouble. I'm in need of the resources at this base as well as needing to get in contact with the rest of my team."

"Right away, sir." The guard nodded and stepped back into the shack and opened the gate. "I'll radio ahead and let your father know you're here. I'm sure you'll want to get him up to speed."

I had to hide my shock at hearing that my father was here. This base wasn't one that any of us visited often, since it was more intel related. "Thank you and good work."

None of us said anything as we rolled through the gate. They both knew how tense my relationship with my father was without the added stress of my mother missing. For him to be here wasn't a good sign and their agreement was deafening even without saying a word.

"Don't say anything until we know what he knows," I ordered as we pulled up to the main building. "My father is a master at getting others to spill their secrets but unfortunately for him, I'm better."

Parker looked at me in the rearview mirror. "You don't think—"

"Doesn't matter what I think, but it would be the first thing that makes sense in all this," I said, cutting him off before he could say it out loud. "Keep those thoughts to yourself for now, only trust each other, and we'll make it through this like we have everything else."

14 - Lailah

It was wise for none of us to drive, since ten minutes into the hour drive, we all fell asleep, trusting that the driver would get us to our destination. It was foolish of us after all we'd been through but none of us seemed to be able to fight how tired we were. After I made contact with the guys, I didn't get any other communication from them. Knowing they were alive and well was enough until we reached them. We'd asked the driver to bring us to another hotel, so it didn't make us stand out like dropping us on some street corner would, especially with us bringing along all our bags.

"We'll be arriving in a few moments," the driver called back to us.

Stretching, I tried to pull myself together enough to get with the program. "Thank you. The jet lag is catching up to all of us it seems. People always talk about it when you travel overseas but man, it's no joke."

"Where is home?" he asked with mild interest.

"The States. We all live in Wisconsin. This is our big summer trip for surviving our first year of college," I answered, trying to make the story simple yet believable. They always said too many details were a dead giveaway.

The driver just grunted as he wove his way through traffic to pull into the hotel parking lot. Hudson and Brayden both seemed tense as we collected our things from the trunk and watched the man drive away. I shouldered my bag and grabbed one of the others as we trudged to the next part of our journey.

"You guys gonna fill me in on why you're so freaked out?" I asked after a few more minutes of awkward tension.

"Something isn't right," Brayden commented. "I can't figure out what it is, but something in my gut is telling me to be careful."

"Do you think the dirty cops could have found a way to reach out and tell them we got away?" I questioned.

We walked past a bar with televisions behind the bar and I caught a glimpse of the destruction we'd left behind in Cape Town. It wasn't in English but I got the feeling that whoever knew about the mission to get rid of us would also know it didn't work. If it was being blasted all over the news, then we were screwed.

"Well, I guess that answers my question." I huffed. "At least they don't have our faces plastered on the news. That would make things even worse."

No sooner had I said those words, images of Jay, Parker, and Micah appeared with the images of a burning building behind them. It didn't take a genius to figure out they were blaming them for the bomb, just as they tried to do with us. Then another set of images showed up with our faces looking back. The image they used was from my student ID at Ryevick. The only way they could have gotten that was from someone on the inside.

"Things just got so much worse," Hudson muttered. "It's better we keep moving."

"You know this proves that it's someone inside the Elementi that has fucked us over, right?" Brayden growled as we hurried along.

It was tricky to move quickly and not draw attention to

ourselves as we did so. "Are you sure we can't take a taxi or something?"

"Not after our faces have been plastered on the news," Hudson pointed out.

"Guess I'm not good at this whole fugitive thing," I mumbled as I realized how stupid that question had been.

"The base is outside the town. It would be much easier to get to if we had a vehicle of some kind," Brayden reasoned. "There has to be something we could try."

Hudson paused and turned to face us. "If we're lucky and that's the first time they've showed the images on TV, we might have a chance, but do you really want to risk it if it's been running for the past hour we've been driving here? They want us in jail or otherwise detained. We can't make it that easy for them."

Brayden cursed and kicked at a cup someone had missed throwing into the trash can. It skittered out into the street only to get crushed by a car driving by. I couldn't think of a better representation of how I felt in this moment right now. Every time we got out of one situation, we ended up in another that was even worse than the last. The Dark Lord was doing a bang-up job in keeping us out of his way, even if we weren't captured. Having a manhunt for us was effective in its own way.

"What if we call Cami and see if she can reach the base and have them send someone to come get us? If the guys are already there, they can make sure it happens," I suggested. "I feel like us running around the streets is going to get us caught faster... unless one of you can steal a car?"

Hudson and Brayden both looked at each other unsure but I knew it was the best option we had. Ducking into a side street, I huddled behind a dumpster and pulled out my phone to call Cami.

"We just saw the news. Please tell me you're at the base," Cami answered.

"Close, but we need an assist. We're in Paarl but we need someone from the base to pick us up so we don't get caught by the police, or worse," I answered.

"I tried calling the guys but knowing Jay, he had them toss their cells." Cami sighed. "Makoto doesn't like to play nice with the Elementi, even though he's one of us, claiming his men are better than ours. Anywho, I will reach out to the base. We might have better luck with the guys there pushing for them to get you three to safety. Hold tight and I'll call you back as soon as I can."

Hanging up, I shrugged as they looked at me questioningly. "She's gonna do what she can. I guess Makoto is a prick to everyone, not just me."

Hudson snorted, shaking his head and Brayden grinned. "Angel, we could have told you that. The good thing is that Cami doesn't play fair and won't give a rat's ass about being nice when it comes to you being in danger. Once Cami claims you as one of her people, she does whatever it takes to keep you alive," Brayden added.

This made me think about her telling me about her girlfriend who died. She'd dealt with so much loss and heartache, I totally understood why she was so protective.

Thankfully, it only took ten minutes before my phone rang. I picked it up right away. "Please tell me they're alright and sending someone to get us?"

"I'm sorry, did you doubt my skills, Lala? I'm offended!" Cami said with a gasp as I switched her to speaker. "Of course someone is coming to get you. It won't be the boys, because they're wanted as well, but they are sending a few men after you. Where are you now?"

"We got dropped off at the Horizon Inn and then we

headed east a few miles," Hudson answered since I had no idea how to answer that question.

"Can you tell me some street names so I can send them right to you? They don't want you wandering about, drawing more attention to yourselves."

Brayden got up and jogged to the end of the alley and rounded the corner. It didn't take long for him to reappear with the information we needed.

"Alright, guys, hang tight and I'll pass this information along. Be safe and text me when you get to the base," Cami requested before she hung up.

Now that I knew we had a way out of this and to safety, I sagged against the brick wall, letting my head rest on Hudson's shoulder. "You know, I used to think I was missing out for not traveling the world. Now I would give anything to be back in Wisconsin with you guys, relaxing on the beach. Is this what things have been like for Jay when he goes on missions?"

"I'm not sure what his missions are like but I don't think he's normally hunted by the police for blowing up a building," Brayden pointed out.

I glanced at him surprised. "That was a very Parker thing to say. What's got you upset, other than the obvious?"

"None of this makes sense," Brayden started. "How did they know we would be here and meeting with Pride? We made those plans on the plane and contacted the company at the last minute so something like this wouldn't happen. We didn't even tell Pride who they were meeting with until they confirmed they could fit us in when we wanted."

That got me thinking. This time when we flew there was only one staff member on board besides the pilot and he'd been on all the previous trips. I couldn't say that I kept track of who the steward or stewardess had been for each of the flights to know if this woman was different or not. Micah wasn't one to leave things to chance though. No one would be on that plane if they weren't safe.

"Brayden, who does Micah use to charter his plane?" I asked, knowing Micah told him everything.

"It's the same company that the Elementi uses. Many of them are Elementi who want to help but don't want to be on the front lines," Brayden answered.

I felt like I was on the cusp of figuring something out but just couldn't put my finger on it. "Who does the background checks on all the members? I have to believe that not every person who wants to join the Elementi would be a good fit or might be working for the demons."

"Well, that is actually a combined effort between Hudson's father and Jay's. Makoto deals with the background checks and mental evaluations, while Hudson's father checks to make sure they don't show any signs of being controlled by a demon with blood tests. There are markers to find out if they've been altered or possessed."

Frowning, I massaged my temples. "Makoto has some odd feelings towards the Elementi for being so involved. He seems to think we Knights are a joke and his people could do a better job dealing with the Dark Lord, but they keep missing them every time they get a tip. Then he's asked to make sure people brought into the Elementi are who they say they are along with being mentally fit for the job and not easily swayed by demons... My other assumption is that he clears the pilots and flight staff as well?"

"Yeah, all personnel gets looked over by him or his people," Brayden confirmed.

My heart clenched as all the pieces finally made sense to me. Shooting to my feet, I looked around wildly, fear coursing through me as the danger we were in hit me in the chest like an arrow. "Guys, we need to leave now!"

They both looked at me confused and didn't seem to follow the same logic I was.

"No, I'm serious. We need to leave before Makoto's men come to get us. I will explain, but you need to trust me right now and get the hell out of here," I begged, my heart thumping in my chest.

Seconds later, an SUV came to a screeching halt at one end of the alley then another on the opposite side, blocking us in. Men leaped out of the first vehicle and waved for us to come to them. "Let's get a move on, you three. The faster we get you out of sight, the better," one of them called.

I turned to face Hudson and Brayden. "We can't go with them. If they take us, we'll never see the light of day again."

"Lailah, what are you talking about?" Hudson asked, his voice tired. "The other three are already there. Besides, Makoto might be a jerk but he's been loyal to the Elementi forever."

"No, no he hasn't. He's one of the Dark Lord's men and has been working behind the scenes to help make all this happen. Who else could know everything and everyone all the time? Jay's mom wasn't kidnapped by chance. Makoto probably gave her up!" I blurted, trying to tell them enough to get them to trust what I was saying.

As I finished talking, I could see them putting it all together, but it was too late. The soldiers could tell something was wrong and advanced. "We can do this the easy way or the hard way, your call."

Whirling on my heel, I brought my weapons to hand, ready to fight. "Sorry, but I never plan on making things easy for the Dark Lord."

This got a grin from the man who'd been speaking. "Seems like you finally caught on to the reality of the situation, but it's too late, Synergy. You're surrounded and we have the other three of your men. If you want to see them alive, then I suggest you come with us."

"The Dark Lord wants us dead so why should I trust anything you say?" I growled.

"Oh, he doesn't want you dead just yet. No, he plans to make you watch him destroy everything and everyone you love. The worst torment for you is to know you failed to save them all," the soldier announced with a bitter laugh. "If it were up to me, I'd kill you right here, right now, for all you've put us through."

"Let me guess, those cops weren't really cops but your men and I left them out in the ocean," I shot back, hoping that as I distracted them Brayden or Hudson would get us out of this mess.

A body crashed into me, knocking me to the ground. As I tried to fight off the person, I discovered it was Hudson with a tranquilizer dark sticking out of the back of his neck.

"If you plan to ever get out of this alive, you're going to need to think faster on your feet. Us demons are masters at playing dirty. There's no way a person as pure as you could ever pull one over on us," the soldier in charge shared as he squatted next to me. "Those darts will make it so they can't use their powers for a while, but Makoto wanted us to leave you intact. Seems he wants to see what you're made of."

Struggling to shove Hudson off me so I could fight, my anger clouding my judgment, but that all ended with the clicking sound of a taser. Pain flooded my body as it went rigid until finally my brain decided it would be safer if we just checked out for a while until this was all over. The Dark

Lord won this round, but I refused to believe this was the end of things. I would find my opening and next time I wouldn't second-guess myself before acting.

122 RESUCING AIR

CHAPTER 14
LAILAH

In the past year, I've been through a lot and waking up after being tased was not an experience I ever wanted to do again. Of course, it could be that I was lying on a concrete floor in a cell, but the bone-deep body ache I knew had to come from being electrocuted. Rolling onto my back, I stared up at the ceiling with bright florescent lights shining down on me, illuminating the jail cell that I was in, not that there was much to look at. The bed that was bolted to the ground didn't even have a cot on it, leaving the springs exposed. Clearly, they didn't give a shit about my comfort and didn't expect me to stay in here for that long.

"Ah, you're awake," a voice I recognized called out, breaking the silence of the space. "If you had just simply gone with my men, we could have avoided all this. But you had to make it difficult."

Slowly sitting up, I found Makoto standing in front of my cell in his typical yukata with his hands folded behind his back. The last time I'd seen him was at Christmas and the past five months hadn't done him any favors. His hair was now silver and there were a few more wrinkles that hadn't been there before. Everything about him looked tired, as if the life had been sapped out of him—which could totally be a thing if demons were involved.

"I vowed never to make things easy for the Dark Lord," I answered, giving him the same response I did the soldier.

Makoto grunted in response before pacing in front of my cell. "The Dark Lord doesn't like to make things easy for those who resist him either. Something you should keep in mind. I've been tasked with keeping you out of his way while the final pieces are set in motion. During this time, I fully plan to see what the great promised weapon of Synergy is capable of. Everything has pointed to the fact that you should be able to defeat the Dark Lord, but I don't see it. You are nothing but a scared little girl who doesn't know when to quit."

It'd been no secret that Makoto didn't like me and thought very little of me. In fact, he felt that way about all the Elementi Knights and tried to do his best to keep Jay away from us, until Jay put his foot down and told his father how things were going to be. Now I was at Makoto's mercy and I had no idea what to expect, other than he didn't want to kill me.

"Where are the others?" I demanded. No sense in being nice when he clearly wasn't going to think well of me.

"They're sleeping off the drugs they were given. It was infused with demon venom to make sure they couldn't use their powers and bring this whole building down around our heads like they did at Pride," he answered.

Did Makoto truly think I would believe that the bombing was their fault?

"Why would you do this to Jay? I know you've had your issues with the Elementi but why force your son to go through this?"

Makoto paused in his movements and met my gaze. "My son could have been so much more but you and the other *knights* held him back. The Dark Lord promised that if I could get him to turn his back on the Elementi and his role, then Jalen would have a place at my side when the demons rule. What I didn't count on was the strong connection that you and my son would have."

"You know we're bonded, right? That if anything happens to me or him, it could kill us both?"

"Yes, the Dark Lord informed me of this information," Makoto spat, his face twisted into a sneer. "Know that you sealed my son's fate to your own and that I hold you responsible for killing him."

The venom in his words hit me as if I'd been slapped across the face. "You're just going to let him die when the Dark Lord kills me?"

"My son chose you over me so there is nothing left to be done. I shouldn't be surprised, his mother chose him over me as well, but Jalen believes it was all my fault because of the lies she said about me."

This conversation was taking a left turn, and I didn't know how to get it back. There was still information that I needed. "Is that why you didn't even bother to look for her when she was taken?"

"Why would I look for her when I know right where she is?" Makoto challenged.

That simple statement confirmed everything I'd hoped wasn't true. Jay's father sold his own wife out to manipulate his son. "What do you plan on doing now that it didn't work?"

"She will be injected with the serum and be useful for once," Makoto stated. "If I could do that to all of your men I would, but the Dark Lord has other plans that he hasn't shared with me yet."

How could Makoto believe a word that the Dark Lord says? He was a Prince of Hell and lied to everyone about everything. There was no way that anyone was surviving to see the new world he was creating.

"Cami and the others at headquarters know we're here. How do you plan to get around that?" I inquired. If he kept telling me things, then I would know for certain that Makoto might not be willing to listen to what the Dark Lord wanted and kill me sooner just to appease his anger.

Makoto gave me a tight smile but didn't share, making me take a deep breath of relief. "I wouldn't put your hopes on anyone finding you before things are set in motion and you can't stop it."

Well that answer gave me mixed feelings...

"So what now? You have me here, as well as the others, but it seems like you're waiting on something," I pressed, feeling like I didn't have the full picture just yet.

What could have happened to make Makoto turn his back on the Elementi? This was in the works before Jay was born, since Makoto had owned his military company for thirty years or so from what Jay had told me. His mother had trouble getting pregnant with him, so it was a happy moment to have had a son, but Makoto never saw it that way.

"I told you, while I have you here, I intend to see what the angels decided to bless you with, even though you have no connection to the Elementi whatsoever. The honor of having Synergy born into the world should have come from one of the legacy families. We've been a part of this war for generations, leading back to the first Elementi Knights. No matter how many times I asked Jalen what your powers were, he never told me. He wouldn't even tell me what your spirit weapons were."

My eyes widened at the fact that Jay would hold this information back when so many others at Ryevick knew all about what I could do. Did Jay really not trust his father to such a deep level?

"Maybe Jay knew you couldn't be trusted but hoped he was wrong about you," I mused. Makoto had shown he had a temper so maybe he would let something slip if I got him angry at me.

"Jalen is smarter than people ever give him credit for. He's quiet so people say things around him, but they also assume it means he's not very bright. Turns out it's quite the opposite. He uses people's perceptions against them."

Okay, well that plan backfired.

"Enough of this. I know you're trying to do your best to get information out of me, and while I admire the attempt, you're not skilled at it," Makoto pointed out as he signaled to a guard. "You seem alert enough to put you through some evaluations. If you choose to fight this, my men won't have any issues reminding you what a cattle prod can do."

The guard unlocked the cell and grabbed my arm, yanking me to my feet and dragging me after him as he headed down the hall. We left the jail area, but I didn't see anyone else in any of the other cells, telling me the guys were in another area. I didn't have much of a chance to take things in as I was muscled around and shoved into a room that reminded me of the warded training room back at Ryevick. It was the only place we could fight and use our powers without worrying about destroying anything.

"It's up to you if you live through these evaluations," Makoto said before he closed the door, leaving me alone in the room.

My gut told me I was not going to like whatever happened next but I didn't plan on dying anytime soon, so I would do what was needed. Another door opened, and a woman was shoved through before the door was slammed shut. She looked to be around my age. Her clothes looked ragged and dirty like she'd been locked up for quite some time. Her body was thin enough you could see her bones and when she lifted her head to look at me, her eyes were completely black. I gasped and involuntarily took a step back from her, feeling a wave of evil coming off her.

"What happened to you?" I whispered.

At my words, her face split into a smile that was all teeth, and those teeth were pointed like a shark, not human at all. "I was freed from Hell only to be trapped in this useless human body. That's what happened to me. Why do you smell so delicious? They've sent lots of people for me to play with but none as sweet as you. What makes you different?"

"They've done this to others?" I gasped. "And you killed them?"

"A demon's got to eat and the souls of those they leave with me are my favorite food," she informed me with a chuckle. "Most of them were failed subjects of the serum but you, you are something else entirely."

She advanced on me, her clawed hand reaching out to me as if she could just pluck my soul right out of my body. Who knows, maybe she could since I couldn't tell what type of demon she was. Nothing I learned seemed to come close to what she is other than the higher demons like the one who tried to poison me back when I first came into my powers. Stumbling back, I tripped over my own feet and fell to the floor, making the demon laugh.

"Oh, you are going to be so much fun to play with

before I kill you and eat your soul for dinner. I can tell it's a powerful one that will help me level up and give me a chance to get out of this fucking place," she snarled.

"Wait, you're trapped here?" I asked. "What if I helped you get out of here?"

"Now what fun would that be? No, I would much rather eat you, then take my chances with the old man," she said, crouching down as if she was preparing to spring at me.

Since the events at the catacombs, the guys have been adamant about my training and felt it would also help me with my panic attacks. Right now, I was so glad that they had beaten it into my muscles because when she launched herself at me, I reacted before my brain could catch up. Rolling to the left, then popping up to my feet with my sai in my hands, I was ready to deflect the kick she sent my way. Now, in no way was I at the level of the guys but I could hold my own, although no matter what, I was always better at defensive moves than attacking.

"Ho-ho! You're an Elementi!" she announced excitedly. "That just made this all the more exciting! Now I know if I eat you, I'll be able to free myself and eat all the souls I desire."

This time when she attacked, it was faster and harder, forcing me to be on the defensive, not giving me a chance to make a move on her. I'd been trying to keep what skills I had to myself but it seemed that Makoto wasn't going to let that happen and purposefully put me with a powerful demon. When a kick glanced off my cheek, I knew I needed to get some space between us so I could recenter myself. Throwing up a shield, I shoved her back from me so hard, she slammed into the wall, leaving a dent.

"Would you look at that, the little girl has tricks," the

demon mumbled, getting to her feet. "Seems like I need to stop playing around."

I gulped. If she'd just been toying with me, I knew defeating her was going to be impossible without using everything I had to my advantage. Taking a deep breath, I pulled on my powers and wrapped them around me like a cloak. I felt my sai shift into my short sword and shield, along with armor settling over my body, offering me protection. Geared up, I settled into a low stance with my shield raised, ready for whatever this demon was going to throw at me.

"Now, if that isn't a neat trick! I'm not sure all the armor in the world could save you from me," she taunted as her claws extended, making me think of Wolverine.

She came flying at me, kicking out with both feet but I was able to deflect her and swing with my sword as she fumbled off balance. The tip of my blade sliced into her side, making her scream out an ungodly sound that made my teeth hurt. Infuriated, she rolled away only to use the wall to shove off of to slam into me. My shield smashed into my chest, knocking the wind out of me. I threw up a second shield, blocking her claws from slicing along my neck. Getting a better grip on my shield, I tossed her off, sending her rolling and giving me a chance to get back to my feet.

I knew what needed to be done, but I hated it. The only way that I could end this was to end her just as I had Ubel. It would give me a fresh set of nightmares to live with. Dropping my sword and shield to reclaim my sai, I ran full tilt at the demon, who grinned and charged right at me, meeting my attack. This time, I ducked low and grabbed her around the stomach, taking her down to the ground. Her claws sliced at my arms as she fought to get me off her but I ignored the pain, pushing through it. Taking one of my sai, I drove it point first into her heart and flooded her with my power.

"I will set you free, just not the way you wanted," I whispered into her ear. "Tell the Dark Lord that I'm coming for him and nothing will stop me from destroying him and removing him from existence. He won't have a place on earth or in Hell. He will just cease to exist."

"He won't let you win, Synergy," she choked out as my power consumed the demon infesting this woman's body. "The time of the Elementi has come to an end."

"On that we agree, but it will be because demons will be too scared to have us hunt them down by the time this is all over. They will know that humanity is protected by me and I won't stand for anyone else fucking with them," I growled as I shoved more power into her, shattering the demon who'd been possessing her.

As I watched the woman's eyes return to normal, a pair of sad hazel eyes looked up at me. "Is it over?" she whispered as blood trickled out of her mouth.

"Yes, it's over. You can rest now. You've been fighting for a long time. I'll take it from here," I answered, stroking hair out of her face as she gave me a smile of relief.

I knew she wouldn't be the last person who lost their life in this battle but it didn't have to happen like this. Makoto was the reason this woman was dead. He had forced me into killing her, which I would never forgive him for.

CHAPTER 15
PARKER

Pacing around the small, warded room with no windows, I racked my brain to figure out how this had all gone so wrong. We arrived at the base and were invited into the war room where Makoto was, along with the men who led this base. They asked us to fill them in on what happened and what we knew about the situation with the tsunami wave. They knew the others had been kidnapped, but it seemed they managed to get away, leaving the people who kidnapped them stranded in the ocean. I was surprised they knew so much already when it had only happened a half hour before. Then again, it was Makoto's whole purpose to keep up with what was going on in the world around us.

Once they got the information they needed, I noticed Jay and Micah both smiling to themselves as if something was going on that I didn't know about. Shame burned within me, guessing it had to do with Lailah and their Bond to her. If she figured out we were in trouble, she would absolutely need to make sure they were okay. Since we ditched our phones, there was no other way to contact us except through the one thing that would never be taken from them. Makoto seemed to notice this as well, giving some hidden signal. It was too late by the time I noticed that his men were coming up behind the others. A sharp prick to the neck and seconds later, I was out like a light, only to wake up who knows how much later in this goddamn room, alone.

How could we have walked into a trap like this? Really though, it wasn't until we started putting all the pieces together that it crossed my mind. When I tried to bring it up, Jay seemed like he'd come to the same conclusion. I had to hope that Lailah and the others were safe and didn't figure out where we were. If Makoto was double-crossing us, then we were well and truly fucked. There was no way they would guess that we were here though. I never would have even considered that there was a base here in South Africa. Although, she had Hudson and Brayden with her and they were the logical ones in the group. If they were trying to figure out where we would run to after the bombing, they would look to see if one was close by. Every turn we made the Dark Lord was ahead of us. Add in Makoto and it all made sense. That man had his fingers in all the pies and made himself invaluable to the Elementi.

The sound of footsteps outside my door made me freeze. I tried to call on my powers but nothing happened, almost as if I didn't have any, which made no sense at all. Taking a deep breath, I calmed myself and looked inward but there was nothing but an empty void for me to fall through. This was what it felt like when I went after Lailah when she was trapped in her dream. This darkness was alive, lurking, waiting patiently for me to step foot in its world so it could pull me under. Could this be the darkness that the Dark Lord was talking about? The evil that now blemished my soul? Had the angels changed their mind, choosing to abandon me to my fate since I betrayed them and Lailah?

"Step to the back of the cell and place your hands on the wall above your head where we can see them," a man ordered.

My first response was to tell him to fuck off, but that wouldn't do anyone any good. If I wanted to find a way to help the other two and get us the fuck out of this place, I needed to think smart. Not my strongest skill, but everyone has a moment when they need to step up in life, and this was mine. Once I did as they requested, there was a lull before the door opened and two soldiers entered.

"Keep still. If you move then we'll have no other choice but to use the cattle prod on you," the soldier warned as he approached.

I didn't move or say a word as he came up and yanked my hands behind me, putting them in cuffs. "Typically, I only let women cuff me but I guess you're cute enough," I commented, unable to keep from saying *something*.

That got me a kick to the back of my knees, dropping me to the floor and my face hitting the wall as I pitched forward, unable to stop myself. "Damn, you sure know how to show a guy a good time. That's alright, I'm good with things being rough."

"Shut your goddamn mouth before I shock you for pissing me off," the soldier snapped. "Makoto wants to see you. If you have any brain cells in that head of yours, I suggest you listen carefully to what he has to say."

Things were getting interesting. I let him heave me up and drag me down the hall that had doors on each side of the hall—ten of them if I had a guess. I'd bet everything that the other two were here as well, but the doors were steel and had a keypad entry, which I could bypass, but it wouldn't be quick. As we walked, I kept an eye on all the security and tried to find ways around it. I had a feeling I was the only one who could pull it off. Jay might know how to deal with his father and the other soldiers but he didn't know security like I did. As for Micah, he would sooner burn the whole building down than have the patience to organize a plan.

My journey ended in an office, where I was once again brought to my knees in front of a desk that Makoto sat behind, looking over some paperwork. "You may leave. I'm sure he won't be any trouble since he doesn't have his powers."

"Yes, sir," the soldier responded, giving a slight bow before leaving.

Once he left the room, closing the door, I got to my feet, not really enjoying the feeling of debasing myself in front of a man I'd known for most of my life. "What the hell is going on, Makoto?"

He looked at me over the pair of reading glasses he wore, like I was some bothersome kid even though he had to look up at me. "Is that how you want to start this off, Parker?" He motioned for me to take a seat in a chair that was in front of his desk. "We need to have a chat, you and me. If my information is correct, then you are the only man out of the group who hasn't tied yourself to a fate ending in death."

My brows knit together as I sank into the chair, which was extremely uncomfortable with your hands cuffed behind you. "I'm not sure I'm following?"

"Parker, you might play the fool but I know you aren't quite as dumb as you pretend to be." Makoto sighed, taking his glasses off to rub the bridge of his nose. "You've already figured out that I'm not loyal to the Elementi and even if you're not sure how or why, you believe that I'm helping the Dark Lord, which is true. I was never convinced that the Elementi were in the right and when I was only able to have one child, the angels decided to take him away from me. Those who are Elemental Warriors give up everything in their pursuit to rid the world of demons. Those idiots don't realize that there will never be a world without demons in it. Good and evil have existed together since the beginning of time. There can never be a world without evil which means demons will never be gone. The angels are just using us in a battle they're tired of fighting. They know we can't truly win, which is why they only created five warriors at a time, with the promise of a secret weapon to end it all. After seeing a sample of her skills, I'm beginning to see that she is something special but there is no way she will ever be able to defeat the Dark Lord. She's too soft, untrained, and well... female."

My stomach dropped as he talked about Lailah. Maybe he was talking about the battles we'd already fought. It didn't have to mean she was here, trapped like the rest of us.

"Lailah is here?" I asked, trying to sound calm.

"Yes, she arrived yesterday along with Hudson and Brayden. It seems that the police are after all of you for the bombing," Makoto commented, like it wasn't a big deal. "I tell you this because if you plan to run away, know they will be looking for all of you. Forever you will be fugitives and will have to live a life on the run."

"You... you set us up?" I demanded.

"Perhaps I was wrong and you are as dumb as you seem. Yes, Parker, I set you up, but I didn't know who would go to the meeting, so I had a team watching the hotel as well to take action once the bomb went off."

"All those innocent people you killed!" I yelled, shooting up out of my chair. "Have you always been this coldhearted and fooled all of us for so long? God knows you've never shown Jay or his mother any love or kindness, so my money's on the fact you've always been a bastard."

Makoto slowly stood and met my gaze. "Sit. Down."

"Really, and what's going to happen if I say no? Are you going to kill me? Well, if the Dark Lord wins, we're all going to be dead as it is, so why not speed up the process?" I challenged, feeling reckless.

"Kill you—no, that would be too simple. I would just torture Lailah in front of you so she knew that you were the reason it was happening. How do you think she would feel, knowing you once again betrayed her?"

Holy shit, Makoto wasn't fucking around. The look in his eye told me he would enjoy every moment of doing it too. Not breaking my gaze with his, I sat back down as I clenched my jaw, hating every second of bending to his will.

"The six of you are too soft." Makoto huffed. "What does it matter what she thinks of you? Didn't she kick you out of the house, rejecting you completely? The only reason they have you with them now is to use you. They all know they can't beat the Dark Lord without you. Why protect them? They've always hated you. Help me deal with them and the Dark Lord will find a place for you in the new world. Your gift of emotional and physical manipulation is something he finds valuable."

"I'm sorry, I think the drugs you gave me have rattled my brain. Did you just ask me to betray Lailah and the others?" I asked, wishing I had my hands free to check to make sure I was really awake right now.

"That is exactly what I said," Makoto confirmed. "The only reason we're having this conversation right now is because you are free from her hold. The Dark Lord will win this battle now that I have all six of you secure on base. No one can get out of this place, though many have tried. It was built to be the starting grounds to the Dark Lord's army."

There was so much wrong with that statement I didn't even know where to begin. Makoto was never looking for the Dark Lord's army because he was one of the people in charge of it. No wonder the Elementi were always two steps behind everything and getting into trouble at every turn. Makoto gave them a direct feed of information about us. Clearly, he didn't have the same grasp in Wisconsin because we didn't have any staff and connected with the other headquarters that didn't use him the same way. Here on the eastern side of the world, he could manipulate everything. Must have been why he dragged us out of the US and onto his turf.

"If I said yes, what would you need from me?" I asked, trying to understand what else Makoto wanted.

Makoto narrowed his eyes at me as if he didn't *really* believe that I would help him. I didn't know what he was looking for in my expression but he grunted and sat back in his chair. "I want to know what makes Synergy so special. What it is that the angels thought to create that would destroy someone like the Dark Lord. From what I've seen so far, there's no way it could happen. The girl only has close-range defensive skills. Sure, she can purge a demon from a human body but it kills the human in the end. None of that could stop the Dark Lord from doing what he wanted, so there must be something else that only activates with the other knights. I can't trust any of the others to show me her skills. They would use them to try and escape or kill me. You, on the other hand, owe them nothing."

"So you keep reminding me," I muttered.

"Only because it seems like you keep holding out hope that she will take you back and forgive you. I wish to keep you from falling into that lie when there is another option that doesn't end in death. A smart man would look at the big picture and choose the winning team. Are you a smart man, Parker?" Makoto asked, folding his hands in his lap, waiting for an answer.

My mind raced with how I could play this to my advantage and what I kept coming back to was that I had to say yes. Lailah was the only person who could end all this, so if I could get her free, the Dark Lord would know he wasn't safe. No one knew the truth of what she could do, not even us, if I was being honest. Hell, she didn't even know, but the angels had come to tell her that she wasn't scratching the surface of what she could do. If this was the way I could help her and the others, then fuck it, I'd lie the best I knew how. If Makoto found out I was playing him, I'd absolutely die, but that was a risk I was willing to make for the woman I loved and the men who were important to her.

"You're right," I stated. "No matter what I do, she won't ever forgive me. I've groveled enough and my knees are getting sore from crawling back into her favor. That's not even touching how the guys feel about things. Micah would gladly see me dead while the others would just watch, believing I deserved it. I'll do what you need me to as long as you promise me that I won't end up on the chopping block next to them."

Makoto smiled, then stood, walking around to uncuff

me. He motioned for my hand, which I held out to him. Before I could even react, he took a small knife out of his sleeve and sliced my palm before chanting a string of words I'd never heard before. The cut burned, and a symbol was branded into my skin from the blood that pooled there. "You've just made a pact with the devil. Break it and you will lose your life. This is the only way to make sure you don't back out of the deal, Parker. Show your loyalty to the cause and you will reap your reward."

I was so fucked.

CHAPTER 16

LAILAH

After the fight with the demon, I was brought back to my cell. This time there was a thin mattress on the bed, along with a tray with a sandwich and a water bottle on it. Seems they didn't want to kill me right away like I thought. I guess Makoto wasn't lying about that. Gingerly, I sat on the bed, not feeling confident that it would hold me with how janky the springs looked. With a loud groan of protest at my weight, it held. Looking at the sandwich, I couldn't remember the last time I ate and my stomach growled in excitement. It was a simple peanut butter and jelly. I guess I shouldn't be surprised they didn't want to put in much effort. Wolfing it down, I chugged the water as the peanut butter stuck to the roof of my mouth.

A guard passed by and tossed a thin blanket through the bars before moving on. With no windows in the building, or at least the sections I'd been in, I had no idea what time it was or how long I'd been here. Getting to my feet, I grabbed the blanket and wrapped it around myself, trying to keep from falling apart. Curled up in a ball on the bed, I stared at the small sink's faucet as it dripped, trying not to fall asleep. I knew the moment I closed my eyes that the nightmares would be waiting for me and this time, I was on my own to deal with them. None of the guys would wrap me up in their arms and tell me it was alright, and that I was safe with them. Worse yet, the Dark Lord could try to kill me again now that I was separated from the only people who could save me.

No matter how hard I tried to fight it, my eyes shut, and I was pulled into the darkness...

"Little Synergy," the Dark Lord purred. "Did you really think you could win? The angels were foolhardy in thinking a mere human, even with powers, could beat me. Now I have you trapped and alone, waiting for the day of judgment. You picked the wrong side, and that is a choice you're going to have to live with until your last breath. Those men of yours are being tortured for information about you, the Elementi, and anything else I feel like knowing. You did this to them. If they hadn't sided with you, binding their lives to yours, I could have found a use for them. Now, it's just a waste."

No, it couldn't be true. I shouldn't trust anything he had to say. Demons lie and manipulate, that was how they gained power in the world, but something in the pit of my stomach questioned if he might be telling me the truth.

"You have me, why bother with them?" I asked, trying to keep the fear out of my voice.

The Dark Lord laughed. "Because you rejected my offer. I'm one of the Princes of Hell. No one throws my generosity in my face. This is all to teach you a lesson and perhaps give you a glimpse of what your life will be like once the angels forsake you, sending you to Hell for all of eternity. There's no way they would accept you into Heaven after failing to save mankind, those made in the image of God."

"Is there anything I can do to save them?" I begged, feeling hot tears trailing down my face.

"You could take the coward's way out and kill yourself, taking that joy from me I suppose," the Dark Lord mused. *"Truly though, you've lost your chance to bargain and now you have to live with that."*

No—killing myself couldn't be the only way out of this. The angels wouldn't create something and come to personally tell me I was stronger than I realized without it being true. The beings of Heaven couldn't lie, even if I was just a human. I was also blessed. I couldn't let the Dark Lord take more from me. Taking my own life would be the easy way out but I would be failing so many people. Sure, I would be free of this whole mess, but then who would protect the rest of the world?

"You're right, I do have to live with the choices I've made, and that is exactly what I plan on doing. This battle isn't over until I breathe my last breath and that moment isn't now," I snapped, reaching for my power.

Normally in this place, I could never find my own power but something told me that was a lie. Sure enough, there it was, glowing brightly within me. This whole time, I'd been able to use it but up until now, I hadn't believed in myself or realized the lie that it was trapping me here with the Dark Lord. The master of lies and deception had planted the idea and fear that I couldn't save myself in this darkness, but the truth was, I was the light. The beacon of truth that would lead others away from the darkness. The true power of Synergy, combining all the elements together to make them stronger, pushing back the darkness in the world. Alone, light could be powerful but when you spread that light, it became unstoppable.

"This will be the last time we're meeting like this, Dark Lord. The next time will be face-to-face in battle when I wipe you from existence. Darkness can't thrive where there is light, and I plan

to shine brighter than the sun!" With that proclamation, I let my power burst forth from me, purging my body of the darkness I let live within me, and the lies that I believed kept me from my full potential. The Dark Lord roared in anger as I thrust him out of my mind and body, sealing the opening he'd been using to get into my mind so he would never again have access.

Gasping, I sat up on the squeaky cot, feeling like I was burning alive as a sheen of sweat covered my body. The burning became more intense, and it reminded me of having the Dark Lord carve all those symbols into my skin, making me scream as I clutched myself. Just when I thought I couldn't take it any longer, the pain stopped, and I was left panting and sobbing into the blanket still wrapped around me.

What the hell happened to me?

I slipped an arm out of the blanket to push my hair out of my face when I noticed that it was back to normal. Scrambling out of the bed, I stood and yanked my shirt over my head and looked over my skin to find that all the marks the Dark Lord put on me were gone. My power had burned them away, just as it had the remnants of darkness I'd let live inside me for so long. It was proof that I was no longer demon tainted, but free from his hold in all ways. This time when I dropped to my knees and sobbed into my shirt, it was tears of joy. Finally, I was free! I'd been trapped in that darkness, letting it fester in me, giving him power where he had none.

The sound of running footsteps echoed in the quiet and I quickly tugged my shirt back over my head.

"What the hell is going on in here?" a guard yelled as he approached my cell with his cattle prod out.

How did I even answer that? Oh, sorry, I was just purging the Dark Lord from my body. It was just a nightmare? Did they even know they were working for a Prince of Hell?

"Sorry, it was just a nightmare. It happens after you've faced down the devil," I answered, getting to my feet and wiping off my cheeks with the sleeve of my shirt. "So sorry to have bothered you as you stand guard, keeping me locked away for no good reason."

I'd reached the point where I would no longer keep silent about what was happening here. Makoto was a traitor and either his men knew it and followed him or they were idiots who believed everything they were told.

"Just keep it down. No one likes to listen to someone screaming like their soul is being ripped out of their body," the guard muttered as he walked away.

"Oh, do you know what that sounds like from personal experience, or have you been allowed to keep your soul? Has the great Makoto kept some of his men out of the Dark Lord's clutches? I wonder what system he uses to choose between who he'll banish to Hell for eternity and who can live as a normal human for just a little longer?"

"You don't know what you're talking about," the guard said as he stopped and turned to face me. "The world is going to change and I plan to be on the winning side, no matter what it takes."

"Really? What makes you so sure that this is the winning side? See, if someone told me I was working for a Prince of Hell, I'm not sure I would trust anything that is promised. Demons are known for being the best liars and manipulators, kind of a rule for them, I believe," I taunted. Clearly, being freed from the Dark Lord had removed all my fears about my imment torture and death with the way I was spouting at this man.

The guard laughed at me. "You think I should put my trust in a group of kids who aren't even out of college yet? Yeah, that sounds like such a better idea. Makoto has saved my life and never steered me wrong in the ten years I've worked for him. Try selling your bullshit to someone who might believe you. Enjoy the time you have left. I hear Makoto has big plans for you and none of them are helping to keep you alive longer."

Not having a response to that, I let him leave and I returned to the cot, feeling a weariness in my bones. I knew Makoto wouldn't bother to keep me around much longer and I had a feeling that it would become an even shorter length of time once the Dark Lord had zero control over me. At least when I slept, I wouldn't have to worry about him visiting my dreams ever again. It would finally be safe for me to rest. I wasn't delusional enough to think all my nightmares would be gone, but I would be safe. This time when I closed my eyes, I pulled up images of the guys and moments that we'd shared with each other as a group and on our own, hoping to lose myself in happier times.

CHAPTER 17
LAILAH

"Time to get up," a voice snapped, shattering my sleep.

Cracking open an eye, I found two men standing just inside my cell door, ready and waiting for me to fight back. Too bad for them I wasn't going to play that game. It was what they expected from me and I wasn't going to give them what they assumed I would do. Instead, I slowly sat up, yawning and stretching before I got up and walked over to them.

"Are you doing cuffs this morning or is the fact you're much larger than me effective enough for you?" I asked before I was close enough for them to grab me.

"Do we need to cuff you or are you going to do as you're told?" one asked, tapping the cattle prod on his hand menacingly.

"Intimidation it is," I answered before stepping forward. "I assume we're going back to the same room I fought the demon yesterday? Makoto did say he wanted to do lots of testing and I doubt he got enough information yesterday... was that yesterday? With no windows it's hard to tell how long I've been held against my will."

"For someone being held captive, you sure are awfully chatty," the man on my left muttered.

I flashed him a smile. "Funny thing about being caged is it puts things into perspective. I figured out that I refuse to die being scared. Honestly, I've gone up against the Dark Lord several times and you're just not all that scary anymore."

"You've gone head-to-head with the Dark Lord?" The right guard scoffed. "I don't think so. You wouldn't be alive if that was the case."

"Ah, so you've met the Prince of Hell?" I inquired, raising a brow at him.

The man opened his mouth to say something but Makoto appeared in the hallway. "What is taking so long? I asked you to bring her to the training room right away and here I find you gossiping in the halls."

"Sorry, sir," they both answered in unison.

That was the end of our conversation as they shoved me forward to follow Makoto back to the scary room where they forced me to kill demons. I tried not to think about how today would go and what twisted test they had for me to see what powers I had. I'd failed last time at keeping my second set of spirit weapons hidden, but I needed the armor to keep from getting beaten to a pulp. The door opened and one of the guards shoved me through so hard that I sprawled on the floor like a baby giraffe who couldn't use their legs yet.

"Lailah!"

My head snapped up, hearing a familiar voice. "Parker!" Pushing myself up, I ran to him and let him envelop me into a hug. "Oh God, I'm so happy to see a friendly face.

Do you know anything about the others or where they are?"

Parker buried his face into my hair, holding me tightly. "No, they've been keeping us separated and drugged so we can't use our powers. They had to give me an antidote for whatever the hell is going to happen in here."

"The last time I was here they released a demon, and I had to kill it, showing them what skills I have. Parker, they don't plan on letting us live. They want to know all they can about me, then when his curiosity is sated, he's going to kill me," I whispered, unsure if they could hear what was going on in the room from wherever they were watching.

His arms tightened around me and his lips brushed my ear. "I will never let them hurt you, Trouble. You might not know how you feel about me but I know how I feel about you. I am not going to let anyone take you from me. Whatever it takes, we will make it through this and we will save the others too. I swear on my life, I will see you through this."

The sound of a door opening had us pulling apart to be faced with a horde of people running into the room with weapons—no guns but knives, swords, and bow and arrows, nocked and at the ready. Makoto was no longer testing out a theory, he had a hunch and was forcing us to prove his theory or die. Parker took a step in front of me and his spirit weapon appeared, glowing with purple flames on the long five-inch blade. I'd never seen it do that before but I didn't think I'd ever seen the look of fury on his face quite like that either.

I knew that my sai wouldn't do a damn thing, so I went right for the sword and shield, knowing it was my best chance. Jay had worked with me to strengthen my body so when I had to use my sword and shield, I could, even if they weighed nothing in the spirit form. Just because they were weightless didn't mean I didn't need the body strength to use the moves required for this skill. As the first person attacked me, I slammed my shield into them, tossing the man back into the rush of people. I couldn't tell if they were demon possessed or not, but I would soon, since our weapons and powers didn't work on humans. An arrow came flying at me and I was able to duck in time to dodge it but the attack was followed up by a woman with a broad sword swinging double-handed at me. My shield took the brunt of the blow but the impact knocked me to my knees as I held the blade off with both hands supporting the shield.

"Lailah!" Parker yelled. "Hang on, I've got you!"

I couldn't see what was going on around me as the broad sword bore down on me, leaving me to trust Parker was coming. The next second, the weight was gone, and I shoved to my feet and backed up, trying to get some space to gather my bearings. The room was full of angry demon-possessed people, with the one goal of killing me and Parker. I had no chance to catch my breath before the next person was making a move. This person was fighting with a dagger so it made it easier and my body fell into its training. I side-stepped the attack and stabbed them right in the ribs with my sword, taking them down. Not that it mattered with other people filling the spot.

Parker ended up at my back and we fought, falling into sync, moving as a team that we'd always been working toward. This was the revelation that we'd been missing the whole time. On our own, we couldn't handle it, but together, we were stronger. Now was not the time to wax poetic in my brain though. We had a battle to survive and the others to save. It was clear that Makoto was in charge of the army that the Dark Lord was preparing and was pulling from them to conduct this crazy experiment. The army must be in the mountains near here or else they had them scattered instead of in one large group.

My arms got tired as we fought, sweat dripping into my eyes, but I couldn't wipe it away. It burned, making them tear up. This wasn't working. I had to change it up but that meant giving more away to Makoto and ultimately the Dark Lord. Did it really matter though? So what if he knew what he was up against? Just because I used a skill here and now, didn't mean it would be the same ones that would take him down.

"Parker, we have to use our powers," I called to him. "We won't live through this if we don't."

"No, Lailah, trust me when I tell you that is the last thing we should be doing," Parker said, his tone adamant. "I know what he's trying to do, Trouble, and we can't give it to him. It's the only thing keeping us alive right now."

I didn't have time to digest all of that statement but what I could tell was he was scared. "Parker, I need you to trust me. There is more going on here than just what Makoto wants us to believe. There are still more people pouring in here. If we can fight to the door, then we might be able to get out of here and save the others."

Out of the corner of my eye, I could tell he was hesitating but with a frustrated growl, he started moving in that direction. He charged forward as I watched his back but it was a losing battle with people being replaced as soon as we took one out. Trusting my gut, I pulled on my powers and channeled what I had done in the first battle with Tabitha, when I was only bonded to Brayden. It took a lot more concentration and willpower than it did now that I was connected to all of them but Parker, yet somehow I managed. I thrust my power into Parker as I grabbed onto his shirt, needing contact with him to get things to happen more smoothly. He gasped as my power flooded into him, making him freeze for just a second before his second form appeared. His armor was purple and his staff now had a blade on both ends instead of just the one, making it even more deadly as purple flames flickered around the sharp edges.

"Holy shit, Trouble, what are you doing to me?" Parker demanded as he cut down our enemy with more power and speed.

Now that I was fueling him with power, I left myself more vulnerable. I pulled my power around me like a shield and knew it would be strong enough to withstand the blades and arrows. "I'm getting us the fuck out of here is what I'm doing. Now, move it and use your own goddamn powers to make them panic or fall in love with us."

"Right, okay, let's see what I can do," Parker muttered as he took a deep breath.

Some of the people closest to us yawned and rubbed their eyes, letting their weapons fall to their side. Others turned on the person standing next to them in a rage that was more aggressive than what they were giving us. The bad part was when we got too far away and they weren't near the bubble of emotion Parker was giving out, they returned to normal. Let me tell you, when they figured out what he did, they were not happy. Knowing that I didn't have a lot of energy to spare for myself, I expanded my shield enough that I didn't have to worry about an arrow or something taking Parker out from behind, but I couldn't do more than that as I added to his power bank.

"We're almost there, just hold on a little longer," Parker

shared. "Let's just hope they don't cut off the stampede of people and lock us in here with them."

"One thing at a time, Parker. Get us out then we'll figure out the rest," I directed, shoving him to keep him moving as I felt him hesitate. "Don't you dare quit on me."

"I told you that wouldn't happen this time. I'll get us out," Parker snapped.

"Don't you dare get pissy with me when you have only yourself to blame for me having doubts in the first place. Especially, in a situation like this," I shot back.

With a roar, Parker shoved back three men who tried to charge him and split us up. "Right now might not be the best time to have this conversation, don't you think? How about when we make it out of this alive, you can yell at me all you want about how badly I fucked up? Trust me, I will be happy to listen to whatever you want to say."

He was right. This wasn't the time or the place for our personal drama when all we had was each other to count on.

"Hold on tight. I'm going to see what this new weapon can do," Parker warned before he lunged forward, spinning his staff as fast as he could.

The flames on the ends grew with the added wind until it was a giant wheel of fire that turned every person to ash as it touched them. It gave us the last upper hand we needed to spill out into the hallway. Parker twisted and grabbed my hand, running off into the hall, slamming people into the walls as we went. The smaller space made it easier for us to manage, instead of being surrounded. He seemed to know where he was going so I just hung on for the ride as I was dragged away with possessed people hot on my heels. Now that I wasn't powering Parker the same way, I created a shield and thrust it behind me, creating a barrier that they slammed into, making me smile as we turned a corner at high speeds.

"Where are we going now?" I demanded as I almost slammed into a wall myself.

"As I was being led to that room, I memorized everything so I could get back to the others. They had us in individual rooms like that one, so it's impossible to use our powers to get out if we managed to bypass the poison they gave us."

"Wait, so even if we free the others, they might not be able to use their powers? How does that help anything?" I asked, frustrated. Makoto seemed to have covered all his bases.

Parker glanced at me over his shoulder. "As the love of my life told me—one thing at a time. The first step is getting to someplace that I can shut the security system down, or at least the cameras. With them blind, it will help to keep us hidden as we break the others out."

"And I'm guessing you have a clue to where that would be?"

"Sure do. They brought us to their command center when we first got here, to have us debrief them about the situation with Pride. If we can get into the room, I should be able to do most of the things I need to," Parker informed me, confidence in his voice.

It seemed that Parker had a solid plan. I just couldn't help but worry that this was too easy. Makoto ran the top private military in the Eastern Hemisphere. There's no way they couldn't just shoot us on site and end this whole thing in a second. Sure, it could be that the Dark Lord wanted us to live but that might have changed since our last encounter in my dreams. I wasn't his scared little puppet anymore. I'd cast him out and purged his hold on me. I decided to do the scariest thing I could right now and trust that Parker could do all that he said he could.

We reached the end of the hall and Parker kicked open a door leading to stairs going up and down. He pulled me up a flight of stairs to another level but this time he let go of my hand and motioned for me to keep quiet and to wait. I nodded my agreement as he slipped out the door. Standing there holding my breath, I tried to listen for any sound of what might be happening on the other side of the door, but it was too thick for me to hear. Then the door was yanked open and there stood Parker, a little worse for wear with a split lip but otherwise just as he left.

"Come on, it seems they weren't expecting us to get out of that training room. With the amount of possessed people he has on the base, most of the men must be down there dealing with them. Demons don't give a shit about who you are or if you work on the same team. If they're pissed, they'll kill you," Parker said, wiping his lip with the back of his hand.

Stepping out into the hall, I saw three men knocked out and their hands cuffed behind them. "You dealt with all of them on your own?" I asked, impressed and equally worried for him. "They could have killed you! What if one of them pulled a gun on you?"

"Easy, Trouble. They apparently are under orders not to kill us unless it's the only option," Parker assured me. "Although to be safe, I did take their guns away from them. Here, you keep one so you can watch my back."

I took the handgun, checking to make sure the safety was on so I didn't accidentally shoot my foot or something. Jay made sure I knew how to handle a gun since we didn't always just deal with demons who were trying to kill us.

"Come on, the room is up here and we don't have much time until they notice the guys in the hall."

The large double doors in the middle of the hall must be where we were headed and just as we reached them, a man stepped out with his gun at the ready. Parker must have anticipated this possibility and got a shot off first, killing the man.

"Shots fired on the third floor. I repeat, shots fired on the third floor," a man yelled from inside the room.

Parker wasted no time moving into the room and shooting the two men in there before I even registered there were people. I always saw Jay as the soldier of our group, but the reality was that all five of them had the same training. Yeah, it was meant to deal with demons but right now, these men were our enemy and helping the demons take over the world. With those two dealt with, Parker settled down before a computer and started to type in gibberish.

"That makes sense to you?" I asked, peering over his shoulder.

Parker grinned. "This is my first language, that of computer code. It's complex but I recognize the style of code so it shouldn't take me too long to make some tweaks and get us hidden for a while. Who knows, I might be able to have their doors unlocked before we get there. It would certainly save us time."

"*War room, come in.*" A walkie-talkie crackled. "*War room, come in, report your status.*"

Well that wasn't going to happen, and I doubted they had a woman working for them at all so it wouldn't help for me to pretend. "How much time did you say you would need?"

"*War room, if you do not report then we are sending backup your way.*"

"Looks like this will have to be good enough. I just need one more minute to shut down the cameras and the lights...."

As he spoke, the room went dark, the only light coming from the computers and blinking lights of electronics in the room. A hand grasped mine, twining our fingers together, letting me know it was Parker. "Come on, Trouble, let's go get the others."

LAILAH

Even with the main lights out, the emergency strobes helped light the way even if I thought I was going to have a seizure. Parker had intentionally set off some sort of alarm so sirens were blaring, making my ears hurt. If his goal was to make it a horribly disorienting atmosphere, then he did the job. If I didn't have him to anchor me, I don't know what I would have done or if I'd be able to make sense of anything going on. He pushed forward, leading us back down two flights of stairs, then down a winding hall to a third set of stairs that only went down. Here, the place was pitch black with only the flashing lights from above giving us any light to see. Parker let go of my hand and light bloomed into existence. On the gun he had in his hand was a flashlight which I was extremely thankful for as we moved through the unfamiliar layout.

"I didn't get the door open like I hoped but I disabled the secondary handprint lock on each of the doors. Shorting out the keypad will be easy enough so we shouldn't have too much trouble getting them out. The only problem I have is there are ten rooms and only four of them. I have no idea who or what could be behind the other six doors," Parker informed me as we stopped in front of one of the doors.

"Do you think he would keep a demon down here? This seems rather specific to dealing with the Elementi," I reasoned. "Either way, it's worth checking all the rooms. One of them could have Jay's mom in it."

Parker's brows shot up at this idea. "Fuck, you might be right. Alright, as I work on getting the doors open, I need you to use the flashlight on your gun and watch my back. This hall is a dead end that way, so if you stand shining the light on what I'm doing and facing the stairs, we should be good."

Nodding, I did as he asked, watching for a moment as he pulled out a knife and got to work prying open the keypad. Pulling my attention, I watched the shadows and listened the best I could with the alarms going off. The reality of my life right now made me want to shake my head. No one would have ever pegged me as the warrior princess type. I was more of the goofy sidekick but here I was with a gun in hand ready to break out the men I loved. That was only the beginning. Once that happened, we still had a dark overlord to kill and then had to save the planet. Maybe I should have taken Cami's advice and read more of those fantasy books she kept pushing on me, then I might have a clue how to end this all.

"Got it!" Parker exclaimed as the door lock clicked. Tucking away the knife, he pulled his gun back out and stood to the side of the door before he pushed it open. Peering around the corner, I let out a sigh of relief that it was just empty and nothing was trying to kill us. "On to the next one. Now that I've done one of these, the others should be easier."

Three more rooms were empty and if our theory was correct, then the next set of doors should hold the people we were looking for. When the lock clicked on the next door, it came bursting open and Jay tackled Parker, slamming him to the floor.

"Jay, wait, it's us!" I yelled, reaching out to stop Jay from pummeling Parker in the face.

Jay paused hearing my voice and looked up but the flashlight was shining right in his face, making him wince before I lowered it. "Lailah, what are you doing here?" Jay demanded, getting to his feet and stalking over to me. "Why are you and Parker running around while the alarms are going off?"

The angry energy that was coming off him had me backing up until I was pinned against the wall. "Ah, well, that's a bit of a story that we don't really have time for."

"No, I think now is the perfect time for you to fill me in on what's happening, or are you going to be a bad girl and disobey me?" Jay whispered. He slid a hand up my arm to my neck, gently gripping it. "Good girls get rewarded, bad girls get punished."

I gulped at the fierceness in Jay's silver eyes. "Dirty cops came and kidnapped the three of us, claiming we were involved in the bombing at Pride. We got away and Brayden came up with the idea you might be here, so we drove to Paarl. Once we got there, they were blasting our pictures all over the news and we knew we couldn't get out of the city without someone noticing us. I called Cami, and she reached out to the base and they came to get us. It wasn't until that moment I figured it all out."

"What did you figure out?" Jay asked even though I was pretty sure he knew.

"Your father is a traitor working for the Dark Lord,

running his army and is trying to kill us," I blurted, not really sure how to tell a man I loved that his father was an asshole.

Jay narrowed his eyes. "What do you mean he's trying to kill us?"

"Well..." I started but Parker got another door open and Micah came out swinging.

Parker got socked right in the mouth before Micah took a moment to figure out what was going on. "Lailah, what the fuck are you doing here with *him*?"

I let out a frustrated growl and attempted to shove Jay away from me. He let me move him, his hand sliding off my neck as I headed for Micah. "Can we cover that in a moment? We need to get the last few rooms open to see if Jay's mom is in one of them along with Brayden and Hudson. Then we need to get the fuck out of this goddamn nightmare of a prison." This outburst had both Jay and Micah looking stunned. "It's been one hell of an experience since you guys went off to your meeting. The next time I tell you guys we don't split up, you better fucking listen!"

Thankfully, none of them took the risk of arguing with me as I went to help Parker with the next keypad. Clearly, he didn't need it since he got the previous one open on his own but it gave me a purpose. He'd been right. Now that he got the hang of it, he was opening the doors much faster. Thankfully, this time when the door was opened no one came out swinging. No one came to the door at all. Sneaking a look around the doorframe, I saw a woman on her side, sleeping on a cot. She was stunning, dressed in a simple green dress with her long black hair flowing out behind her. This woman had to be Jay's mother. There was no other reason she would be here.

"Jay," I called to him. He was in a heated discussion with Micah. "You're gonna want to handle this, I think."

I don't know if it was the look on my face or the tone I was using but horror crossed his face as he dashed into the room and knelt beside his mother. He started to whisper to her in Japanese as he lifted her out of the bed, her head falling to rest on his shoulder. None of this woke her and I had to wonder what Makoto did to her, and why. There was no reason to keep her locked away like this if the plan was to turn her into one of those mindless demon-possessed people. Unless he was hiding her from the Dark Lord to keep her from that fate—but why?

Parker had moved on to the last two doors, freeing both Hudson and Brayden in quick succession. Now that we were all out, it was time to get moving.

"I don't have time to explain everything but here's what you need to know. Makoto is working with the Dark Lord. He's trying to get me to show off all the powers that I have by having demon-possessed people attack me. Somehow, he figured out that me working alone wasn't all I could do, so he pulled Parker into the mix. I'm guessing because he isn't bonded to me. If he died, he wouldn't take me down with him. Makoto unleashed a massive amount of them on us but we got out of there and did what we needed to set you guys free. Now that we're all up to speed, can we please leave before something else happens?" I asked, talking as fast as I could.

"Why can't I feel my powers?" Micah asked, staring at his hand as if he was trying to do something with it.

"Makoto gave us all a drug laced with demon venom, blocking us off from our powers. Before he sent me to fight, he gave me an antidote," Parker answered.

That did not make Micah's mood any better as he spluttered at the information. "How the fuck do you expect us to get out of here if we don't have our powers to use?"

"If you'd given me a moment, I would have told you," I grumbled as I walked up to him and grabbed his face with my hands to pull him into a kiss.

Clearly, I didn't need to kiss him for this to work but right now I wasn't going to take the chance that I might never get to again. Letting my power flow through him, I searched for anything that shouldn't be inside him. When I came across the demon venom, I was able to burn it away, making him whimper as he held onto me for dear life. I knew this didn't feel good, but it was what needed to happen if they wanted their powers back. As soon as I felt the last vestiges of the venom were gone, I pulled back my power, giving him one more brush of my lips before looking him in the eyes.

"Holy shit, why did that have to hurt so bad?" he wheezed as he rested his head on my shoulder.

I let my hand comb through his long hair for a moment as he collected himself. "I'm sorry, I know just how awful that is, but it was the fastest way to get your powers back." Nodding, he let me go, and I faced the others. "Who wants to go next?"

None of them looked thrilled but Hudson stepped up to the plate, resting his forehead against mine. "Let's save the kiss for a reward after you do whatever it is that made Micah sweat."

"Fair enough," I said, letting my hands wrap around his neck so I had more contact with his skin.

Now more comfortable with this new trick, I could manipulate the process faster. But no matter how fast I went, it would still hurt like a bitch. Yeah, it was a cleansing fire, but fires still burn and blister whatever it touched. The moment he was free from the venom, his lips descended upon mine as if it would give him life. "Thank you, Sunshine."

Hudson moved and let Brayden take his place. He wrapped me up in a hug, tucking my head under his chin as I completed the process. He let out a grunt as I got to the venom and his arms pulled me tighter against him as if he was going to draw me into his body. When the deed was done, he peppered my face with kisses before landing on my lips in a quick but searing kiss. "Go help Jay so we can get out of this hellhole."

Jay only had eyes for his mother at this moment, worry creasing his brow. "Can you check her too? She shouldn't be like this. Even if she was drugged with something normal, she's too quiet."

"I'll see what I can do but no promises," I warned as I clasped one of his mother's hands in my own.

Closing my eyes, I let my power trickle into her through our physical connection. This was the first time I'd done anything like this to a person who wasn't possessed or one of my men, and I was scared to hurt her. Instead of filling her with my power, I just let a small wisp float through her body, exploring to see if there was anything there to deal with. When I got to the area around her heart, I knew we were in trouble. It felt like it was enveloped in something dark and oozing, as if it was slowly strangling the life out of her. My eyes snapped open and met Jay's concerned gaze.

"I can help her but I can't do it here. The amount of power I'm going to extend will knock me out of commission. We have to hurry though, she doesn't have a whole lot of time," I said, keeping my voice soft for only us to hear. "Will you let me heal you so you can protect her?"

Jay nodded his agreement, and I saw him set his jaw,

ready for the pain he knew was coming. "Don't go easy on me. Get it out of me."

Biting my lip, I let go of his mother and grasped his arm. Doing as he requested, I slammed my power into him, hunting down the venom so I could purge it from him. Jay dropped to his knees, clutching his mother to him as he endured what I was putting him through. Moments later, he was cleansed, and we both gasped as I pulled my power back from him. Tiredness swept through me and I knew healing all of them after the battle Parker and I fought was putting me close to being useless. Taking a deep breath, I reached out to all the men I was bonded to and pulled some of their power to me, giving me temporary strength to make it through this.

"I've done the best I can for all of you right now but we need to get out of this place if we plan on seeing tomorrow," I shared, feeling my body sag even with the pick-me-up I'd given myself.

An arm slid around my shoulders and a kiss was pressed to the side of my head. A sense of peace enveloped me and I knew that Parker was influencing my emotions to help get me through this. "Come on, Trouble, let's give 'em hell."

CHAPTER 19
BRAYDEN

Watching Parker with Lailah told me that something shifted between the two of them while we were locked away. While I was still pissed that he hurt her and created even more wounds on her heart and mind, I knew they wouldn't be able to walk away from each other. They loved each other even if they needed to work on things. Trust had been broken and it couldn't be fixed overnight or with a few sweet words. By no means did I think things were fixed, but I could tell that she was willing to accept his affections and allow him to step up. Right now, it was more important for us all to put our personal drama aside and focus on getting the hell out of here alive and in one piece.

"Jay, I know you don't want to hand off your mother but you're the only one out of all of us that knows this place," Hudson pointed out. "Allow me or Brayden to take her for now. Once we're out of the building, you can take her back."

I could tell he wanted to argue but then he looked between his mother and Lailah, and begrudgingly handed her over to Hudson. Lailah held something out to me and I was shocked to see it was a gun.

"Not everyone in here is possessed and the guards knowingly work for the Dark Lord, so I consider that making them our enemy," she explained.

Taking the gun, I let my hand linger against hers. "I agree completely with that logic."

She nodded absently and turned away from me to follow Jay as he led the way back up the stairs. Someone had turned the alarm off but the strobing lights were still flashing, making everything seem to move in slow motion. The whole place was overrun with people destroying everything around them. It made me think of a zombie apocalypse, if the zombies were intelligent and could fight. Soldiers were fending off swarms of these possessed people and we dove into the thick of it, falling into formation just as we'd been trained. Never in the years we'd been working together had we ever worked this seamlessly but everything flowed like a well-oiled machine.

They kept telling us this was how all the other groups functioned but we'd never figured it out. With Lailah added to the mix, it seemed to connect that missing piece. Seeing as we were surrounded by more of the demon people, I used my spirit weapons, leaving the gun tucked into my pants at the small of my back. The one bonus of being in the basement was that we were already on the floor we needed to be on to get out the front doors—if that's where Jay was leading us. I caught a glimpse of the door but Jay headed the opposite way.

"Where are you taking us, Jay? The doors are behind us," I called out.

Jay just gave me a look, telling me I was clearly being an

idiot. "Yeah, what are you gonna do once you're out there? Run all the way to the city or maybe back to Cape Town?"

Fuck! Okay, so clearly he had a plan, and I needed to get with the program and follow wherever he led us and shut the fuck up.

As we fought our way out of this mess, I could feel a tug on my powers as Lailah drew more strength from me and a few of the others. She was bone tired and reaching the end of what she could do without a break. Who knows what she'd been through before she got to the point she and Parker saved us. What I wouldn't give to just collapse this whole building and crush those within it and end this whole mess. Only right now, I couldn't, not with us inside. I was saving the idea for the moment we got into a car and out of this hellhole. Then we had to find a place to lie low and let everyone rest for a little while before we went toe-to-toe with the Dark Lord.

It was a good thing that Jay knew where he was going because I was completely lost, unsure of where the hell we were going and where we'd just been. We reached the end of the hall with double doors that Jay kicked open, exposing a back lot full of various vehicles and other equipment. Lights illuminated the parking lot, seeing as it was well into the evening and the moon was only a sliver in the sky. We didn't head for the first vehicle we spotted. Instead, Jay kept pushing us to the back of the lot where older jeeps and trucks were lining the chain-link fence.

"Everyone, get in the back of the tarp-covered truck. I'll get it started and bust us out of here," Jay yelled, motioning us to hop into the back of the green military truck.

Micah all but tossed Lailah into the back of the truck and climbed up behind her, reaching out for Jay's mom. Hudson joined them as Parker and I stood watch for anyone who might be lurking in the shadows. He must be thinking what I was, that this was going too smoothly. Makoto and his men might be overwhelmed, but this was what they trained to do. If we could make our way out of it then why couldn't they? He had more people, and they were fresher, not having been battle tired or locked away, drugged with venom. No, there was something else we were missing.

The truck rumbled to life. "Everyone in. We're getting the hell out of here," Jay called from the front seat as the door slammed shut.

"Let's go," I said to Parker, motioning with my head for him to get into the back of the truck.

He shook his head. "No, Brayden, I'm going to hold them off while you guys make a clean getaway."

"What are you talking about? There's no one here to stop us," I challenged, looking around the space like I was missing something.

Parker grabbed my arm and pulled me to look at him. "I know you don't have any reason to believe me but I'm not safe to be around you guys. There was only one chance to get Lailah out of here and I took it, knowing it would mean giving her up forever. Please let me do this. Let me love her and protect her the only way that I can since I'm not bound to her."

"Nothing you're saying is making any sense," I argued. "Just get in the damn truck."

"No," Parker stated firmly and took a step back. "I told her I would protect her with my life and that is exactly what I'm going to do."

Realization dawned on my face as the horror of what was about to happen made my stomach twist into knots. "She won't survive that, Parker. If she loses one of us, she won't recover from that. It will be the last straw and she will shatter."

"You don't know that. She's stronger than all of us combined and the world needs her to save it. I'm a fuckup, always was, always will be, but this, this I can do for her," Parker explained through gritted teeth. "Please get in the truck and leave. Don't let her see me go down. Once I do this, I'll have broken another oath and it will kill me, dragging me down into hell because I lost all rights to go to Heaven. Don't make me beg, Brayden. Take care of our girl. Be her rock and hold her together. You're the only one who can do that."

My eyes burned as I realized he was right. We couldn't take him with us and I refused to let Lailah watch as Parker paid the price for setting us free. There were no words that I could say to comfort him. All I could do was what he asked of me. Jay blared the horn and waved at us, leaning out of the driver's side door. "Get the fuck in. We've got to go!"

Parker pulled me in for a hug that I returned, squeezing him tightly. I let go and pulled myself into the truck and pounded on the cab wall so Jay knew we were all clear.

"Wait!" Lailah demanded. "Parker isn't in yet."

She rushed to the back of the truck but I snatched her around the waist, pulling her to my chest. "He's not coming, Angel. He's keeping his promise and making sure you get out of here alive."

"No! No, not like this, never like this. I won't allow him to take the easy way out. He promised that I could yell at him when all this was over and he would listen to every word I said. He can't stay back because that would be breaking a promise," Lailah rambled, frantically trying to fight my hold on her. "I won't forgive him. If he stays there and leaves me again, I won't *ever* forgive him."

I watched as Parker stood there crying, watching Lailah fight to get back to him, but all he did was smile and raise his hands to make the symbol of a heart over his chest before collapsing to the ground.

"What just happened? Why isn't he getting up? He should be getting up and fighting to get to me. If he lays there much longer, we'll get too far and he won't be able to find us," Lailah babbled, on the verge of hysterics.

Dragging her back from the sight of Parker crumpled on the ground, I pulled her down with me as I sat. She stopped fighting me as she continued to say nonsense, rocking back and forth as tears hit my hands, falling from her cheeks. None of the others said anything, even though questions were written all over their faces, but I didn't even know what to say to them at this point. When she stopped rocking, I pulled her onto my lap and cradled her. She pressed her face into my neck, like a child, as I held her. Parker had paid the ultimate sacrifice to get us out of there, knowing he wouldn't be coming with us. Whatever his agreement was with the Dark Lord, he made it with the understanding he would never follow it and instead used it to his advantage.

I lost track of how far we drove or how long we were on the road, but the early morning light shone into the back of the truck, telling me it had been hours. Jay pulled into a motel parking lot and cut the engine, waking Lailah and the others up. There was no way I could fall asleep and not keep an eye on things back here. In truth, I was waiting for the breakdown I knew was going to happen once I explained what happened to Parker. We'd seen Lailah in a lot of situations but I truly meant what I said to Parker. I wasn't sure she would make it through this and be able to look us in the face. I don't know that I could look at myself. I hadn't even tried to find a way to work around the fact that Parker just sacrificed himself for all of us. Instead, I just let him die. What kind of person did that make me?

Jay appeared at the back of the truck with a hotel key in his hand. "I got us connecting rooms. Figured we could all use some sleep before we make our next move. Wait... where's Parker?"

"I think it's best if we get to the room before I explain that," I answered.

Hudson handed off Jay's mom to him and we made our way to the second floor into room seventeen. Lailah didn't speak. She just trailed after me listlessly, eyes blank as we entered the room and I sat her on one of the beds.

"Okay, what the hell is going on and why is she like that?" Jay demanded, his voice sharp.

"Parker didn't get into the truck," she whispered. "Why didn't he get into the truck? We were leaving, all of us. He promised me he wouldn't leave me again and that we would make it through this. That he wouldn't let anything happen to me."

The four of us stood around the double bed, looking at her then each other, unsure of how to even react. Jay turned to me, his hands on his hips. "Explain."

"I don't know the whole story, only what he told me moments before we left. It appears he made an oath with the Dark Lord. What the oath was, I don't have a clue, so don't ask. He told me he never planned to follow the oath, only using it to get Lailah and us out of there alive. If he broke the Oath, it would kill him and send him to hell," I explained, watching Lailah out of the corner of my eye as I talked.

"Dead... did you just say he's dead?" she asked, her voice cracking, more tears streaming down her face. "No, you're lying Brayden. It's not good for you to lie. Tell me the truth, where is Parker? Is he going to meet us here later?"

Now that Parker was gone, I was the only one who could deal with this. He'd been right that Lailah saw me as her rock but I didn't think that was what she wanted at the moment. No, the person who was missing was her heart, the man who could always make her smile or laugh with a stupid joke. Even if I wasn't who she needed right now, I had to make good on my promise to Parker and try to hold her together, even if she didn't want me to.

"Angel, he isn't coming," I told her as I kneeled in front of her. "He kept his promise and made sure you got out of there alive. If he hadn't done what he did, I don't think we'd be free right now, and God knows if we'd have ever made it out of there alive. Parker saved all of us because he loved you and would do anything for you."

That statement finally made her snap.

CHAPTER 20
LAILAH

D ead.

That's what Brayden just said to me.

Parker was dead. He died to get us out of that prison of hell.

No—I refused to believe that. There was no way he could be dead after all we did to stay alive. Parker wouldn't betray me again by making a deal with the Dark Lord even if it was to ensure my freedom. Obviously, Brayden was wrong, and we needed to go back and get him or make sure he had a way to find us.

"Angel, he isn't coming," Brayden said, kneeling in front of me. "He kept his promise and made sure you got out of there alive. If he hadn't done what he did, I don't think we'd be free right now, and God knows if we'd have ever made it out of there alive. Parker saved all of us because he loved you and would do anything for you."

Fuck that!

"Stop talking about him in the past tense! He isn't dead and there's nothing you can say to convince me otherwise. Parker is *mine,* and I didn't tell him he could leave me!" I roared, shooting to my feet and knocking Brayden on his ass. "Say he's dead one more time and we'll see who's going to join him in the afterlife!"

The devastated look on Brayden's face made me even more furious.

"Don't you fucking look at me like that, Brayden. I am not to be pitied. You want to know why, because that motherfucker isn't dead. I didn't tell him he could die and I own his ass right now. He betrayed me and that means I own his life, not the Dark Lord—*me!*"

"Lailah," Jay barked, drawing my attention. "Sit. Down."

The urge to fight him on this was strong, but I knew Jay was being serious and wouldn't have second thoughts about making sure I followed his order. Rage burned in my veins and I needed an outlet, which right now seemed to be picking a fight with the one man I knew I couldn't win against. "Make me."

"Oh fuck," Micah muttered, running his hands through his hair as he shook his head. "Come on, guys, let's go find some food."

Hudson reached down and helped Brayden to his feet, ignoring the standoff that was happening between Jay and me. A few moments later, I heard the door close, but I refused to let my gaze drop from Jay's, knowing he would see it as weakness.

"What are you hoping to get out of this, Lailah Mackenzie?" Jay asked, using my full name, telling me he wasn't happy with me. "Do you think you're the only one who is hurt at the loss of Parker?"

I scoffed at that. "After what he did to me, you all hated him and turned your back on him. Hell, you told him he better not come around again unless I asked for him and made sure all his bags were packed. How upset can you be?"

"I might not express my emotions like you do, but I'm not so cold and unfeeling to be unaffected by the death of a man I knew almost my whole life," Jay growled back. "Don't you stand there and act like you aren't at fault for rejecting him either. You wanted him out of the house and out of your life. He didn't just betray you that day, he betrayed us all when he chose Lilith over us. We are the *five* Elemental Warriors and today we lost one of our own, who I stood shoulder-to-shoulder with in more battles than you know of. You've been in this world for not even a year and you think you have the right to take your anger out on the rest of us?"

Jay's words stung as they landed too close to home and the guilt that I was feeling, but they also fueled my anger. "If it wasn't for me showing up when I did, you would have succumbed to your father's wishes and ended up one of those mindless people fighting to make the world a living hell for other demons. I might not have the same skin in the game but in my short time, I've been asked to give up everything and everyone I know and love for this—even my own life! Fuck you and your superior logic. I've been head-to-head with the Dark Lord more than any of you, giving up part of my soul that I wasn't sure I would ever get back. Tell me, how am I not as invested in this as you. Please, tell me. I would love to know."

As I spoke, I'd been resvancing on him until we were an inch apart from each other. I could feel his breath on my face as he stared me down, unflinching at my words, only crossing his arms as he waited to see if I was finished speaking. When I let the silence stretch, he just continued to study me as if he was waiting for something to happen.

"He can't be dead," I rasped. "Parker isn't gone. He can't be gone because I didn't get the chance to tell him that I loved him and that I would forgive him. He needs to know that I wanted to work things out, that he was mine. Jay, he can't be gone. He.... no.... I didn't tell him."

This must have been what Jay was waiting for. His face softened and he caught me as my legs gave out. Lifting me, he climbed onto the bed and sat against the headboard, letting me sob into his chest. I could no longer deny what they were telling me. I thought I knew what it felt like to have my heart break when Parker betrayed me and the Oath broke, but this pain was unlike anything someone could even try to describe to me. It was as if I'd lost something integral to who I was as a person and there was no way to get it back. It was just gone.

When I finally cried myself out, Jay scooped me up and carried me into the bathroom and set me down to turn on the shower. I couldn't remember the last time I'd taken one and the idea of being able to wash the filth away from this experience was exactly what I needed. Unable to extend the effort to do anything, I just stood there watching the water shoot out of the showerhead. As if sensing that I needed someone to just take charge, Jay had me lift my arms and peeled my shirt off me. Next went the bra and then he kneeled to help me out of my pants and undies as I rested a hand on his shoulder so I didn't fall over. Naked, I started to shiver in the cool tile bathroom until he steered me into the shower and under the warm water. When he stepped back, I thought he was leaving me and I clutched his arm desperately.

"Don't leave me," I whispered. "I can't handle being alone right now."

"I'm not going to leave you, Beautiful. I just need to get

out of my clothes. Showers aren't as effective with them still on," Jay assured me as I released his arm. "I'll be right here in your sight the entire time. I won't disappear on you."

Was it that obvious what I was worried about? Of course it would be. This was Jay, the man who knew everything about me, even things I didn't know about myself. He would give me what I needed, even if I didn't yet know what that might be.

Moving quickly, he stripped out of his clothes and stepped in behind me, guiding me to the middle of the shower and turning me so I was facing him. He took the small bottle of shampoo and worked it into my hair, scrubbing my scalp with his strong fingers. When he was done, he tipped my head back so the soap didn't get into my eyes as it was rinsed out, then he repeated the process with the conditioner. Once done with my hair, he moved onto washing me with a bar of soap and a washcloth. The movements were confident and to the point, not lingering or being suggestive in any way that would make me think he was alluding to more.

When he was done taking care of me, he switched places with me. For himself, he just used the bar of soap to wash from head to toe. I guess with not really having any hair to wash it made sense. Watching the water ripple over his muscles had me rubbing my legs together to gain some kind of friction. Even though he acted like he didn't notice me watching, he took the time to stroke himself since he was already rock hard. When he moved on, I couldn't help but reach out and grasp it in my hand, feeling it pulse at my touch. He hesitated but didn't stop me as I ran my hand up and down slowly, letting my thumb swirl over the tip that was already weeping out precum. Jay and I hadn't had much of a chance to be together since we bonded and I ached to feel him inside me again. Right now, I think it was the only thing I could feel since I was numb to everything else and too exhausted to cry again.

Jay reached down and gripped my hand, stopping me from moving, drawing my attention to his face. "I'm willing to offer you a distraction but we will do this my way."

"What does that mean?" I asked, needing him to spell it out for me.

"It means that I will be in charge of what is happening and how. Of course, you will always have the chance to stop things with a simple request but if you will allow me, I will be the master of your body," Jay explained.

Once again, this man proved to me just how much he loved me by giving me exactly what I needed, even if I didn't know what that was. "Yes."

"Then turn around and put your hands above your head as far as you can reach," Jay ordered.

Without question, I did what he asked, reaching far above my head, grasping the top of the glass shower wall.

"You are not allowed to move unless I tell you to. If you do, there will be consequences. Do you understand?" Jay asked.

"I understand."

"Sir is how you will respond to me while I'm in control," Jay corrected as he trailed a finger down my spine.

Licking my lips, I rested my head against the shower wall, feeling weak with the wave of lust rushing through me. "I understand, Sir."

"Good," Jay whispered into my ear as he swept my hair to the side and kissed my neck just under my ear. "Shall we see how good of a girl you can be?"

Jay's fingers caressed my ass before slipping between

my legs to skate over my slit that was begging for attention. I let out a moan and pressed back into his touch. Seconds later, a stinging slap descended upon my ass. I let out a yelp as I looked over my shoulder in surprise at Jay.

"I warned you there would be punishment if you didn't follow the rules, Beautiful," Jay pointed out. "Now that you understand how this is going to work, I suggest holding still."

"You've been looking for a reason to spank me and now I've let you talk me into a situation where it can happen," I said.

Hearing me, Jay pressed his body to mine and slid a hand to hold my throat in a gentle grip. "Does that mean you don't want to play my game anymore? Tell me now and this will be over, otherwise as I requested, this will be played by my rules. I can feel how much you don't want to be in control of your life right now and I'm offering you a reprieve from having to make any choices. Instead, you just have to listen to what I'm telling you to do."

Silence fell between us as I took a moment to decide whether I was up for this right now. Jay was right. The last thing I wanted to do right now was to deal with anything happening in the real world. If I stayed here, I would be taken care of and given what I needed.

"I will follow your rules, Sir. Please give me what I need," I said, relaxing completely against him, submitting to his will, knowing I was safe with him.

Jay let his teeth run along the shell of my ear as his free hand slid across my belly down between my legs. "That's right, Beautiful. I'll take good care of you as long as you promise to be a good girl."

A finger swirled around my clit twice before it sank

inside of me, making me cry out at how it wasn't enough. I needed more. "Please, Sir," I begged.

"Good girls are happy with what they're given. Are you unhappy with what I've chosen to give you?" Jay asked, his voice deep and commanding.

I shook my head as he stopped moving his hand, leaving his one finger still inside me as my body begged for him to do something with it. The hand was removed and another slap on my ass echoed in the small bathroom.

"You will use your words, Beautiful," Jay commanded.

"No, Sir, I wasn't complaining about what I was given." I panted as his fingers returned but they only seemed to glide over the opening.

Jay hummed in my ear at my response, kissing down my neck until he reached where my shoulder joined. He latched on and sucked the skin there as he thrust two fingers into me this time. I gasped but held myself still, even though all I wanted to do was grind on his fingers that he hadn't moved since entering me. He knew exactly what he was doing with this type of torture, making it impossible to think of anything but what was happening right here in this shower.

When he released my neck, he must have decided that I was being a good enough girl to warrant a good finger fucking because that was what happened next. "Remember to keep those hands on the wall," Jay instructed.

Without warning he started to work those fingers like it was his sole purpose in life. He told me I couldn't move, but he never said anything about keeping quiet, which was good. I wasn't sure I'd be able to do that too. "Fuck yes!" I moaned.

My legs shook, as an orgasm started to build, and he took his fingers out and slapped my clit with his hand, shocking the hell out of me. I yelped, but I didn't let my hands move from the wall. Another two slaps followed, making me grunt as they sent shock waves of pleasure through my body. He shoved his fingers back inside me, using his other hand to flick my clit as he hooked them, stroking my G-spot. I felt something building, and it was different from all the other orgasms that I'd had before. Granted, before the guys, I was practically a virgin and ignorant to the wonders of sex, so this might be normal, but something told me it might not be.

I could feel myself clenching around his fingers, warning him that I was close to coming. The hand that had been working my clit like a DJ then slapped hard down on it. That was the tipping point. I shattered, screaming out my pleasure as my legs gave out on me, and no manner of willpower would have kept them working. My whole body convulsed and I'm pretty sure I just pissed myself as well with how strong that climax was.

"Oh my God," I gasped as Jay held me to his chest. "That was amazing."

He nipped at my ear before using a hand to turn my face so he could capture my lips with his own. The kiss was passionate as he sucked my lower lip into his mouth, nibbling it with his teeth before kissing it better. His tongue claimed mine as he deepened the kiss, taking what little breath I had away.

"We've just gotten started, Beautiful," he shared, nuzzling his nose behind my ear. Pressing on my back, Jay had me bending over until I was folded in half. "Grab onto those ankles, Beautiful. Don't let go or I'll stop."

I peered up at him from between my legs, getting a great view of his cock bobbing with excitement as he grabbed my hips. Getting me into place, he grabbed himself to slick it up before giving it a good solid thrust in until he was balls deep. "Holy shit!" I yelled, not fully prepared for that swift action. Thanks to the prep work he'd done though, I wasn't uncomfortable. He knew that he was the thickest of all my men.

Jay pulled back and slammed home twice more. I was thankful he had a good hold on my hips or I would have crashed into the glass at the impact. Finally, he fell into a steady rhythm that wasn't a pace for the faint of heart and I just hung on for dear life as he pistoned in and out of me. As distracted as I was by things, I didn't miss the fact that he was playing with the second entrance that was in clear view while I was bent over so fully. Using his thumb, he massaged it and pressed the tip in but didn't push any further, allowing me to relax into the feeling of it. When he did finally slide it into the first knuckle, I was more than ready for the move. He continued to work both entrances until he pulled his thumb out and pressed two fingers in, making me stiffen, unsure that I was ready for that, but he just took his time working them in just as he had his thumb.

The two fingers found their way in and the feeling of being so full of his dick and fingers working me over was overwhelming. It was a whole new level of sensation, even more than when Hudson had introduced it to me. I could feel another orgasm beginning to build and I had to fight the urge to press against him to deepen the movements, knowing he would stop and I would be left wanting. His fingers moved much more freely in my ass and I welcomed the sensation, feeling much more confident about anal play. As if he sensed my change, he removed his fingers and pulled out of me completely.

"Please, Sir, let me come," I pleaded, an instant reaction to being left empty.

"I would like to try your delicious ass, if I can?" Jay asked as I felt his blunt head pressing into the entrance. "You're ready but I won't do it if you aren't interested. This choice is yours alone."

Risking that we were taking a break from the rules, I reached back, grabbed his dick, and pushed myself back onto it, letting it slowly enter past the tight ring. Standing up a little straighter, I grabbed his hips and held him still as I worked the rest of his cock into me. Once we were back to chest, I leaned my head back to rest on his shoulder, looking up at him. "My choice is hell yes."

Jay grinned at me, his eyes shining with heat and love as he dipped his head to kiss me. "You are a naughty girl, aren't you, breaking the rules like that?"

"Seems like you're going to have to punish me," I purred.

He shoved me forward until I was pressed against the glass wall once again, only this time he held the back of my neck as his way of controlling me. His grip was tight but I could still breathe easily enough with the pressure. His other hand spanked me on each cheek until I could feel it throbbing and I whimpered as he rubbed them lovingly.

"I can't tell you how long I've waited to see these cheeks bright red from my hand," Jay shared as he slid in and out of me. The ache added a whole new level of pleasure to this moment I didn't think was possible. I was beginning to see why people were so into this type of thing.

Now that he finished my punishment, he turned his attention on bringing me back to the brink of an orgasm. This feeling was so different. I kept wanting to push against him but I just kept telling myself to relax and let the feeling pass. Feeling me struggling, he used a hand to work over my clit, stroking it into a frenzy but not letting the damn break as he worked to catch up. Finally, as I felt him struggle to keep it together, I risked breaking the rules and worked in tandem with him, urging him deeper and faster. He hissed in my ear and as punishment he pinched my clit with his fingers, making me scream once more as I climaxed, using the wall to keep myself steady as he draped over me, grunting and urging short thrusts into me as he spent his load.

CHAPTER 21

LAILAH

Spent emotionally and physically, I didn't really remember much after Jay and I dried off and he tucked me into one of the beds, curling up beside me on top of the covers. Neither one of us had extra clothes, but he waved off my arguments of him putting his dirty pants back on. Not having the energy to really argue with him, I let it be and let him hold me as I drifted off to sleep, silent tears rolling down my cheeks. My moment of forgetting about the world around me and that fact that Parker was gone ended the second we left the bathroom. The pain of his loss punched me right in the chest but Jay was kind enough not to comment, only holding me tighter. The guys returned, and I cracked open an eye but I didn't have the energy to wake up, so I didn't. It had been one hell of a day and I didn't want to participate in it anymore. Tomorrow would be another day and I would have to deal with the reality of life soon enough. But for now, I could hide in a dreamless sleep.

Only, it wasn't a dreamless sleep because as soon as I drifted away into the darkness of my mind, I found myself back in the void where the Dark Lord used to come visit me.

This time, my mind decided that it wanted to cause me the worst amount of pain possible and there stood Parker. His hands were tucked into his jean's pockets, wearing his favorite purple shirt that read—*All You Need Is Love.* Everything about him was so perfect and lifelike that I almost believed that he was standing here with me and it wasn't just my mind, desperate to have one more moment with the man I loved and lost.

"What are you doing here, Trouble? You know it's not safe to do this without someone to protect you," Parker warned. "None of the others can sense that bastard like I could."

Clearly my own mind wanted to cause the maximum amount of pain, having him say shit like that to me.

"If you were that worried then you shouldn't have fucking died on me, Parker. You promised me that you would get us through this and that I could yell at you all I wanted once we got out of that hellhole," I snapped, hands on my hips. If my brain was going to be an asshole, I wasn't going to take it lying down.

Parker's brows raised at the venom in my voice. "Wow, you aren't going to pull any punches, are you?"

"Why should I? You left me, *again!* You didn't even say goodbye or warn me that something was wrong. Instead, you just let me watch you die right there in the dirt as we drove away!" I yelled, throwing my hands up in the air.

Parker rubbed the back of his neck as he looked down at his feet. "Yeah, well, as usual, I didn't really think through it all. I just focused on the fact that I was keeping you safe and alive."

"What good is that when I'm left to live this life without one of the people I love? Oh sure, I have the others, but who's going to have the patience to teach me how to play those video games you all love to play. Or who's going to eat all the pies I make in the middle of the night when I can't sleep? No one else is going to understand my love of sugar cookies the way you do or tease me mercilessly about the dirty books that Cami makes me read to get *ideas* on how to have group play time with you all," I demanded, my voice getting louder and louder as I spoke. "Parker, you left me before I could tell you that I forgive you and I want to find a way to make things work, that my life isn't complete without you in it. How could you do that to me?"

Now my shoulders were shaking as I was gasping for breath and the tears I was fighting back won out. "You're mine, and I didn't tell you, you could leave."

Parker just stood there looking at me utterly shocked, but I couldn't wait for him to figure his shit out. I ran right into him, wrapping my arms around his middle. How could he feel so real when I knew he was gone? If this was my brain's way of giving me a chance to say goodbye to him it was too real. He even smelled like he always did, with his spicy aftershave and hints of grease from working on that stupid truck of his that was always needing to be tweaked. Thankfully, he returned my embrace and enveloped me in his large body, dropping to his knees, clinging to me.

"I didn't know, Trouble. I didn't know how you felt about me. What I did was the worst thing that I could have ever done to hurt you. I don't deserve to be given a second chance or to be loved by someone like you," Parker said, his voice cracking. "You are everything to me and saving you so you could save the world was the only way I could think of to show you how much I loved you and atone for my sins. I shouldn't have left you though, because you're right. I did promise you I wouldn't leave you again."

Pulling back, I lifted my arms to hold his face as I looked

into his stunning green eyes. "Parker, you are my heart and I don't know how I'm going to do this without you. It was never supposed to end like this. We all live together. We all die together."

"Lailah," Parker pleaded as if I was causing him physical pain with my words. "I hope you won't ever doubt how much I love you ever again. That you will forever remember that I would literally give my life for you, even though you didn't ask me to."

"Fucking idiot," I muttered and slammed my lips to his, cutting him off from saying anything else equally stupid.

If I was going to be stuck in this dream, then I was going to make it a happy one that I would be able to think back on as my last moments with him. I shoved him back so I was straddling him as he looked up at me, dazed. My hands fisted in his shirt and I dragged it up and over his head with his help once he figured out what I was trying to do. Now that his chest wasn't obstructed by clothing, I let my hands wander over his sculpted muscles, tracing all the dips, making him shiver under my touch.

"Trouble, what are you doing?" Parker asked as I reached to undo the button of his pants.

Rolling my eyes, I looked at him. "If you have to ask then clearly I'm not making my intentions known. I plan to make the most of this time we have together regardless of if it's just in my dreams."

"Yeah, about that—"

"Parker," I cut in. "You owe me this after everything you've put me through. Let me have this, please. I want a memory of us together more powerful than when my heart shattered watching you crumble to the ground like a puppet with his strings cut."

"What if we can keep meeting here like this? That it's

not the last time you could see me… do you still want to do this?" Parker pressed.

"Are you telling me you don't want to have sex with me?" I huffed, sitting back and crossing my arms.

"Fuck no, but I also don't want you to regret this someday," he explained.

Leaning forward, I pressed a kiss to his heart. "The only thing I will regret is that we never got to have this moment in real life. Yes, you hurt me, but I would endure that pain again if it meant that I could have you back."

Apparently, that was all Parker needed to hear before he turned the tables and flipped us over so I was on the bottom. "I refuse to let you experience any more pain at my hands or actions. You, my beautiful bundle of trouble, are only going to lose your mind in the pleasure I plan to give you."

Parker slowly pushed up my shirt, kissing along my skin as he worked the clothing off. In this dream world, I was wearing a t-shirt and sweatpants and not naked like I was back in the hotel room, small wonders. I lost sight of him as he yanked the shirt over my head, leaving us a matching set of bare chests. His hands skimmed down my shoulders until he reached my hands, which he grabbed and lifted to kiss, holding my gaze as he did.

"Lailah Mackenzie, I broke one oath to you so I won't even try to give you another. Instead, what I give to you is all of me, mind, body, and soul. You alone hold the essence of what makes me who I am and even though I doubted myself, you never did, always pushing me to be more. I failed because I believed what everyone in the world told me—that I was a fuckup and always would be. Then, you literally crashed into my life and changed it, turning everything upside down, knocking me off my high horse and showing me life could be more than fun games, and goofing off all the time. Forever and always, I will be yours if you still want me."

"If I had the power to do it, I would make it so you could never leave me again, Parker. I love you, all of you, just as you are - the good, the bad, and the in-between," I answered, pulling him down to kiss him, adding to my point.

Parker wrapped his arms around me and held me tight, our chests plastered together, our hearts beating in time as we lost ourselves in the feel of each other. At some point, we both shed our pants, and I hiked a leg up over his hip and let him slide into me. It felt like coming home, perfect beyond words, reinforcing that this was just a dream and I needed to make the most of it. There was nothing rushed about this as we stroked each other, absorbing all that we could from this moment. Parker pulled me up to sit in his lap, my legs wrapped around his waist, and he buried his head into my neck as he hugged me to him, holding me as he thrust up into me. I tossed my head back, reveling in the feeling of him inside me, making sure the moment and feeling was seared into my brain.

As I leaned back slightly, he latched onto one of my nipples as he supported my back with his other hand, letting me trust in his ability to keep me from falling. In this moment, there was nothing but trust and love flowing between us, wrapped up in what felt like a magical hug. Why would I ever want to return to the real world when I could have this in my life forever, have him with me forever? Needing more from him, I hooked a hand around his neck and pulled myself to him, kissing him deeply before I pushed on his chest, asking him to lean back. Once I was on top, I moved with a little more purpose. I'd enjoyed the slow sensual moment between us, but now I was craving him. I needed to have him fill me to the brim until I couldn't take anymore of him in, and he wouldn't do it for fear of hurting me so I was gonna have to take matters in hand.

Riding him, I rocked my hips in such a way that I didn't have to lift myself off of him and lose that contact. My hand spread out wide on his chest, feeling his heart thundering as he panted, telling me he was getting close. I cupped the side of his face and leaned down to rest my forehead on his, speeding up, knowing we both wouldn't last much longer. With one final thrust, we both fell over the cliff and exploded with pleasure, moaning and clinging to each other.

As we caught our breaths, a tear trailed down my cheek, knowing that this dream was going to end soon. It broke my heart that when I woke up, he wouldn't be there with me.

"Don't leave me, Parker," I whispered, my lips brushing his. "I can't do this without you. I don't want to do this without you."

Parker opened his eyes and I could see the sadness and fear in them. "What I wouldn't give to do this all over so I never had to leave you."

He tilted his chin up so our lips met and I could feel him pouring every ounce of love that he could into me, and I did the same, needing to believe this was real. There was no way a dream could be this real, and if it was real, then I wasn't going to let him go. Watching him walk away from me twice in a lifetime was enough for me. I didn't plan on letting it happen ever again. The world around us started to glow so bright it drew my attention, breaking our kiss. The air around us was alight with gold and purple energy, wrapping us up in a cocoon until it seemed to hum and vibrate as if it was alive. As the power level continued to grow, I noticed there was a haze of dark energy floating between our powers. It looked the same as when I purged the others from the demon venom. There was something clinging to Parker's powers.

Sitting up, I looked at the man below me. "This is real..." He looked hesitant to answer me but he nodded that I was correct. "Is it true you made an oath with the Dark Lord?"

"Well, it was with Makoto but it was on behalf of the Dark Lord. He even made me spill blood over it to ensure that if I betrayed them, I would die for that betrayal."

Hope bloomed in my chest at his answer. "I think I can save you."

"Lailah, I'm dead. I felt my heart stop the moment I helped you all get in that truck and leave the base. Trust me when I say that I am definitely no longer a part of the world of the living."

Rolling off him, I grabbed my shirt and pants, pulling them on, needing to think clearly, and I couldn't do that naked. "I don't think you're dead-dead. I think you're in purgatory or something because that's what this place is, the thin veil between our world and Hell. That's why the Dark Lord could pull me here to talk to him when he can't enter the real world. What if the Dark Lord has to come here to get you before you're totally dead, unable to come back? Will you let me try to save you?"

Parker sat there looking all mussed from sex and incredibly distracting so I tossed him his clothes. "Trouble, you know I can't say no to you but I don't want you to be hurt worse if it doesn't work. That is the last thing I want."

"I'll take that under advisement. Now, put your clothes on so I can do this and not want to jump your bones again.

Knowing that you're not my imagination changes things and I want nothing more than to try out all the crazy things I'm sure you have saved up in that brain of yours."

He just grinned as he got dressed and came to stand before me. "Alright, now what?"

"I have a theory and it has to do with how I was purged of the Dark Lord's hold on me and how I got the venom out of the others."

"So what you're telling me is this is going to hurt—a lot." Parker grimaced but took a deep breath. "If this is the price I have to pay to get my life back then fuck it, the pain will mean I'm alive, right?"

"That's the spirit," I answered, popping up on my toes to kiss him. "Ready?"

"As ready as you can be to hopefully return from the dead."

Nodding, I took both of his hands and closed my eyes, centering myself and reaching for my powers. When I went slower, it hurt less, but I used more power in the long run. On the other hand, when I blasted Jay, he was in a world of hurt but I could burn out the venom faster. Maybe I could try what I did with Jay's mother and seek out the poison and then destroy it. Sending out a whip of my golden power, I let it flow through Parker's body until I found what I was looking for. It seemed that his whole right arm was full of the dark energy and it was growing the longer it was left to its own devices. This must be the hand that he'd bled from. Could this be why he was still here? Was the Dark Lord waiting for the curse to take over his whole body, turning him evil?

"So this is a good news, bad news moment," I stated, opening my eyes to look at Parker. "I've found what I need to get rid of but it's more than I've ever managed before. This is going to hurt like a bitch for me to burn out of you."

"Where was the good news in that, Trouble?"

"That I'm going to get rid of every last drop of it and set you free to bring you back with me," I answered with a bright smile. "I'll just pull from your powers when I feel like I'm reaching a point I can't manage on my own."

He looked skeptical but a resigned look settled onto his face. "Can I at least sit down for this? I'm afraid if I'm standing, I won't be able to endure it as well."

"Smart call," I agreed.

Sitting cross-legged in front of each other, I took his right hand in both of mine, knowing this was where I had to concentrate my powers. "I love you, Parker Jones. No matter how this goes, I need you to know that."

"I love you too, Trouble, and I'll see you on the other side. I have no doubt."

CHAPTER 22

JAY

By the time the guys came back from getting us supplies and reaching out to the Elementi, Lailah was in a deep sleep. I felt like I could move now without fear of her waking up and feeling alone without one of us in bed with her. Shushing them, I waved them over to the room my mother was sleeping in, knowing we wouldn't wake her if what Lailah said about her was true, which I didn't have any reason not to believe.

"How's she doing?" Brayden asked.

"Well, she cried herself to sleep, but it looks like she'll sleep soundly, which is all I can ask for right now," I answered with a shrug. "I got her cleaned up and showered, so that seemed to settle her some. You didn't grab any clothes by chance, did you?"

"Yeah, we found a little shopping area to get food and grabbed some basics. Hope she doesn't mind wearing a dress. It was easier to grab that than pick out a whole bunch of clothes," Hudson explained as he unpacked some of the bags, tossing me a pair of pants and a simple t-shirt.

I quickly changed before we got further into our

conversation, then snagged a water bottle. "I know we all need sleep but we need to make a plan first. Rest will come easier if I know what the hell we're gonna do when we wake up."

"I was able to get in touch with Beth and filled her in on what happened. Let's just say the news about Makoto didn't go over well. But now that we know his role in things, it helps her to keep information to herself. There are networks he doesn't have access to so that will help as long as there aren't any of his people in the mix. Beth said she is going to keep it to just Cami, Maggs, and herself for now, while we try and figure out who else is trustworthy," Micah shared.

Nodding, I chugged down the bottle of water as I tried to determine what my father's next steps would be. He lost all of us and that would not make the Dark Lord happy. I also didn't think he learned what he wanted to from Lailah. He could deduce some things from how we all got out of there, but that was still limited information. The Dark Lord wanted to move up his plans, but it still seemed like he was missing something vital to making that happen and we were part of it. Something to do with Lailah was keeping him from ruling the world, but he was being cautious on how he went after her, not knowing what powers she truly had. I'd noticed that all the marks from her skin that the Dark Lord put there were gone, while still leaving all the other scars she got. Could it be that her powers removed them like she did the venom in us? If she could do that and heal my mother, was it possible that she was the antidote to the serum as well?

There were too many questions and not enough answers.

"Do we think it's safe to say that the Dark Lord's army is

here?" Hudson inquired as he opened a bag of beef jerky to gnaw on.

"If there is one thing I don't have doubt about, it's that," I stated, crushing the empty water bottle in my hand. "My father has been protecting it from the Elementi for at least two years, leading us on a wild goose chase all over the fucking world. It makes me sick to think he's been helping that bastard of a demon for who knows how long."

Hudson reached out and gripped my shoulders. "Jay, there is no sense in beating yourself up when he had us all fooled. No one blames you for wanting to think the best of your father. I don't think any of us would have done things differently. What is important is that we know now and we'll deal with the fallout. It doesn't change the mission."

He had a point, but it wasn't their father who would have to be killed or arrested for their crimes against humanity. All I could do at this point was keep moving forward and make sure we didn't lose anyone else to this battle. "We need to call Parker's family. They deserve to know he's gone."

"Should we try and go back to find his body?" Brayden asked. "Seems like we owe it to him to at least try. He saved us all at the cost of his own life."

"That fucking idiot shouldn't have ever made a deal like that," Micah snapped. "Who the hell would make such a stupid choice?"

Brayden shot to his feet and got up into his best friend's face. "You cut that shit out right now and be grateful for what he's done for us. If Lailah hears you talking like that, she's going to lose her mind, asshole. All of us know you hated the guy, but she loved him, even after all he put her through. So take a moment to think before you say something that will hurt her."

My brows climbed in surprise at how aggressive Brayden was being about this. He wasn't wrong and Micah should take a moment to deal with the fact that Lailah would mourn Parker for quite some time. This wasn't something he could ignore.

"Fuck you, Brayden. You think I'm not pissed that he killed himself for me? I don't deserve a sacrifice like that from someone I was never even nice to," Micah snarled, shoving Brayden back. "I would never say shit like that in front of her. She's been through enough. It doesn't change that Parker was selfish and in his last moments hurt her again. Only this time, there's no chance for him to make it up to her."

Ah, now I understood where this was coming from. Micah was feeling like shit because Parker did the one thing no one else could to protect the woman we all loved. If one of us died, we would kill her and take her down with us. Parker wasn't bonded to her, freeing him to make such a choice. It could also be that Micah had a heart and was actually feeling bad about treating Parker the way he had the whole time we'd known him. Not that Micah would ever admit that to a single soul, because heaven forbid the man was wrong about something.

"Fine, then get out whatever snarky bullshit things you need to before she wakes up," Brayden shot back, not letting Micah get out of this easily. "Parker was a brother to us and we need to honor him. I think we should try to find his body before we tell his parents. It will help if we can tell them the truth and have all the answers before we destroy their world."

"That is a fair point," I answered in agreement. "It's best we have everything we can give them and not show up empty-handed."

"You want to leave and head back to Ryevick?" Micah asked, a challenge clear in his voice. "We're right where we need to be to end this. Why would we leave?"

I stabbed a finger in the direction of the other room. "You're telling me if she wakes up unable to do anything but put one foot in front of the other, you're going to make her fight a battle she doesn't even want to be a part of? God, just when I didn't think you could be a bigger jackass."

"Fuck!" Micah swore, getting to his feet and pacing. "When did I become the punching bag?"

"Do you really need an answer to that?" Hudson asked, getting up from the bed. "I know we didn't figure anything out yet but I need some sleep, so you'll just have to fill me in on things later."

"Truthfully, I think we all need sleep before we can be of any use. I'll stay in here with my mother. You guys can have the room with Lailah," I offered, wanting to keep an eye on mother as it was.

The guys all mumbled their agreement and headed back into the second room, leaving me alone to my thoughts. I brushed a hand over my mother's forehead, brushing the hair out of her face, making sure she wasn't too warm or cold. Her skin felt clammy and her breath was shallower than it was before, making me uneasy. Lailah said that whatever was done to her was constricting her heart and we were short on time, but I didn't know how to ask the woman I loved to burn herself out to save Mother. Two women that I promised to protect and both of them were hurting in their own way and I couldn't do a damn thing to fix it. I was the person who protected others, now I was helpless, and I didn't like that feeling one bit.

"Jay!" Micah yelled. "Get the fuck in here, now!"

I flung the door open and found the entire room

glowing with a golden light that was emanating from Lailah. Her body was pulsing with so much power it was blinding. It was almost like you could feel it vibrating through the air. The hair on my arms stood up on end and the air was thick, making it hard to breathe as I got closer to her. I fought through the urge to back away from her and grabbed her hand, making me crumble to my knees, grunting at the feel of my power being ripped out of me. Whatever she was going through, she needed lots of power and I'd just given her access to mine.

"Touch her," I bit out. "She needs us."

Even though I couldn't see the others and if they were doing what I told them to, the moment they made contact with her, the wave of power fluctuated. This was just like the feeling of when Lailah pulled our power during the drive to Paarl. Only this time, it was all four of us giving her power and creating a perfect circuit, connecting all of us making a pass-through for the power to grow stronger and stronger. In my mind's eye, I could see the red, blue, green, and silver energy intermixing with her golden aura. What surprised me was the fact a purple energy was appearing and growing as the power pulsed.

Why would Parker's power be showing up in this? It's never shown up before. Even when we created the barrier to protect the property, it didn't flow with ours. I assumed it was because he wasn't bonded with Lailah like we were, but now I wasn't sure of anything. Just when I didn't think the power could grow even more, it pressed against my skin as if it was just to the point of bursting out of my very skin, and it popped. If it had been a bomb, it would have leveled the whole town, if not the next one over. As the power shook the ground under us, I clung to her, trying to keep from breaking the connection we still held, feeling like the process wasn't over yet. There was still more to be done and I couldn't break the circuit.

Just when I didn't think I could hold on for a moment longer, my fingers convulsing around her wrist, I was pulled into a blinding white light. I remember Lailah telling us what it was like when the angel came to talk to her and it made me curious if that was what was happening now. Why else would there need to be so much power gathered? Was it to combat the darkness that was around us, being so close to the Dark Lord's army? As my vision normalized and adjusted to the brightness, I found Lailah standing with someone, holding their arm and leaning into their body as if they were a part of her. I noticed this person's hair was ginger, glistening in the bright light like a beacon.

"Parker?" I asked, taking a step forward. "How...?"

Lailah's face shone with pure joy and excitement. "We saved him, all of us together. We brought him back."

"Are we dead?" Micah asked from beside me.

I snapped my head in his direction, not having noticed he was even there. To my left were Hudson and Brayden, meaning all six of us were back together in this strange place.

"No, you're not dead," Parker answered. "Trust me, I know what that looks like and it's not this."

"We're in Heaven's limbo, just like the darkness is Hell's," Lailah explained. "This is where the angel brought me in my dream to tell me what was going on."

As if talking about them caused one to appear, a flash of white light faded for us to see a being with large white wings and a white shapeless dress. I couldn't tell their features or anything else about them as they stood there, but I could feel their eyes on us.

"Knights, I have brought you here because it is finally

time for Synergy's true powers to be unlocked. Each of you have shown great sacrifice and stayed true to your Oath and nourished your Bond with Synergy to the point that you can now defeat the Dark Lord. Trust in each other, for Synergy's purpose is to take that which is singular and combine it to make it all that much stronger. You have done well, our brave knights. You've survived more than any before you have had to withstand. God smiles on you, extends his favor. Be blessed and remember my words when the outcome looks bleak."

Finished with what they had to say, we were sent back to our bodies with a flick of a wing, causing me to gasp as I landed on my back, looking up at the ceiling of the hotel room. "Holy shit," I wheezed.

Slowly, I sat up and found the others in the same state of shock as myself but when I glanced at the bed, I froze. There, holding Lailah to his chest was Parker, in the flesh, looking just as he had when we last saw him. I knew without question that the two of them were bonded.

"Jalen?"

Spinning on my heel, thinking I must be crazy to hear what I just heard, I decided not to question it as I rushed forward and pulled my mother into a tight hug. "Oh thank God, she did it. She saved you, too."

CHAPTER 23
LAILAH

When I opened my eyes, I found myself back in the real world—at least I hoped it was. Parker was wrapped around me as if he was scared to let me go, my face smothered in his chest. The sound of his beating heart made me tear up, and I came to terms with the fact he was alive. I'd managed to do the impossible and with the others' help, we brought him back! Another thing I noticed was the hum of a Bond between us, telling me that all five of the men I loved with all my heart were connected and whole. I'd been crying so much the past several hours, but I couldn't hold back the happy tears that were soaking his shirt.

"Jalen?" a woman's voice called out, pulling me from my own revelations to turn my head.

Standing in the doorway between the hotel rooms was Jay's mother. She was awake and looked perfectly healthy, which made my already happy heart overflow with joy. Whatever I'd done to help Parker must have been enough to purge her of the curse that had been put on her as well. There had been so many losses in this journey, it was healing to have won a few battles today. Jay rushed to his mother and wrapped her up in a hug, surprising her since he wasn't normally a man to show such strong outward emotions.

I started to sit up but found that even the effort of trying was too much. My whole body hurt like I'd run farther than my body could handle and passed out for the effort. Groaning, I just rolled onto my back, my breath coming in shallow pants as nothing about my body wanted to listen to me.

"Trouble, you okay?" Parker asked, leaning over me, his face scrunched with concern.

"I think bringing you back from the dead took a little more out of me than I expected," I joked and attempted to laugh but it hurt too much to do that. "Do you think it would be okay if I take a nap?"

Parker reached out and brushed my hair out of my face. "Yeah, I don't think anyone will be upset if you close your eyes and rest. We'll all be here when you wake up."

Only having the effort to hum my response, I let my eyes closed and fell into a deep sleep.

"Guys, it's been two days," Micah's voice rang out, harsh with anger. "Are you telling me we shouldn't take her to a hospital or get her help?"

"Look, I know you're upset but think of the power she used to heal Jay's mother and bring Parker back. It makes sense that she would need time to rest and restore her powers," Hudson reasoned.

I could hear them moving about the space. I was thinking we were still in the same hotel room but anything could have happened while I was out. Taking a deep breath, I was pleased to notice that my body wasn't in pain and as I stretched my muscles, rejoiced at being able to move, giving that euphoric feeling. With a large yawn, I opened my eyes and found the guys all hovering around my bed, looking at me with varying degrees of excitement and concern.

"Good morning?" I asked, unsure of what to say.

Parker flashed me his signature grin followed by a wink. "Afternoon, if you want to get technical."

Slowly, I sat up and rested against the headboard, taking in the room around me. "Jay, was I hallucinating or was your mother awake?"

"No, Beautiful, you're right about that. She's in the other room napping. Whatever they did to her sapped a lot of her energy. You healed her from the curse but she still has some recovering to do," Jay answered.

That made sense. Her body had gone through a lot and I remembered how bad the curse was strangling her heart. "I'm glad she's safe." Pausing, I took a moment to look at all of them together and my heart burst with happiness. "So, what have I missed?"

"You've been asleep for two, almost three, days without moving a muscle, scaring the shit out of us," Micah grumbled.

Brayden glared at him as he climbed up on the bed to sit next to me, taking my hand and setting it in his lap. "Do you remember everything that happened?"

"I think so... I found Parker in limbo and then saved him with all your help. Then an angel came to meet with us. The details are a little fuzzy on that but pretty sure it was something about my true power being unlocked?" I answered, ending it with more of a questioning lilt.

"That would be the basics of it, yes," Hudson assured

me. "While you were sleeping, we worked with Beth and Cami, trying to figure out just what information Makoto has access to and how to get around it. Unfortunately, he has inserted himself in almost all areas of the Elementi, making him the perfect mole to funnel information in and out."

"In?" I questioned.

Jay's jaw clenched at my question. "It would seem that he used his access to cover the Dark Lord's tracks, which is why we didn't know anything about him until he came after you directly. This whole thing has been years in the making and we are so far behind. I'm disgusted to even call that man my father after all he's done."

My heart ached for Jay, knowing how he'd spent most of his life working to gain his father's approval. "Okay, so we're playing catch-up. What about the fact that we're fugitives?"

"Thankfully, Beth and the power of the Elementi were able to make those accusations go away since we were able to tell them what really happened. All our names have been cleared and charges dropped so that isn't anything to worry about," Hudson explained. "Actually, the local government was pleased since we helped them root out a section of dirty cops that had been doing all kinds of messed-up shit."

I let out a sigh, my shoulders relaxing, glad to know that one thing was going well for us. "So, now what? All of us are back together, bonded, and my powers have been unlocked..."

Jay turned to face me, a stern look on his face. "It's time to end this. We take out the Dark Lord's army and seal off any chance of him coming back."

"Great, I'm all for it. How exactly do we do that?" I

pressed, knowing he had an idea but was hesitant to share it.

I could feel him fighting against himself, so I crawled to the foot of the bed and settled my hands on his hips, looking up into his eyes. "There is no one that I trust more than you to make this call. You know your father. You know war, and I have all the faith in the world you know the right move to make. So what's it gonna be, Jay? How do we bring down the Dark Lord?"

Wrapping his arms around me, he pulled me close, resting his head on mine as if he was going to fall apart if I didn't hold him together. I felt him come to terms with what he needed to do. "We go after my father. If we have him in custody, we will have all the information we need, and with Parker's help, he *will* tell us everything."

"Crazy idea here—but what if Makoto is the Dark Lord's conduit?" Parker asked. "How else could he have made an oath like that with me, if he didn't have some connection to the Dark Lord? We know from Ubel and Tabitha that willing people can become conduits without the serum."

This thought had me pulling back to gape at Parker for the sheer brilliance of the idea. "Holy shit, you could be right!"

Parker just grinned and dusted his knuckles off on his shirt. "Yeah, well maybe coming back from the dead changes a man. Who knows, I might be the smart one in the group someday."

Micah scoffed at this but didn't voice his thoughts, which was oddly mature of him.

"Okay, so let's pay with that idea. If that's true, then if I can purge him out of Makoto, it would limit his ability to interact with the world. Then, all we would need to do is find a way to seal Hell to prevent this from happening again," I reasoned. "What if once we sort things out here, the angels can finally act?"

"They seem really hung up on that whole freewill thing," Micah muttered. "Seems all we've been going through since you arrived has been one big test to see if we could handle this battle. Makes me wonder how many Synergy's have come before you and failed, so they all died."

My jaw dropped at that idea and the horror of it. "You don't think they would really do that, do you? Angels are supposed to be good and pure, doing the work of God."

They all looked at me like I was missing a screw to believe that.

"Whatever helps you sleep at night, Cookie Monster, but I'm gonna live in the real world about this. They've done nothing but put us through hell and back. Fuck, they were even holding back your powers when they let the Oath break between you and Parker. They most definitely don't have our backs about shit. We need to do this on our own with whatever they gave us. That's the real purpose of that meeting in magic land. Wish us good luck and cross their fingers we stop the world from being turned into a second hell."

The anger and venom in Micah's words had me blinking at him for a few moments in surprise. Clearly, he'd not been taking this well and the fact that in his eyes I almost died again might have pushed him to the edge. Reaching out for him, I wiggled my fingers to get him to come closer, he finally gave in with a dramatic sigh and sat on the bed next to where I was kneeling. Without hesitation, I curled up on his lap and rested my head on his shoulder, wrapping my arms around his chest.

"None of us want to do this, but we don't have a choice. We can't run and hide, sticking our heads in the sand. All we can do is push forward. There is no guarantee that we'll make it out of this but I have to believe that they aren't going to send us into this battle without some way to win. Call it blind optimism, or naivety, but I won't lose without giving it all I've got. No holding back. We either live through this or die trying and that's a lot to accept," I whispered, my lips brushing against the skin of his neck. "All I know is that as long as the six of us do it together, then there has to be hope."

Micah groaned, hiding his face in my mess of curls. "How the hell did I fall in love with a woman who is all sunshine and rainbows?"

"How did I fall in love with a man who is all doom and gloom, believing that all hope is lost?" I chuckled, pressing a kiss to his neck. "As the angels said, we need to trust each other and give it all we've got."

"Can we start with you taking a shower? Two days in bed makes you smell a little stale," Micah teased, causing me to pull back and punch him in the arm.

"Rude!" I laughed. "Do we have some clothes for me to change into? Not that I'm ungrateful for the oversized t-shirt but I can't really go out in public like this."

"Yeah, we got you clothes. I suggested we forget about the underwear since some of us like to rip it off you anyway, but I got outvoted," Micah grumbled, setting me on my feet.

Hudson grabbed a few shopping bags and handed over basic hygiene supplies and fresh clothes. "We'll get some food. I'm sure you're hungry after not eating for two days."

As if on cue, my stomach rumbled at the idea, making

us all laugh. "I'll be out in a flash then we can get down to business."

"Take your time. Cami is supposed to be meeting us in an hour," Hudson shared. "She's going to take us to the Elementi branch out here. Surprise, it's located at another university in Stellenbosch."

"Guess if the system works, then why change it. Do we think Makoto will try to hit them there?" I asked, a little hesitant with the idea.

The guys all frowned at the question but Jay was the one to share his thoughts. "What we have going for us is that he might not know Parker is alive, and we didn't head there right away. We have to assume he has people watching the place but we need the resources there. My mother has also said she has things to share with me as well once you were awake again. Beth is doing all she can to change codes and access to something only we can get to but it's a risk we're gonna have to manage."

None of this was going to be easy since we were so far behind on things. Better to cut our losses and deal with what we could while trying to put an end to this battle. "Okay, I'll be ready to head out and face whatever happens in about fifteen minutes."

Micah kissed me on the cheek and Jay swatted my ass as I passed by, making me glare at him over my shoulder.

"Don't make us wait. Get a move on it, Beautiful," Jay ordered.

Rolling my eyes, I fought to keep a grin off my face as I headed to the bathroom. He did that on purpose so I would remember what happened the last time I was in here, the bastard.

"I'm beginning to think that I shouldn't ever let you leave my sight," Cami grumbled as she waited for us to pile into the minivan she was driving. "I've been gone for what, a week, and you guys end up on the most wanted list, get kidnapped, and bring back someone from the dead. What the fuck is wrong with you people?"

I was unable to hold back my laughter at hearing just how absurd our lives really were compared to the rest of the world.

"Careful there, short stack, you're the one driving the mom mobile," Parker teased. "Did you need to put down a few dictionaries to sit on so you can see over the wheel?"

Cami flipped Parker off and stuck out her tongue. "If you hadn't just died and come back to life, I would kill you myself."

My anger flared at her comment. I knew she wasn't being serious, but it was too soon for that kind of crap. "Cami," I warned.

Catching the look on my face, she tossed up both hands as if I was going to attack her. "My bad, I shouldn't have gone that route. There are plenty of other ways to insult that idiot that don't involve killing him or him being dead."

"That is the world's worst apology," I pointed out.

"Oh well, that's because it wasn't an apology. More of a recognition that some jokes aren't welcome at this time," Cami reasoned, giving me a smile and a wink. "Everybody in and buckled up?"

"Yes, Mom," Parker teased, kicking the back of her seat.

"Don't make me come back there," Cami growled. "Fuck, I'm glad you're not really dead."

Parker chuckled and reached around to slap her shoulder. "Me too, tiny-tot, me too."

Rolling my eyes, I let them bond over their strange way of showing love as we pulled away from the motel we'd been staying in. The drive was only a half hour but I couldn't help but feel tense, ready for something else to happen to us now that we'd left the safety of our little hideout. It was irrational, and I knew it. Besides, we needed to get Jay's mother somewhere safe and get the chance to find out what really happened. Other than having a few conversations with Jay, she refused to share anything until she felt she was safe from her husband. I didn't have the heart to tell her that I didn't know if that was really possible, with how deep his ties to the world around us were. Of course, I had no doubt that Jay would do whatever it took to make his mother safe. This had been too close of a call for him on top of thinking we had lost Parker.

No one really spoke as we drove. Instead, we all looked out the window lost in our own thoughts. When we finally arrived, it felt reminiscent of when I first showed up to Ryevick, only it was summer and there were no students on campus. Cami drove us to the back of the school property to a rundown warehouse that looked like it was for groundskeeping. It would just be like the Elementi to make a blind cover just as the Manor was for them back at Ryevick. Before we got out, Cami made a call, letting them know we were here. Apparently, they were sending someone out to meet us.

"Just be prepared, you guys. This facility isn't one of our top priorities so it isn't as fancy and updated with tech as Ryevick is as our HQ. They will be able to help us with what we need but just lower your expectations," Cami shared, looking mostly at Jay and Parker with a cocked brow.

Before either of them could say anything, a door on the side of the building opened, and a woman dressed in jeans and a t-shirt came out to greet us. "Hello, I'm Blessing and I run this facility. It's a pleasure to meet you all even if it is under unfortunate circumstances. Please follow me. I'll show you where you can set up and get you situated with all you need. We might not have the fanciest of things but we still know how to get the job done."

Grinning, I knew I was going to like Blessing with her no-nonsense attitude. She guided us into the building, which indeed was for maintaining the grounds, but led us to another door that opened to a flight of stairs leading down under the building. In true Elementi fashion, they preferred the whole underground facility vibe. The actual Elementi part of the building made me feel like I was in a normal office with offices, drab carpet, and an open space with cubicles. Blessing led us past all that into a large conference room that had long vertical blinds that could be closed if we didn't want people to look in at us. A large whiteboard and corkboard were set up like we were in some cop shop and needed a murder board or something.

"How many computers will you need?" Blessing asked.

"I didn't want to pull from our resources until I knew who could go without for now."

My jaw dropped at that statement and turned on Cami. "They don't even have enough equipment for themselves, let alone us? What the hell is with that? How can they do their jobs monitoring what's going on when they don't have the things they need? No wonder the Dark Lord picked to have his army here with Makoto so close by."

"Lala, I get why you're upset but, girl, you're yelling at the wrong person. Take it up with Beth and others on the council. They decide who gets funding and how much," Cami said defensively.

Letting out a calming breath, I relaxed. "I'm sorry, Cami, that was unfair. With all that's been going on, I'm just finding that I have extremely low patience with things like this."

"You're preaching to the choir, babe," Blessing commented. "I've been trying to tell them that we're missing things but they don't want to hear it. Kept saying that the feedback from other sources told them this area was a dead zone for demon activity."

My teeth ground as I clenched my jaw. "Let me guess, Makoto made that judgment call."

"Funny how he seems to keep coming up and fucking us over, isn't it?" Cami muttered.

Jay stepped forward and extended his hand to Blessing. "Thank you for being here and not giving up, even if they didn't listen." She took his hand, shaking it. "If you could do without two computers, we'll manage just fine. If there is a printer available as well, then we don't have to worry about using a tablet or anything to share information."

"I can work with that," Blessing answered, giving him a

slight grin in response. "You are nothing like your father, you know that."

Jay bowed his head to her. "I take that as the highest compliment."

"You should. He's a prick." Blessing huffed as she turned to leave the room. "I'll send someone by with drinks and snacks for you. Brain's gotta have food to work their best."

Now that we had the room to ourselves, none of us seemed to know where to start. So in true Jay fashion, he took the lead and gestured for us all to sit down as he guided his mother to sit beside him.

"*Okasan*, will you please share with us what you know?" Jay asked in English.

Up until this moment, he had only ever spoken to her in Japanese, so I assumed that was all she spoke. I shouldn't have been so simpleminded. I'd also found out that her name was Hina, not that I ever planned on calling her that. It seemed so informal even if she was practically my mother-in-law. Hina gently placed her hands in her lap and looked over the rest of us before she settled on me. Her eyes, so much like her son's, seemed to be able to see into my soul but I wasn't scared, just unsettled to be so vulnerable. Thankfully after a moment or two, she broke her hold on me and turned to face Jay before she spoke.

"It all started before I was pregnant with you," she started, her voice soft as if it was floating on a breeze. "Your father woke up one night, claiming that he had been visited by an angel who promised him that his child would save the world. Now, all of us knew the rumors that Synergy could possibly be a person and that's what your father believed that angel meant. From the moment you were born, he pushed you to be the best on the promise that you would fulfill this great destiny. When you came into your power and we discovered you were not Synergy but the element of air, he was crushed. He disappeared for a month, claiming it was for work and I believed him since he hardly ever spoke to me about such things. It was always made clear to me that I was his wife, but that didn't mean I deserved more from him than a life where I was looked after."

My heart clenched, knowing it must have hurt so much to be brushed off like that when it was clear she loved Makoto in her own way. Jay had told me he never planned on being married or loving anyone so he didn't end up like his father, but the Heavens decided otherwise.

"When he returned one day out of the blue, he told me that he secured our son's fate and would give him the power he was promised. That's when he took you from me," Hina said as her voice cracked. "The only part of Makoto that ever loved me was what he gave me through you, my son. I knew if I tried to stop him it would only make things harder on you, so I let you go, hoping one day he would give you back to me."

Jay took his mother's hand and pressed it to his cheek before kissing the back of it in the largest show of affection I'd ever seen him give to someone other than me. "There was no way I was going to abandon you, *Okasan*. I will see that you are forever free from him and able to live your life once this is all over."

Hina gave Jay a sad smile but didn't say anything before returning to her story. "It was just after Christmas that I heard about you, Lailah. Jalen told me he wasn't going to make it home because you needed him." The guilt I felt hearing that made me frown. When she saw my expression she reached a hand out to me, clasping my hand in hers, giving it a squeeze before pulling back. "No, please, don't feel bad. I was so happy he found someone to love enough to drop everything to save her. It's something I've never gotten the chance to have. Word spread through the family of what happened at the Christmas Eve party and the whole mess of the serum getting taken from the labs. I was surprised that Makoto hadn't come back to question what I knew or what my family might know."

"Forgive me, but why would he come to you about that?" I asked, not understanding the connection.

Her eyes flicked to Jay, a little surprised. "That would be because my family runs the largest port in Japan, controlling all the import and export of goods. If anyone was smuggling things, we would hear about it through our connections. It's one of the reasons I was selected to be Makoto's bride, along with the money I inherited when my father passed away twenty years ago."

"So why did Makoto work with Pride, instead of with your family, since you own it?" Hudson asked. "Wouldn't it make more sense to have things like the serum smuggled with a company you have control over?"

"I suppose it would if he had any control over it," Hina answered. "My father made sure in his will that it was left to me and me alone. He hated how Makoto treated me after we were married, completely changing into a different person. My father would have supported me in leaving Makoto, and by leaving the company to me, he insured I could do so whenever I wanted and be fully supported. You see, I'd just graduated from college with an MBA in the hopes of working alongside my father. Once I was married, Makoto forbade me from doing so, which led my father to blackball him from many companies he partnered with.

This forced Makoto to find suppliers elsewhere in the world, and most of them were not reputable."

Parker leaned back in his seat and let out a whistle, expressing how we were all feeling.

"Okay, so that clears up that question, but why did he kidnap you?" Brayden pressed. "If he couldn't use the ports and Jay was already bonded, then why curse you?"

"He wanted me to sign over the company to him. The longer I refused, the stronger the curse would be and eventually kill me. But I knew what he was up to so I refused to help in any way," Hina explained. "While he had been gone for that month, he'd made a deal with the devil and they promised that Jay would have an important part in their new world, along with him. All the power the angels led him to believe he would have could be his if he was their man on the ground helping them. If he was going to get the serum distributed how they needed it to be, having access to my company would change everything."

"What a bastard!" Cami fumed, kicking at one of the empty chairs next to her, sending it shooting across the room to bounce off the glass window.

"Easy on the furniture, it's hell to get replacements," Blessing remarked as she entered the room with two laptops in her arms. "I've got computers for you. I made sure they were our most updated and secure but you might want to do a check on it before doing anything too illegal."

Another man followed on her heels with a box that he set on the table. It contained a printer and other supplies we would need. He glanced around the room at us but when he saw me, he paused and broke into a wide smile.

"Well, they didn't tell me there was a babe who came in with the Elemental Warriors. Are you their mascot or some-thing, because you're all I would need to be cheered on," he said, making me almost want to gag at how cheesy that line was.

All the guys tensed and I could feel the murderous thoughts they had toward this man. Cami, on the other hand, burst into a fit of laughter, almost sliding out of her chair onto the floor. "Bro, you better run before you have five men with magical powers coming after you for hitting on their wife."

The man looked from me to the guys and back again, his face losing all its color. "Their *wife*... she's married to all of them?"

"Yeah, took me a minute to wrap my head around it too," I teased. "Guess it's a perk of being Synergy. I get all the sexy magic men to myself."

Apparently, I'd pushed the man too far, and he fainted upon hearing I was Synergy. Blessing let out an irritated groan and grabbed the guy by his shirt, tossed him in the chair Cami kicked, and rolled him out of the room. She returned quickly with another box. This one was full of water bottles and snacks.

"I'm sorry about Chad. Clearly, he didn't get the memo on who was going to be here today," Beth apologized. "I'll make sure he steers clear, although I don't think that will be a problem after that interaction—idiot. Anything else you guys need, just send me an IM. The program is on both computers and it's secure."

"Thank you, Blessing," I said with a smile.

CHAPTER 25
LAILAH

Jay and Parker made quick work of setting up our information center and getting down to business. Rolling my chair over to Cami, I leaned in and whispered, "What are the rest of us supposed to do who can't find all the things on the internet?"

"Did you practice your cheer routine?" Cami asked, resulting in getting a smack from me. "What? I think you would look super cute in one of those mascot costumes. What would you be? A teddy bear, bunny, oh I know! An elephant since they're your favorite animal!"

"Really, this is how you want to act when the end of the world could be right around the corner?" I teased.

"Fine, what do you think would be more productive, Miss Synergy?" Cami shot back.

Before I could answer her, Micah walked up to us and reached out a hand to me. "Come on, Cookie Monster, we're going to find out if they have a sparring area. I want to make sure your skills aren't rusty if we're going into battle."

Instantly, my memory flashed back to the battle where Parker and I managed to survive before we freed the others. I hadn't spoken about it with all that had happened between now and then, but I knew for a fact I wasn't rusty. When I reached out to our Bond though, I could feel that what Micah really needed was some time with me and this was his solution. "Sure, and if they don't, we can explore the place so I can make sure the council of whoever gets these people what they need."

"Won't all this be over once the Dark Lord is defeated, though?" Cami interjected. "I mean, that's what they said, right? Synergy will appear when needed most to banish evil from the world."

"I would really love to believe that but I'm not feeling particularly trusting of angels or demons at this point. Better to be safe than sorry, I think," I responded as Micah pulled me out of my chair and we left the room.

"Do you really think it's possible that this could all be over when we kill him?" Micah mused. "If we can take out a Prince of Hell, I feel like that would be a pretty big warning to others who might try."

"Yeah, but what happens when we die? I don't think we'll suddenly live forever and protect the world from disaster just because we're the six people who saved it once," I said with a snort.

Micah glanced down at me with an odd look on his face. "Lailah, you brought back Parker from the dead—"

"Only because he was cursed! It had nothing to do with him getting stabbed or his head chopped off. If you die in a normal way, I wouldn't put any hope in the fact I can bring you back."

He grunted in response, intertwining our fingers together. "I put all my hope in you, Lailah. Hell, I put the fate of the world in your hands because I know it will be safe."

It was moments like this that reminded me why I loved this cranky asshole so much. They didn't happen often, but in these rare moments, he could be so utterly vulnerable and sweet.

As we searched the place, we didn't find anything that looked like a sparring area or even a workout room. Just when we gave up hope, my good buddy, Chad, stepped out of an office and stopped us. He froze like a deer in the headlights, eyes wide and worried.

"Chad, what do you know, we were just looking for someone who might be able to help us," Micah called out, a wide grin plastered on his face. "This place doesn't happen to have a workout room or training area does it?"

Chad opened and closed his mouth like a fish a few times before he managed to get words out. "Lower level."

"Great... how do we get there?" I encouraged when he didn't expand on that information.

He turned and started to walk away from us then paused and looked over his shoulder, waving for us to follow him. I leaned into Micah and whispered. "You scared that guy into being mute."

"If only it was that easy with everyone," Micah muttered. "The world would be a better place if people knew when to keep their mouths shut."

Chad led us to an elevator, and we discovered that we were on the top floor out of three subterranean floors. It seemed that the second level was the facilities for the staff like a cafeteria, workout space, and other utilities, while the third and lowest level were the apartments. The elevator door opened on the second level. Chad led us out and pointed down the hall to the left. "Take it until it ends and the gym will be past the double doors."

Micah patted Chad on the back, making him flinch as if he'd been shocked. "Thanks, man, we'll take it from here."

"That was mean," I whispered harshly.

"Asshole, remember," Micah answered with a wink. "Seems I've gone soft if you've forgotten that little detail."

Rolling my eyes, we entered the gym to find Brayden and Hudson already there, dressed in matching gym shorts and white t-shirts. "What are you guys doing here?"

"What took you guys so long?" Brayden asked, his brows scrunched. "We've been waiting for almost fifteen minutes."

"How did you know how to get here?" Micah challenged.

"We asked Blessing when we saw her in the office," Hudson said, cocking his head to the side confused by our question. "Have you guys been wandering around this whole time?"

"Whatever, we're here now so it's best if we just get down to business. The other reason I wanted to spar was to see what happens now that Lailah's powers are unlocked. It's smart for us to know what we're dealing with before we end up face-to-face with the Dark Lord," Micah shared.

"Yeah, that's great and all, but I don't think they have warded rooms like they do back at Ryevick," I countered.

Brayden walked up to me and grabbed me by the hips so I was facing him. "Why don't you put up a shield for us to work in? You're bonded to us all now so it should be way easier to do."

Pausing at that thought, I realized he had a point. "Guess there's only one way to find out."

Closing my eyes, I gathered all six balls of power and pulled strings of energy from them, weaving them into a net. I'd never done anything like this before but it just seemed to be instinct and flowed easily between my fingers. When I felt like I'd woven it tight enough, I tossed it out around us and made sure to cover the floor since there was another level to this place. Then I sealed up the last bits of it, creating a perfect containment for the space.

"I think that should work," I commented, looking around as if I could actually see what I just did. "I don't think anyone else can come in or out of the space I just blocked off though."

"That was fucking amazing, Cookie. You did that so fast and I can feel how powerful it is," Micah said with a grin. "Let's see what other things you can do."

Without missing a beat, he materialized his swords, and they burst into flames. "Holy fuck!"

Next Brayden and Hudson produced their weapons as well, each of them glowing with a fire that matched their powers. It seemed that they all had a power upgrade, and it made me curious as to why Parker's staff had done that. But then I remembered how much power I was pouring into him when it happened. Now, I didn't have to do anything but be connected to them to give them a solid boost. Skipping my sai, I went straight for the sword and shield but instead, I got two small crossbows with golden tipped arrows that glowed with my power.

"So, is this an upgrade?" I asked, waving them at the guys.

"Whoa, don't wave those around like that until you know what they can do!" Micah barked, ducking out of the way. "Didn't Jay teach you anything with those gun lessons?"

Seeing as they all had a slightly panicked look, I dropped the crossbows to my side. "Better?"

They all gathered around and examined them, taking

my hand, turning it this way and that to get a better look. "I have to admit, Sunshine, those look far more impressive than my guns. Try one out and see what happens." With a wave of his hand, Hudson made a water target that floated in the air opposite of us.

With a shrug, I lifted one arm, aimed down the sights and pulled the trigger. The short arrow flew from the crossbow faster than my eyes could track and when it hit the water, it exploded like a bomb of golden light, knocking us back on our asses.

"Yup, that is definitely an upgrade, Angel," Brayden groaned as he sat up. "Look at that. It reloads itself. Just like Hudson's guns, they never run out of ammo."

"Oh, those are going to fuck some demon asses up!" Micah crowed, smiling like a fool as he helped me to my feet. "If all of us have gotten upgrades like that, then I'm not so worried about this fight."

We all laughed at feeling the same sense of relief, knowing we had a fighting chance for this battle. It all came to a halt when the gym door was thrown open and Blessing stood there her face filled with panic. "You need to get back upstairs now!"

"What happened?" I demanded as I pulled a string in the net, unraveling the whole thing in a second, allowing Blessing to enter.

Her eyes were wide, and I didn't have to be bonded to her to sense the fear that she was feeling right now. "They're almost here. Makoto and the Dark Lord's army. They're attacking the school. The wards are keeping them at bay but they haven't been renewed in a long time. I'm not sure how long they'll last."

That was all we needed to hear before we bolted out of the gym and headed for the stairs next to the elevator. None of us wanted to risk the chance we got stuck in it. How the fuck did Makoto know we were here? We'd been right under his nose for three days, why wait to hit us here? Could it be that he finally figured out that Parker wasn't dead? None of it really mattered, the fight was upon us and we had a date with the devil.

CHAPTER 26

LAILAH

Just like how things were at the base, it was pure chaos as everyone ran around the facility, trying to get prepared for battle. While all Elementi members were trained in self-defense, there were not many who were actual fighters. All of them knew how to handle a gun but that didn't mean they could hit the broad side of a barn. Each of us were given tactical gear to change into—thick black cargo pants with black t-shirts and bulletproof vests. It made me feel like I was supposed to be SWAT instead of an Elemental Warrior, but I was thankful for the added protection. I knew Makoto had normal humans working and fighting alongside him, as well as the demon possessed. This could mean guns along with traditional weapons, making this getup a safe bet.

Blessing was in full control even if the rest ran around in a panic. She directed everyone into the areas they needed to be, including making sure the women and children got the hell out of here. The guys and I did a sweep of the third level, making sure it was clear before we locked it up, ensuring no one got crushed if something happened to the facility. Jay, as always, fell into being the leader of our group when it came to battle and we listened to whatever he told us. Blessing also was wise enough to listen to his advice as he suggested the better fighters be out front and the rest remain as backup while the six of us went right up to meet the jaws of evil.

I couldn't imagine what it must be like to know your father was leading the enemy army and the chances of having to face off with him were high. Although, if he was the conduit for the Dark Lord, then I had a feeling the real fight would be between the two of us. Somehow, I'd found a moment to pull Jay and Parker aside to tell them what we discovered as we were sparring. Of course the others followed, refusing to let me out of their sight with the impending attack.

"Wait, you mean I get the double-ended staff back? That's awesome. It was so much easier to fight off the swarm," Parker said, clapping his hands together and rubbing them in excitement.

Jay didn't really comment, just nodded his head. "Thank you for the warning, now I'll be prepared for any changes that might happen."

"Another thing we found, is that I can work with all of your energies together seamlessly. There is no more struggle or fear of passing out, trying to force them together. I don't know what all I can do though. Most of it feels like instinct," I shared.

Jay reached out and cupped my face in his hands, pinning me with his gaze. "Trust yourself. If you feel the need to make a move, don't second-guess it. We'll follow your lead without question. You are Synergy and this fight will be won or lost by your choices or actions."

"Fuck, man," Parker snapped. "Way to freak her the fuck out."

Jay glanced at Parker for a moment then returned to me. "I will never lie to you or put you in danger. You understanding the truth of this battle is the best thing I can give you. Lailah, you were born for this and so were we. Together, we will get through this or die with the knowledge we did all we could."

Fear sat in the pit of my stomach like a stone at his words but I also understood where he was coming from. There was no sense in pretending like this wasn't a fight for our lives and the rest of the world as we knew it. Giving false hope or platitudes wouldn't do us any good. Honesty and trust would be far more powerful. "Anything else I should know before we go face the devil himself?"

"Only that I love you with all my heart, mind, body, and soul. I am and will forever be thankful that you showed up in my life and changed everything," Jay murmured before capturing my mouth in a searing kiss that set my body on fire. I could feel through our connection how his words didn't even begin to describe how much he loved me.

He pulled back first and stepped to the side as Micah moved to stand in front of me. "No matter what, there's nothing left unsaid between us, right?"

"Nothing. We've never been good at holding back from each other," I answered, giving him a smile. "Only know that if we live through this, you and Parker have to figure your shit out because I won't have you guys hating each other for the rest of our lives together."

"I can deal with that," Micah agreed, tipping my head back and biting my lower lip before he soothed it with a flick of his tongue. It made me gasp, and he used that opportunity to deepen our kiss, leaving me breathless. He handed me over to Brayden.

I wrapped my arms around his neck and nuzzled into his neck, letting him ground me the way only he could. "Thank you for always being here right beside me since the very beginning."

"There isn't any other place I'd want to be, Angel. You have been such a gift to me and my family, it will take a life-time to repay you," he whispered into my ear.

"That's funny, because I don't ever remember there being a debt between us that needs to be repaid. We are family, Brayden, and I know you would do the same thing for me in a heartbeat, so I call us even," I countered.

Brayden chuckled as he pulled back enough to see my face, running his fingers down my cheek. "You drive a hard bargain but I'll allow it." The kiss between us was tender and full of love, making me feel like the most treasured woman in the world.

Someone coughed and nudged Brayden, making him laugh as he pulled away from me. "I'm sorry, was I taking too long for your liking to express my undying love to our girl?"

Parker scowled at him. "You've been able to express your feelings far longer than any of us and I want to get my moment in before something crazy happens. I refuse to go last anymore. It got me killed the last time."

His logic was hard to argue with and Hudson didn't seem bothered about having to wait, so I stepped up to Parker taking his hand and drawing his attention. "Alright, I won't make you go last."

"Don't get me wrong, Trouble. You are absolutely worth waiting for, but I've got shit to make up for still," he explained.

"So dying wasn't enough?" I asked, tilting my head, slightly frowning. "I'm not sure I want to know what else you have in mind."

"What I did wasn't nearly enough to make up for things. Trouble, any one of us would give up our life for you, if it meant you would be safe and alive. No, I plan to spend the rest of my life for however long that may be, making sure you never doubt me or my love for you again," Parker shared, kissing me on the forehead. "Besides, I haven't gotten a chance to spoil you rotten or make some grand gesture like the old eighties' movies. What do you think about me hiring a full-time baker so you can have sugar cookies on demand at any moment?"

I snorted at that idea. "Parker, I can make my own cookies."

"So I shouldn't tell you that I might be the owner of Ann's bakery..."

"You did not!" I gasped.

"Look, you love her cookies and she loves you. Besides, she didn't have anyone to take over once she decided to retire," Parker defended. "How about we save this argument for later and you can scold me all you want while I try to convince you how this is a brilliant idea." I pouted at him but he just grinned, scooped me up into a bear hug and peppered my face with kisses before landing on my lips, sending shivers of delight down my spine. All too soon, he set me down and nudged me over to Hudson, who reached out a hand to me.

"Sunshine." Hudson sighed as he pulled me to his chest, resting his head on top of mine. "No matter how this battle goes, I will forever be thankful for the time I was given with you. Should the heavens bless us with more time, then I don't ever want us to miss a moment of life together. We will leave the Elementi and start our own adventure. The six of us, just like you wanted. Like you said at the start, we are no longer fighting for anyone but us and the future we want to have."

"How do you always know what I need to hear?" I asked, sinking into his hold.

"Because you are the other half of my soul, the sunshine that lights up my world," he answered. "Now it's time to shine that light over the world and banish the darkness that is trying to take it from us." Hudson pressed a firm kiss to my lips but didn't linger like the others had. This was more of a normal everyday kiss for us, and when he saw my expression, he smiled. "I'm not going to say goodbye. I have faith in us that we will all make it out of this."

My heart melted at his words. Knowing that he had that much trust in us as a team gave me the fortitude I needed to turn and face the others. "Alright, let's go say hello to the Dark Lord and his army."

Jay led the way, while Brayden took one of my hands and Hudson took the other, with Parker and Micah flanking us in the rear. We headed to the main room where all the cubicles were and found this is where everyone had gathered to listen to Blessing address the whole group. It seemed that we missed most of it but then again, it wasn't really for us.

"Know that no matter what happens at the end of this, I am proud to have served with all of you. No matter what, we all persevered and did everything we could to keep the world we live in safe. The heavens have shined down upon us in the gift of having the six Elemental Warriors here with us in our hour of need. Listen to what they tell you. This isn't their first battle with the Dark Lord, therefore making them experts on the matter." Turning her gaze to us, she asked, "Do you have anything you wish to share before we all head above ground?"

I squeezed both Brayden and Hudson's hands before I released them and stepped forward. "Hello, all of you, my name is Lailah and I'm the element known as Synergy." I paused, letting everyone get out their reactions to that statement. "You are all well aware of the serum and what it does, along with how the demons are using it. I want to put your minds at ease about something though. Even if we could find a way to banish the demon possessing them, they will forever be vulnerable to another taking its place. There are people working tirelessly to find a solution but right now, their best fate is to be put out of their misery. They are aware of what is happening even when controlled by a demon so all the atrocious acts that the demon has done, they have witnessed. All that to say, death isn't the worst thing that can happen to them. It will set them free."

The room filled with murmurs as they decided how they felt about what I'd said. Jay came to stand beside me, placing a hand on my lower back for support as he addressed them. "You all have weapons that have been blessed and ammo that has been christened with holy water, allowing you to fight both human and demon possessed. This battle isn't just about our survival or stopping evil for now, this is the final battle to determine who will rule mankind. Fight for yourself, your family, friends, and other loved ones, because we're all that stands in Hell's way."

Alarms began to blare and lights flashed all around us, causing people to scream. A few bolted from the room toward the exit, knowing this meant that Makoto had finally broken the wards around the school. They were here and there was no more time to prepare. Jay clasped my hand tightly as we headed to the surface, knowing we needed to be the first ones to greet the army. They were here for us after all.

Back in the warehouse, Jay dropped my hand and yelled for Micah. "Help me get these doors open so that people can get out easier."

Soon, the large rolling doors were open, illuminating what was in the space and revealing an ATV we could all fit in, with the open space in the back for hauling things. The keys were in it and Parker started it up with ease. "Everyone, get in!"

I spotted Cami standing alongside Blessing and motioned for her to join us. "No, Lala, my place is here. Go be the badass I know you are and save the world, alright? I'll find you after all this is over."

Seeing that she wasn't going to budge, I let Micah pull me up into the ATV and hung on as Parker slammed on the gas, sending us rocketing out of the building. Clearly, he'd gotten his driving skills from the same person who taught Cami. I thought we were going to die before we even made it to the front of the campus.

"Lailah, can you send your power out and tell us if they're just coming in through the front or if they're attacking on all sides?" Hudson yelled over his shoulder.

Upon his request, I took my power and tossed it out around me, sending it far and wide, coating the whole campus as I looked for demon signatures. The hard part would be if they had two groups since I wouldn't be able to track the humans this way, but it was better to try than not try at all. My power shone brightly as it hit the army that was in front of us, but I could also feel smaller groups coming from the left and the right sides of campus as well.

"Looks like they have teams on either side but they aren't moving. They must be waiting for a signal."

Parker slammed on the brakes almost tossing me from the vehicle if Micah hadn't caught me. "What the fuck, man?" Micah yelled.

"Look, I know you might cut off my balls for this idea, but I think we should split up and hit the groups that are waiting. If three of you go and distract the main group while Micah and I lead teams to the right and left, they won't expect it," Parker pointed out. "Jay, you know I'm right. They don't know that she can find them, and if we keep them from flanking us, it could make all the difference."

Jay sat there silently for a moment processing before he spoke. "Lailah and I will meet the front lines while Parker and Hudson go to the left and Brayden and Micah go to the right. I know how to stall my father and if he is the conduit for the Dark Lord, then his real target will be Lailah. The faster you can defeat the smaller groups, the better. Go back and get Blessing and Cami to help you with their people. Play their game against them."

I hopped out of the ATV and Jay followed. "Be safe and come back to me or I'll bring you back and kill you myself. I'm pretty sure I can do it, too."

They all nodded and Parker whipped the ATV around, heading back to the warehouse. I looked up at Jay, squared my shoulders, and pulled my new crossbows into existence. "Let's go play chicken with the Dark Lord and see who blinks first."

CHAPTER 27
LAILAH

As Jay and I made our way to the front lines, I couldn't allow myself to worry about the others. They were trained to fight, and they now had stronger powers than ever before. The Dark Lord knew none of this. Taking Jay's lead, I stood tall when we reached the front entrance to the school. I could hear the sound of many feet thundering through the air as they approached. We stopped and let them come to us. What I found interesting was that they were on foot. If it was me, I would have used large vehicles to bust in and drop a large amount of people off, flooding the space. Instead, they walked in like they owned the place or they'd already won the battle.

The first wave of the enemy came to a halt and parted, revealing Makoto dressed in all black with a hood pulled up, shadowing his face. I could feel the darkness in him for the first time. He was, without a doubt, the conduit for the Dark Lord and had been for quite some time. The energy that pulsed out of him smacked into me but I lifted my hand, allowing a shimmering wall of my power to block it from pressing on me further. I didn't put too much strength into it, not wanting him to know how strong I was just yet. We needed to give the others time.

"We finally get to meet in person, Little Synergy," the Dark Lord's voice boomed, filling the space. "My servant has told me much of your visit with him and how you let one of your own men die so you could save yourself."

"Parker died trying to save me, the way no one else could since he wasn't bonded to me," I responded, playing along. Did he really not know that Parker was alive?

"I suppose it wasn't a hardship to let him die after he betrayed you like that," the Dark Lord mused, as he turned his head to face Jay. "Yet you still keep this one with you, even though his father had been betraying the Elementi for decades. Makoto is a man after my own heart, a lover of power, willing to do whatever it takes to have it and keep it. They say children don't stray far from their parents. Is that really someone you want to have fighting alongside you?"

A smile tugged at my lips. "Then it's a wonderful thing that he takes after his mother, isn't it? She refused to bow to Makoto's wishes even if she wouldn't abandon him. Jay has proven to me time and time again who he is and trust me, he's exactly who I want at my side right now."

Snarling came from the shadowed hood as twin green flames glowed but still revealed nothing of his features. "Then I will cherish the tears you spill as I take the soul from his body and eat his heart so that he will never return to this world."

"Only God can wield that kind of power," Jay snapped. "All demons are created from angels that have been cast out of Heaven. They were all of a lower status, unable to act without his permission. Even when demons attack now, they must bow to his rules. I don't think trapping a soul in Hell for eternity is a power you have."

"It seems that you have paid attention in school, but who's to say what you learned is the truth?"

I scoffed. "Why would we ever believe a word that comes out of your mouth? Demons thrive off lies and half-truths. They are master manipulators, getting humans to do what they need by making it their choice. I don't doubt that you've managed to change things in the history books but the Elementi have followed the truth for generations, ensuring that things won't be tainted by the likes of you."

"Such courage and passion," the Dark Lord sneered. "It's no wonder why the angels chose you to be Synergy, with all that hope and promise flowing through you. Do you think Makoto is the first person of the Elementi that I've turned? A mission like this isn't one that you win by moving fast. It's the long slow game, moving the right pieces in the right places. No one will ever know who is truly loyal and who isn't. People will do just about anything when they are given the right motivation."

His words made my mind race, trying to figure out what he was telling me. He had a hidden weapon, I knew it. He was alluding to it, but I couldn't figure out what the hell it was.

"Why would the angels have sent me if the Elementi didn't follow the rules they set for them?" I demanded, trying to get more information.

Makoto advanced, his hands clasped behind his back as he moved slowly. "Because they believed they were doing it for the right reasons. As you said, Little Synergy, we are the masters of deceit. Makoto believes an angel came to him in a dream, telling him his son would be the savior of the world. When it didn't happen, he turned to me. There was no angel. It had been me all along, driving his need to gain power and prestige. Before your dear Air Knight came into his power, Makoto believed in the Elementi, and did all he could to make it protected against the likes of me. Only when the heavens let him down did it create the perfect opportunity for me to provide my help. Now I had a man who had more control over the Elementi than the Elementi did."

"Who else have you manipulated?" I gasped, realizing that it wasn't just one person he was talking about, it was many.

"Ah, now she understands." The Dark Lord chuckled. "You know about Tabitha already, then there is your Water Knight's stepmother, the Fire Knight's aunt, and as for the lost Heart Knight, I had a few people step into his life. Phoebe was only one of them, but I made sure each one made him believe that he was *nothing,* would always be *nothing,* now he is *nothing.* Even you tossed him away in the end, leaving him to die alone and painfully."

I knew the Dark Lord was trying to hit me where I was most vulnerable and if I didn't know that half of what he said was a lie, it would have destroyed me. Parker was alive, I'd saved him, and he had never been nothing to me. "So, what now? Here we are, laying all the cards on the table, spilling all the secrets, knowing that one of us won't make it out alive."

"Do you really think you can defeat me when I've been the master of this game the whole time? You're crippled without all five of your knights. Look, you only have one standing beside you. There is no question how this is going to end but I wanted to take the time to introduce you to someone that you got to know extremely well." The Dark Lord waved a hand and someone else stepped forward cloaked in darkness, but I could see strands of neon pink hair peeking out.

No, no, no, no, no—this could not be happening. There was no way she would turn against me in this. She couldn't be one of his pawns. There just wasn't any way that could be true.

"Allow me to introduce to you the person who kept you right where I wanted you to be," the Dark Lord boasted, yanking back the hood to reveal Cami.

I dropped to my knees, unable to hold myself up a moment longer. She stood there still and stiff as a statue. Her normally vibrant eyes were black pools of nothing. Everything that made Cami, Cami, was missing, leaving only this shell of a person cloaked in darkness and evil. Just when I thought I was safe from whatever the Dark Lord could throw at me, I was so incredibly wrong.

"Your beloved best friend has been mine since the day I killed her first love. I, of course, promised that they would be reunited when I brought Hell to Earth, but that would only happen if I was able to bring you to my side or destroy you. As I said, *everyone* can turn their backs on the world if given the right motivation."

"No," I whispered, dropping my head into my hands, unable to wrap my mind around this. "It doesn't make sense. She wouldn't."

Jay's hand rested on my shoulder and gave it a squeeze. "Trust your instincts, Lailah." He said it in a low, quiet voice, ensuring that I was the only one who heard him.

Closing my eyes, I sent a strand of my power out toward Cami, letting it wrap itself around her. I knew my best friend. She had been right beside me through all the ups and downs, helping me when the guys couldn't. She had always been in my corner. If she had been an agent to the Dark Lord, I would have known. There had to be something I was missing because none of this made any sense.

Pressing my power into her deeper, I discovered a barrier sitting over her, blocking me from being able to touch her. It hovered close to her skin, so it felt like it wasn't really there. But as I probed at it, it pushed back. My eyes snapped open, and I shot to my feet, arm raised with my crossbow in hand once again, and I fired a shot.

The arrow hit home, dead center in her forehead and whatever had been wrapped around her splintered, revealing a woman who was the same size and stature but absolutely wasn't my best friend. "Lies! Everything you say is *lies!*"

Anger flooded me and all the fear and worry I had vanished, leaving me filled with a righteous anger. No more talking, it was time to fucking end this.

CHAPTER 28

BRAYDEN

It didn't sit right with me to leave Lailah behind with only Jay to face down a Prince of Hell but Parker was right, we needed to take advantage of the element of surprise. When we arrived back at the warehouse, Parker skidded to a halt with Micah leaping out of the ATV before it was fully stopped.

"Cami, Blessing!" he bellowed. "Fuck, tell me you're here."

People were still pouring out of the facility downstairs, so I think it was a safe bet they were still here. They wouldn't have taken off and left them on their own.

"What the hell are you doing back here? Is Lala okay? You didn't just abandon her to face that fucker all by herself, did you?" Cami demanded as she stomped up to us.

I couldn't help but grin at how she looked all pissed off, glaring at a man who was almost twice as tall as her. "No, we've come to help you out. There are secondary groups waiting off to the left and right of the campus and we need your help," I explained.

Hearing all the commotion, Blessing joined us, a scowl

on her face that could rival Micah's. "What do you mean, how could we be any help? I'm willing to do what we can but I'm not sending my people on a death mission unless you tell me there is no other option."

"That's not what we want. Lailah and Jay are holding off the Dark Lord and his army while we deal with these smaller groups so we don't get boxed in. They don't know that Lailah sensed them so they wouldn't be prepared for us to hit them first," I expounded.

Blessing and Cami looked at each other and seemed to come to an agreement as Blessing gave us her answer. "Alright, but I'm only having my advanced fighters come on this mission and leaving the others here to protect the base."

"Why not send them with the women and children?" Hudson asked.

"Because this is their home and they want it to stay that way. None of these people, fighters or not, want to give up anything more than we have to, to those fucking demons."

Parker nodded. "Hard to argue with that. We'll take what we can get and make it work. Blessing, you're with me and Hudson. Cami, you'll go with Micah and Brayden. You guys know how to work together as a team the best."

The change that had come over Parker since he came back from the dead was astounding. Yeah, it had only been three days but never would the old Parker have said something like that, or even considered it. Hearing what he told Lailah before we left to face off with the Dark Lord told me that he truly understood what he'd done was wrong. Not that I ever doubted he thought otherwise, but this time it showed in every action that he made. He didn't goad Micah and actively tried to be of value before being asked. The man that Parker was finally turning into was who Lailah had seen all along, while the rest of us just expected him to live up to the standard we'd set for him. If we made it through this, I knew without a doubt, we could find happiness and the friendship we'd always strived for.

"What's with the dopey smile? We have a war to win," Cami teased, punching me in the arm. "Come on, let's do this."

Blessing was working quickly to divide her people into groups of who would be going and staying, then splitting them again to give us about fifty people each. Our best guess was the demons were hiding in the hilly groves on either side of the campus. We didn't want to use the ATV or other vehicles that might give away our location, so we were hoofing it and moving as quickly as we could in smaller groups so we didn't draw attention to what we were doing. I pulled on my powers and my Elemental Warrior armor appeared, along with my upgraded daggers that were more like short swords, flickering with a green flame. Micah did the same, his curved blades glinting deadly in the fading sunlight.

Could it be that they were just waiting for darkness to fall before they struck us and boxed us in? I didn't have time to worry about motivation as we darted from tree to tree, trying to keep hidden as we got closer. I could hear the sound of people rustling in the woods and low talking voices. Without bothering to listen to what they were saying, I saw a large group of them arguing and opened the ground under them. Shrieks filled the air as they were swallowed up by my power. As our people converged on them, I knew I couldn't use that trick again or I would risk killing them as well. Now it was time to fight head-on.

Micah dove into the thick of it, his blade moving incredibly fast along with sending out fire balls. I scanned the area, knowing he would be fine for the moment, and saw a group of our people getting overwhelmed by a swarm of demons. These weren't demon-possessed people, these were straight-up lower-class demons with wings, dive bombing and trying to blind people. With a flick of my wrist, I grabbed a bunch of pebbles and hurled them at the demons, scattering them. Jay always had better luck with this type of demon since he could shoot them in the air but I switched to my smaller dagger, knowing they wouldn't hurt the non-possessed people. Then I heard the snarl of a higher demon as they skulked in the shadows, the sunlight too much for them to attack us just yet.

"Micah, we got trouble!" I yelled, knowing his fire was the best solution to deal with things quickly. He whipped his head around as I boxed the demons in with rock walls, which was our typical method.

Understanding lit up Micah's face as he caught on to what I meant. I was trying not to freak out our people since the horror stories of the venomous higher demons were well known in the Elementi. "On it!" Micah answered and charged the rock prison I made, leaping up as I created an opening for him.

Leaving that to him, I returned to dealing with the lesser demons who were wreaking havoc and making it harder for our people to fight those they could win against. *Fuck, this was worse than we thought. I hope Parker and Hudson are faring better than we are.*

CHAPTER 29
HUDSON

Demons, there had to be actual demons in the mix, didn't there? The Dark Lord was making use of all that he controlled in this world, not just on those injected with the serum. It made sense that the Elementi helping us couldn't kill demons the same way we could with just blessed weapons. They needed holy weapons, and they didn't have those. In reality, there were only a few hundred of them to go around so it wasn't surprising. The sound of gunfire filled the air as we fought.

We hadn't been able to catch them off guard, having an open field in between us and them, so they came out charging, ready for a fight. The only good thing about that was I could hear the roars of higher-level demons trapped in the forest, unable to come into the light. It gave the Elementi a fighting chance, while Parker and I went to deal with them. My newly improved weapons shot faster and with the flaming bullets, they were one-hit kills if I hit a vital spot. Winged demons darted around us but I used water to swallow them up into a whirlpool where I could shoot them easier.

Parker moved lightning fast with his double-bladed staff, cutting down our enemy as if they were nothing. It gave me peace of mind that we were paired together since our weapons and fighting style meshed well. The problem we were running into was there were far more to fight against than we anticipated. Were the others dealing with this as well? These groups were not meant as backup. They were equipped to make sure that everyone was dead and stayed that way. The higher demons alone made that clear since they leach the soul right out of you. Memories of when Lailah was attacked by one flashed through my mind, marking the beginning of our journey to this point. That was when the Dark Lord marked her and started to torture her mind with nightmares.

"It's been awhile since we've faced one of these, you ready?" Parker asked as he gripped his staff tighter.

Taking a steadying breath, I nodded. "Let's do this. The sooner we kill them, the faster we get back to Lailah."

"Yeah, this was far more intense than I thought we would be dealing with."

As we entered the forest, we found three higher-level demons prowling about. I created a water whip and sent it slamming into two of them, tossing them back and allowing us space to deal with one at a time. Parker charged forward and dropped to his knees at the last moment, dodging the long-clawed arms of the demon. He sliced up and across, effectively gutting the demon while I sent off as many shots as I could into its skeletal face. To our shock and amazement, the demon burst into smoke and evaporated, returning to Hell.

What once used to take all our power and strength, now was something we could defeat rather efficiently. Never would I say it was easy, but this was a far better outcome than we were used to. The other two recovered from my attack and boxed us in. The most dangerous part of the higher-level demons were the claws. They were attached to long spindly arms that could reach while leaving their bodies a safe distance away. I fired off two shots, watching it stumble back then I pulled on my power, wrapping it up and freezing the water so its arms were trapped at its sides. Never before had I been able to freeze without Jay's help, but clearly our powers were changing now that the bonding was complete and Lailah had her powers.

Just as I was going to get off another few shots, a body slammed into me, knocking me to the ground. Shoving back with my elbow, it slammed into something hard and a person cried out. There was a shattering sound as the demon broke out of my ice bindings.

Fuck, I need to get this man off me.

Using my power, I tried to shove him off me but it didn't work, which meant it was a pure human. This also meant my spirit weapon guns wouldn't work either, and my real gun was trapped on my hip against the ground. Thrashing about, I nailed him again with my elbow but he wouldn't let up. It was as if he was trying to hold me down long enough for the demon to get me. But that would mean he would steal the soul from this person too. "It'll kill us both!"

"Hail the Dark Lord. May he reign the world forever," the man answered.

"Sorry, asshole, that's just not going to work for me and I'm gonna need you to get off my friend here," Parker commented from somewhere above me. "Hudson, would you mind shooting that demon while I deal with this prick?"

There was a grunt and the weight of the man on me was gone. Glancing over my shoulder as I got to my feet, I found Parker wrestling the man to the ground in a choke hold. Not wasting any more time, I called on my weapons but instead of my handguns, a large crossbow appeared. If this was anything like Lailah's, then this was going to be a one-hit-and-done moment for the demon. Sure enough, as the bolt shot out of the crossbow and struck the demon, it exploded. The force of it shook the ground, bringing along with it shrieks of lesser demons as they got swept up in the aftershock.

"Holy shit, dude, why didn't you use that to begin with?" Parker demanded as he stepped up next to me.

Glancing down at the crossbow and then back up at him, I blinked a few times. "I didn't even know I could call on it."

"Well, now that we know you can, let's skip the *pew-pew* guns and go for the big boom, alright?" He patted me on the back and started to jog back to the main fight, a reminder to me that this was far from over. We'd just begun.

CHAPTER 30
MICAH

Five, there had to be five fucking higher demons running around in this goddamn forest, trying to kill us. For once, I was thankful that Parker pushed us to do this, because if they had run free once the sun went down then way too many people would have died. Higher demons didn't give a fuck who your allegiance was to, if you were in their reach, they would kill you. I saw it right before my very eyes moments ago. Brayden had trapped two of them for me to deal with but when I was done with the second, I almost impaled myself on one of their clawed hands, jumping down from the stone jail.

Blasting it in the face with fire, I blinded it long enough to get the fuck out of its way and slice its head off. With our power levels where they were at now, it was so much easier to kill the motherfuckers, but getting close enough still took skill. Brayden wasn't that person, which is why we came up with the method that we were using now years ago. Three down, two more to go, but I couldn't spot them anywhere, and the sky was getting darker every minute that passed.

"Where the fuck are you ugly bastards?" I grumbled as I pulled up a fireball, trying to get more light into the area.

I heard someone scream from deeper in the woods so I took off running. I found a woman with the claws of the demon piercing her chest as she thrashed, trying to free herself. It was too late to save her but I could stop the demon from taking any more souls tonight. Charging forward at its back, I released my weapons so I could move silently without drawing attention to myself. Leaping, I kicked off the demon's back as I materialized my blades, removing its head in one swift motion. The demon disintegrated as I dropped back to the ground and made my way over to the woman who was gasping for breath, blood trickling out of her mouth.

"Where... am I?" she managed to get out, her voice garbled with blood.

It struck me that when the higher demon went after her, it removed the demon that had possessed the woman, leaving her back to her normal self. Kneeling beside her, I took her hand, squeezing it gently, trying to comfort her which was not a skill I had. "You're safe."

"I..." Tears started to stream out of her eyes. "I hurt people.... why? Why would I do that?"

Each breath sounded worse than the next as she muscled her way through, asking that one question I couldn't answer for her. "You didn't do those things. The demon who took over your body did. Don't worry about that, everything's going to be fine now, No need to worry."

God, where was Brayden when I needed him? He did so much better at this emotional shit.

Straightening up, I looked around the area, trying to find anyone else who wasn't me to help this woman in the last moments of her life. "Don't leave me," she begged. "I don't want to die alone."

Dropping my gaze back down to her, I sighed and got more comfortable next to her, even though there was a battle raging on. If this was my mother, I wouldn't want her to be alone no matter what was going on. "I'm not gonna leave you, I promise."

"Thank you..." she whispered as her breathing became erratic and she grimaced in pain.

Soon those halting, stuttering breaths came to a stop and her body let go of one last breath as life left her. A mix of anger and pain sparked through my body as I relived the moment they told me my parents were dead. The demons kept taking from us and all anyone could offer was their stupid fucking sympathy—well, this time was different. We were going to end this. This woman and the others like her wouldn't die in vain. They would be avenged no matter what it took.

"Micah, look out!" Cami yelled, her voice filled with panic, yanking me back to my surroundings.

Without questioning the warning, I rolled to the right seconds before the last higher-level demon struck out its claws, impaling the earth where I once was. Shooting to my feet, I created a massive fireball and slammed it into the demon, causing it to scream in pain. Our elements might not kill it but I hope it fucking hurt. This one I took head-on, dodging its arms, using my swords to fend them off as I got inside its reach. I stabbed my swords into its chest and thrust them upward until it split the damn thing in two. Panting, I wiped the sweat off my brow, finding Cami heading toward me with worry written all over her face.

"What's wrong? What happened?" I demanded.

"We're too late. They already started fighting at the

front lines. It's just Jay and Lailah out there," Cami said, her voice cracking, telling me how worried she was.

I looked around the woods and didn't see anything the Elementi couldn't handle. We'd taken care of all the demons who were the biggest threat. "Then let's get the fuck out of here and help them. Where's Brayden?"

"I was looking for both of you and found you first."

Nodding, I charged forward back in the direction of the school. I'd noticed that now we were all bonded to Lailah. I could feel that connection. Taking a chance, I reached out, thinking of Brayden, trying to see if I could track him down that way. A zing went through my body and I felt an answering tug as if Brayden knew I was looking for him and was answering. The feeling came from the right so I changed course and went after my best friend with Cami hot on my heels.

Bursting through a group of thick bushes, I found Brayden facing off with two demon-possessed people trying to manage how inhumanly fast they were. Weapons in hand, I blocked the attack of the second opponent trying to hit Brayden in the back. The impact of our blades hitting each other sent a shock wave up my arms. Gritting my teeth, I shoved the man back, kicking out to hit him right in the gut to get some breathing room. Shaking out my arms, I squared off with him. "Why don't you play with me instead of my friend? I'll make it interesting for you."

The demon sneered, baring its razor-sharp teeth at me, ready to tear my flesh off my bones. "This one is cocky. I bet it will make you taste even better."

"Sorry, bro, I'm not into dudes like that. Guess you're gonna have to taste someone else," I taunted while whirling my blades, keeping my muscles loose but ready to jump into action.

He charged me with his blades, moving so fast it took all my concentration to keep up with him, but there was no chance he would win against me. The thing he seemed to forget was that I was an *Elemental* Warrior. We locked blades, and he snapped at me, trying to freak me out but I just laughed as I let my fire burst from me, covering my whole body. "Did you want your meat well done or extra crispy?"

Letting my weapons disappear, I grabbed the demon in a bear hug and let my fire engulf him until he turned to ash moments later. Brushing myself off, I looked over at Brayden to see he'd finally taken care of his guy as well. "You good?" I asked when Cami entered the open space, knowing better than to get in our way.

"Yeah, what took you so long?" Brayden asked, breathing heavily as he wiped his brow with his shirt.

"Just taking care of five higher-level demons is all. No big deal," I answered, shrugging my shoulders. "Come on, Cami said the real fight's started and we need to provide backup."

"Guys, I won't be any help. You go to the front lines and I'll make sure things get handled here," Cami instructed, waving us off.

"Shit! Why did we think separating was a good idea?" Brayden growled as we started to run back to the school.

"Don't say that around Lailah, she'll never let us do anything on our own ever again," I joked, needing to be able to laugh at something.

Brayden just gave me a look, telling me he didn't think it was all that funny. When we made it back to the main school ground, I waved for Brayden to follow me back to the warehouse, no way were we going to make it on foot fast enough to be of help. There sat the ATV, waiting for us just as we left it, with the keys still in it. Cranking the engine, it rumbled to life, and I flipped it into gear.

"Wait!"

Snapping my head in the direction of the call, I found Parker and Hudson running up to us, waving their arms to make sure we saw them.

"Get in, fuckers," I called, revving the engine to prove my point.

As soon as I felt like they were in far enough, I slammed on the gas pedal and we rocketed off to the front line to save our girl and the world.

CHAPTER 31
LAILAH

Once that first arrow hit, the world exploded as the demons surged forward, swarming us while others blew past us, going deeper into the school property. They must be going after the Elementi that stayed to fight. I hoped they would be alright, but I didn't have the luxury of worrying about them at the moment. Taking aim, I shot anyone that wasn't Jay, and the explosions that came with it took out at least three or four more at a time. In the madness, Makoto seemed to have slipped away but this day wouldn't end without seeing his life snuffed out. Even if I didn't believe the entire story as true, I knew Makoto chose power over his son and the oath the Elementi made to the angels. That was enough to warrant his death.

Jay and I fought back-to-back, shooting anything and everything we could that moved. I sent out a shield blocking the demons from getting too close to us, but the pressure of their attacks on it while I was focusing made it hard to keep it up. As I took in the people around me, I noticed that it wasn't just humans. The Dark Lord had brought his brethren with him to this fight. I wouldn't put it past him to have Lilith show up. What I'd done to her would slow her down but if she had a few Princes of Hell backing her up, it wouldn't be too far of a stretch to believe she would grace us with an appearance.

"Lailah, we have to move to. Staying here is going to get us killed," Jay called over his shoulder. "You can't keep that shield up forever."

"I know, but how do we even begin to move in all this?" I asked, stumbling as someone hurled demon fire at my shield. "Goddammit, what the hell can do that?"

Jay didn't answer, and I didn't blame him. Talking took effort that we didn't have. What we needed was a break in the horde of bodies to make a run for it, and I thought I could make that happen. Pooling my power together without drawing on the others, not knowing what they were dealing with, I thrust it out around us, blasting demons back and giving us a ten-foot circle. Jay grabbed my hand, and we ran full out toward the nearest building. It had a solid canopy over the door and I caught on to what Jay was gonna have me do. When we got close enough, he dropped to one knee, hunching his back, ready for what I was about to do next.

Taking a running leap, I shoved off his back and caught onto the edge of the awning and pulled myself up. Jay took a few steps back to give him a running start as he vaulted himself up next to me. He landed with a grunt, as I grabbed his arm when I saw him starting to pitch backward, preventing him from falling off back into the hungry arms of the demons. Once I felt he was safe, I let go and quickly fired off a few shots at demons who tried to follow after us. No matter how many I put down, three more seemed to fill the space, making me wonder how the hell we were going to make it out of this.

The wind around us started to pick up, whipping around, pulling at my clothes and hair. A gust almost shoved me off my feet but I dropped to my knees to create less wind resistance. Looking behind me, Jay stood tall and proud, his eyes closed and his hands out as if he was calling all the wind to him... which I guess he was. Trees started to wave in the wind, some bowing to the pressure as I saw the beginnings of a tornado starting in the middle of the quad. It made me think back on the research I'd done when I first came to Ryevick about how the Elementi would show up and natural disasters would happen shortly thereafter. At least we were keeping to tradition. When the tornado touched down, it scooped up a large amount of the enemy as it swept through the space, carrying them out into the open area behind the school where a large vineyard was. I felt bad for the crops getting destroyed but it was a casualty of war and fewer people to fight, the better it was for everyone.

Jay pushed the tornado out as far as he could while trying to avoid any home or more damage to innocents, then he released it, scattering the enemy to the four winds. Once it was released, he crumbled to the ground, making me scream out his name. I pulled on our Bond and I sensed that he'd overused his power and hadn't drawn from any of us, draining his own storage.

"Idiot," I muttered. "We will talk about this when all this is over."

Tossing up a shield, I had it surround the whole building; that way I could focus on Jay. Placing a hand over his heart, I opened myself up to all my bonds and gave them a warning tug before I started to draw from them. I didn't have time to waste, so I slammed the power into Jay's body, filling it to bursting, faster than I ever have before. I cycled it through all of us, recharging everyone all at once, adding to the improved power they now had with us all being bonded. As we had learned before, this only supercharged them for a short amount of time but since it recharges me as well, I could do it an unlimited number of times. Jay gasped like I'd just shot him through with adrenaline, which I guess I did in a way.

"What the hell, Jay?" I snapped. "Why didn't you tell me you were running out of energy?"

"You were dealing with the shield earlier," he answered with a groan as he slowly got to his feet.

Standing, I steadied him as he got his center of gravity back. "Did you forget that I'm the never-ending battery? All I need to do is cycle through our power and it fixes everything."

"Sorry, I guess I haven't wrapped my head around the changes yet," Jay muttered as he looked at the path of destruction his tornado made.

"Don't you dare feel bad about that. We needed to even the playing field," I pointed out. "Besides, if we lose, I don't think the world as we know it will exist. Better to leave behind some damage than the alternative."

We were both taking in the amount of demons we still had to deal with when a shrill whistle sounded in the air. We both turned to find the guys in the ATV come tearing in with Hudson pushing a wave before them, knocking people out of the way. Seeing them had something in my soul relaxing just a bit, knowing they were okay. Brayden used the cobblestones from the quad to pelt at people while Micah let a stream of fire out, hitting the flying demons that seemed to be chasing after them. Now we could end this. Jay and I had held them off long enough to take out their backup so we just had to deal with this swarm of people.

Dropping down off the awning, I used my crossbows to blaze a trail to the rest of my men. When we converged, all the energy we held within us sparked to life, arcing between us in an endless loop of power. This was what it meant to be Synergy, combining all the elements to make something stronger. I looked them all over making sure they were all in one piece. "Everyone good?"

"You know it, Trouble. Thanks for the pick-me-up. That shit is crazy!" Parker commented as he took down two women charging at him. "So, do we have a plan here?"

"We need to find Makoto. He's the Dark Lord's conduit. If we can take care of him, then I think the demons will follow," Jay informed them. "I don't know that it will help those who have been given the serum but Lailah can do that trick she did back at the warehouse."

"Any reason she can't do that now?" Micah asked, looking over at me.

I thought about it, but the moment I considered it, I knew it would be too much even for me. "Too many to deal with. If we can get the numbers smaller, then I can make it happen."

"Great. Now, how do we find the demon bastard?" Parker asked. "I'd really love to have a chat with him."

Trying to strategize as you fight for your life was a lot harder than you thought. There was no time to just let your mind process things as it was reacting to what was happening around you. I couldn't keep the shield up since we had more of us with close-range weapons, so we had to face what was right in front of us. Then a thought struck me. "Parker, can you manipulate any of these people into being pissed enough at the Dark Lord to bring him to us?"

"Guess we're gonna find out!" Parker said with a wicked grin on his face as he shifted to the center of our circle. "Put a shield around me. I need to focus on this. Give me as long as you can."

I did as he requested, enveloping him into a bubble of safety as we handled things.

Time passed slowly as we fought. The only thing that caught my attention was the fact the streetlights came on flooding the area with their light. Sweat coated my body, making my shirt stick to me and the bulletproof vest chafed my neck. The sting of it rolling into my eyes didn't help, but I couldn't afford to stop and wipe it off. We used a combination of elements and weapons, but it was clear that any information we had about this army of the Dark Lord was wrong. It seemed like we were fighting half the world. I knew true demons intermixed, but I couldn't distinguish them as I kept moving and fighting.

Just when I didn't think I could keep pushing my body, the crowd parted and men dressed in the uniform marking them as Makoto's arrived, guns at the ready but they weren't here for us. All fighting around us stopped as if they were frozen. Makoto was chucked out of the mass and stumbled to his knees. The hood he was wearing was now tossed back, showing his normal features. I reached out to sense him with my powers but he was empty and the Dark Lord had left him.

Without thought, I stepped up and decked the man right in the face, shattering his nose and causing blood to splatter on his face. "You motherfucking monster! How could you sell your soul to the devil? All for what, this?" I asked, spreading my arms out. "Is this the world you wanted? The deaths of innocent people littering the ground?"

"In all times of change, there is a culling of the herd. These people were weak. They deserved to be possessed. If the demon within them couldn't protect them, they don't deserve to have a host," Makoto spat.

Jay walked past me until he was standing in front of his father. "Is the Dark Lord gone?"

"Yes, he is free from any demonic influence," I answered.

He nodded, walking behind his father. In a move so fast I didn't truly believe it happened, he snapped his father's neck. I tried to smother my gasp at the shock of the action but Jay held my gaze as if challenging me to be horrified at him. Letting go, his father's body crumpled to the ground, lifeless and unmoving.

"Great, now he has no conduit to use and we can't get rid of him," Micah grumbled under his breath.

"Now, the Dark Lord will have to show himself in his true form. No more hiding in a human shell," Jay countered. "If he's strong enough to be here with us, then he can manifest some type of form."

There was a glint in Jay's eye that told me he had an idea. Cocking an eyebrow, I waited to see what he would say next.

"What the hell, Jay? Are you trying to bring him down on our heads?" Micah snarled.

Jay scoffed. "As Lailah told him earlier, everything about him is just a lie so why should we believe he is a Prince of Hell?"

The guys looked at him like he'd lost his mind but I figured out what he was going to do. "Really. Look at this army of his. They're frozen without a leader. Maybe I should just expel them all. I think we've killed enough people that I can purge them, setting them free from his hold. Once I do that, then poof goes his army. Then what does he have?" I taunted.

Wrapping us all in a shield, I closed my eyes and reached out with my powers, mapping just how far I could stretch the barrier I would need to remove all the demons. It was at the edge of my ability but I could do it. I wasn't alone in this. Reaching my hands out to either side, they were immediately grasped, and I felt them all connect with each other, making a perfect circle. Taking a deep inhale, I readied everything and breathed out, pushing our combined power over the whole campus and out into the forest, where I still felt the Elementi fighting. Some of the stronger demons fought my power, but I didn't buckle. Instead, I sent out a tendril of power to grip them around the throat and yanked them out of the person. When the whole area was free of demon-possessed people, I felt a pang in my heart and the mass casualty that I'd just caused.

If I was able to bring back Parker from the dead and heal Jay's mother, why couldn't I cleanse them too?

This time, instead of pushing out a shield, I sent my powers out, flooding the land. I pulled from Micah, using his fire to add to the cleansing while soothing with Hudson's water. To renew them, I blended Jay's air and Parker's heart to create a new beginning, breathing new life into them and removing all memory of the horrors they had experienced at the hands of the Dark Lord. As I added to the mixture, the combined powers continued to extend past what I'd intended. In my mind's eye, our woven powers stretched far and wide, gaining strength the further it went, gaining momentum.

"Lailah, what are you doing?" Hudson asked, his voice full of awe.

Without opening my eyes, I answered, knowing the truth of it. "I'm saving the world—correction—*we* are saving the world."

My head hummed with the power that I was wielding right now but I trusted in the fact that the six of us were doing exactly what we were created to do.

"*Stop!*" a voice thundered, shaking the ground under our feet. "You shouldn't be able to do that without all your knights!"

Ah, it would seem that the Dark Lord had finally made his appearance.

Ignoring everything that was going on around me, I focused on the most important thing I would ever do in this lifetime. The ripple of my powers could be felt around the world as I destroyed everything that the Dark Lord had spent centuries creating. He would no longer hold any power in this world when I was done. Now, that didn't mean there wouldn't be any evil, but the serum and the havoc it caused, along with his minions blessed with his power, would be cleansed. The Dark Lord would be a blip in our history books of the Elementi when I was finished. The sound of attacks on my shield, that I shrunk down to just shelter us, echoed in my ears. I knew it would hold. The strength we had in each other, along with the love we shared, would keep us safe until I was done. As the angels said, trust and love had the power that could change the world. When this was finished, I would be completely depleted of power, but I trusted there was a way to end the Dark Lord without it.

Finally, I'd rid the world of the Dark Lord's mark. I felt my power fizzle out, and the shield dissolved, leaving us vulnerable to his attack. Opening my eyes, I came face-to-face with the being of my nightmares, and his mother at his side.

"What now, Little Synergy? You have nothing to defend yourself with, making everything you just did pointless. I will live forever. All I have to do is start again, only this time I won't have to worry about Synergy coming after me because you'll be dead," the Dark Lord taunted.

Slipping my hands out of the guys' hands, I took a step forward. "Do you really believe that Heaven will allow you to go unpunished for this act? They couldn't stop you once you involved humankind into the equation, but now that factor has been removed. I wiped you from the face of this planet, healing everything you touched, now you're their problem."

"No! No, there is no way you could have removed every trace, that's not possible!" Lilith screeched, knowing that if what I said was true, they were both in trouble. "I won't go back there. I'm the Mother of All Demons. I deserve to rule what I created!"

The Dark Lord looked down at his mother who was so much smaller than himself. "You rule? This was my kingdom!"

I glanced over my shoulder at the guys and gave them a wink and a smile which did nothing to remove the pissed-off worried look from their faces. "This will all be over soon."

Brayden opened his mouth to say something, but I was engulfed in a pure white light as Heaven's light filled me. A sword materialized in my hand, casting off that pure light that I saw each time an angel came to speak with me. Just like when I went through the bonding process, I was but a vessel for the angel.

"*You have broken the laws of Heaven and in doing so, you will be brought before God in judgment. If you refuse, then all things will end here,*" the angel said, using my voice.

Lilith burst into hellfire, producing a sword, and attacked me. My skill combined with the knowledge the angel provided for me made it possible to hold my own against Lilith. Our swords clashed, sending sparks flying as light and darkness fought.

"Watch out!" Jay bellowed, but his worry wasn't necessary.

I flicked out a hand, sending a ball of light to hit the Dark Lord right in the chest. He had his massive sword in hand and tried to block the holy light but it cut right through the weapon, ripping out the other side of his chest. Locking swords with Lilith, I pulled her close, dropped the sword, and clamped my hand around her head, holding her still as I flooded her with holy light. She screamed and thrashed, trying to shake me off her, but I knew there was no way she could defeat me. I was filled with an avenging angel and it had been sent on a mission which only God could remove it from.

"*You have chosen against judgment, therefore, you shall be cleansed in atonement for your sins,*" I informed Lilith as tears of blood poured down her face. "*May the blood of Heaven free your soul.*"

With one final scream, Lilith shattered into a million pieces of sparkling light that was carried away on the breeze. Turning on my heel, I faced the Dark Lord and approached him, sword in hand.

"One day, there will be hell on earth and you won't be able to stop it," the Dark Lord said, spitting at me.

"*That will never happen. We will always make sure the children of God are protected by any means necessary,*" I intoned moments before I sliced his head off, watching as he dissolved just like his mother.

With the threat gone, my guys watched me with a wary eye. "Can we have Lailah back now?" Brayden asked hesitantly.

"First, you have a choice. Remain the Elemental Warriors blessed with elemental powers or give it all up and be removed from that world entirely. If you choose to give up being our warriors they will not be reborn, leaving the world vulnerable to attack as it just was. On the other hand, if you continue, then you will have our blessing and support to ensure this world is safe."

The guys all looked at each other, then at me and I could see the choice wasn't as hard as one would think. Even though I couldn't share my thoughts, the guys knew me well enough. I trusted them to make the right call.

"We want to give it all up and move on from this life, to have a chance to create our own future," Hudson answered with complete confidence.

"We honor your choice and the service you have done for this world. Go with Heaven's blessing and live long happy lives together."

The angel left my body and took my powers along with it, leaving me once more a normal human. I couldn't hold back the grin at the giddy feeling bubbling up inside me, knowing that we were free. After everything we'd been through, we could finally start our lives and live it the way we wanted to.

Now that was an adventure I was more than happy to experience!

EPILOGUE
LAILAH

T*hree years later...*

"Trouble, we're gonna miss it if you don't hurry!" Parker said, tossing me over his shoulder and giving my ass a slap.

"Parker Jones, you put me down right now! What will people think if they see someone carrying me around like a caveman?" I laughed, pushing myself up so I didn't get a face full of his ass, even if it was a nice ass.

A snicker had me glaring at Micah who was watching all this and doing nothing about it. "Sorry, Cookie Monster, I'm not going to be any help. You know how he gets about things like this."

"He knows we aren't going to miss it, right?" Hudson asked, frowning. "The whole event is ten days long, and we arrived only two days into Carnival."

"Just be thankful he isn't making us wear the costumes until later," Jay muttered. "We need to put limits on what you can choose to do for your birthday."

"Bro, you made us all go skydiving for yours last year." Brayden laughed. "Since we know how short life can be, the agreement was all of us live life to the fullest, and this was part of celebrating life and all."

Upon hearing Brayden's words, Parker set me down so I could go to him, wrapping my arm around his waist in a half hug. He kissed the top of my head, returning my hug and letting out a contented sigh. Even though it'd been three years since we faced down the Dark Lord, all of us carried scars from it that would take a lifetime to heal. The first thing we did after that fight was to fly back to Wisconsin, where we spent the whole summer playing and enjoying our new lease on life. No longer tied to the Elementi in the same way, we needed time to decide what we wanted to do with our lives.

Jay inherited his father's military company, and he decided that instead of keeping it what it was, he was going to join forces with Parker and create an international security company. They downsized the operation, and no longer worked alongside the Elementi, setting out on their own path. The surprise was Hina was their biggest customer, helping her beef up the security for her shipping company. With Makoto gone, Jay finally had the relationship with his mother he always wanted and she was a delight to have as a mother-in-law.

Hudson was now working on his medical projects, trying to find new inventive ways to save people's lives through research. Things with his father were still rocky, but he kept trying. Somehow, we managed to convince his father and ex stepmother to let us spend time with the twins. This past Christmas they came to spend a week with us in our Wisconsin home. We also had Brayden's family there too with all his siblings, enjoying time together. It was a blast having everyone from our families at our lake house, playing in the snow and warming up with hot chocolate.

Brayden was our ecowarrior, working tirelessly to find ways to protect our earth and make it accessible to everyone. It'd been fun to see him blossom into his own person, free from the expectations of being an Elemental Warrior. His parents were even collaborating on some things with him.

Micah's transformation was the most surprising, now that his aunt was no longer connected to his life in any way. His mind for business was astonishing, and he took a real hands-on approach to helping this small country he basically owned. While Hudson, Parker, and Jay finished up school at Ryevick, Micah and I spent some time exploring his kingdom, as I affectionately like to call it. Micah didn't really want to go back to school, and I decided that I didn't either, feeling that what I wanted in life couldn't be found in a degree from a fancy school like I once thought.

Parker did in fact buy the bakery from Ann, but after he explained his reasoning behind it, I couldn't have been more thrilled with the idea. So now I was learning everything I could from her since I would be taking over the company when she retired. Getting lost in the kitchen covered in flour, trying out new recipes, was exactly what made me the happiest woman in the world. Of course, Parker loved that he could be the taste tester on all my new ideas. Unfortunately, he loved everything that I made so he was no help.

"Guys, I realize you want to enjoy the sights and all but we really will miss something important if we don't hurry," Parker begged, giving me puppy dog eyes.

Accepting defeat, I tossed my hands up in the air. "Fine, lead the way. We'll keep up."

Parker led us to where the stadium-sized bleachers were erected so we could watch the parade. Around us people were shouting, dancing, drinking, and living life like they might die tomorrow. Parker had gotten us a reserved space with prime viewing of the parade. When I wasn't moving fast enough, Parker dragged me to the front of our little seating area, settling his hands on my hips as he kissed my neck. I could feel the excitement oozing out of him and I just couldn't figure out what it was stemming from.

We'd promised each other that even if life got busy, no matter what, we would all be together for whatever the birthday boy or girl wanted to do. Sometimes, it was trips like these or doing an activity like skydiving with Jay. None of us could back out of it. We all had to experience it together, building forever memories before something came up in life that would prevent us from going on adventures.

The floats for the parade were out-of-this-world insane and the most amazing thing I'd ever seen. Anything and everything might appear on a float but when the next one rounded the corner, I gasped. The float had five people standing in a circle holding hands with another person in the middle of it. Each of the figures was covered in flowers that matched the five elements, while the middle figure was covered in gold glitters and sparkled like the sun. On the side of the float was written, *Synergy, the power to change the world as we know it.*

Gaping up at Parker, I felt tears flood my eyes. "It's amazing, but I don't understand?"

Parker just grinned and used a hand on my jaw to turn

my attention back to the float. There was an explosion of light as sparklers burst into flames, etching out the words, *Three Years into Forever.*

"I told you I would never stop repaying you for saving my life, or have you doubt how much I love and treasure you," Parker reminded before capturing my lips in a searing kiss. "Happy anniversary, Trouble. I'm beyond blessed to have you as my wife."

"I love you so much," I said with a sniffle, trying to hold back my tears.

"Alright, we let you have the big reveal for your birthday. Now hand over our wife so we don't look like assholes who didn't do anything," Micah grumbled.

Laughing, I was swept up in the rest of them, getting showered in love and kisses. When we gave up being Elemental Warriors, it meant we gave up everything connected to it, along with our Bond. So we decided that the first order of business was to have a wedding. Legally, I was married to Micah, helping to ensure we both held the majority of his business to prevent anyone from messing with it. On that magical day though, I'd married them all, each of us giving our vows to each other, regardless of what the marriage license said. It had been a small affair with our close friends and family in Bali so we could all enjoy the trip together and relax.

"This is amazing, you guys. I don't think it could be more perfect." I sighed contentedly, wrapped up between Jay and Brayden as we toasted our anniversary.

"Bitch, you better not say that when I flew all the way out here to spend time with you!" Cami's voice cut through the noise.

Whirling on my heel, I spotted my best friend and her wife, Maggs, grinning at me. I let out a squeal of delight as I rushed to hug them. "What are you doing here? Didn't you tell me you wouldn't be able to make it?"

Cami also left everything to do with the Elementi, and her sisters gave her their blessing. Maggs worked with Parker on his side of the company, while Cami worked with Jay training all of our security. It was amazing to have her always around and part of our lives, adding to our family.

"Seriously, that's a stupid question. I'm always around for big moments." Cami scoffed. Maggs elbowed her with a glare that had me raising a brow.

Maggs was normally the laid-back one out of the two. "Am I missing something?"

"Sorry, it's the hormone treatments. They're making me crazy," Maggs apologized.

They'd been trying for a baby the past year and so far hadn't had any luck, but they were far from giving up hope. "I'm sorry, girl, a normal cycle is rough. I can't imagine getting injected with more. Do they think it will work though?"

Maggs and Cami looked at each other with an odd expression before Cami seemed to burst with excitement. "Oh hell, I was gonna wait because I didn't want to steal your big moment, but I can't do it. We're having a baby!"

"Wait, seriously?" I cried, tugging Cami into a bear hug before doing the same to Maggs. "I'm so excited for you both. This is going to be so amazing. You guys will be the best moms!"

Maggs placed a hand on her belly and looked at me with tears in her eyes. "I can't believe it's really happening." I gave her another tight hug and stepped back, clapping my hands.

"So, Lala, when are the boys putting a bun in your

oven?" Cami asked, wagging her brows. "You know it has to be soon. Our kids need to be best friends."

Glancing over my shoulder, I looked at the guys. The excitement and heat in their eyes told me it was time to open it up for discussion. "We'll see. I'm not making any promises. It would be a huge life change for us and it's only been three years of freedom. Kids will happen eventually and I know no matter what, they will become the best of friends like their mothers did."

"Fine, be that way, but don't think this is the end of this discussion," Cami grumbled.

The rest of the night was filled with so much love and fun I thought my heart would burst. If I'd known what awaited me when I received that acceptance letter from Ryevick, I don't think I'd change a thing. We went through hell and back. Literally. But the outcome was more than I could have ever dreamed of. My life now was well and truly blessed with people I loved and who loved me in return... What more could you ask for in life?

* The End *

About the Author

Elizabeth is an International Best Seller, originally from Illinois but now living in sunny Phoenix, AZ. Elizabeth has been writing for nine years and started out in YA Fiction but recently found herself loving the Reverse Harem genre. Like her favorite books, Elizabeth loves to write about strong women of all varieties. Not all strength is flashy or apparent at first glance—some lies just under the surface.
Don't Miss Out!
Be the first to know what is coming next by following Elizabeth's social media! You never know when or what will be coming next!
Facebook: Elizabeth Knight's Unicorn Queens
Instagram: elizabethknightauthor
TikToc: elizabethknightauthor
Newsletter: https://landing.mailerlite.com/webforms/landing/i0m1g8

ALSO BY ELIZABETH KNIGHT

Omegaverse

Knot All Is

Knot All Is Lost Duet - Complete

Knot All Is Ruined Duet - Complete

Sunshine & Rainbows Omegaverse

Bailey-Rose duet:

Clouds & Daydreams + Petals & Promises

Lyra/Eli duet:

Knot Now Knot Ever + Yes Now Yes Forever

Mafia Royalty Shared World

Caprioni Queen

Glitter & Guns

Blood & Heartache

Revenge & Truth

Love & Power

Gun Runner Princess

One For The Money

Two For The Show

Complete Series

<u>Hidden Empire Series</u>

Two Tricks

Three Tricks

Four Tricks

More Tricks

Our Tricks

<u>Hidden Empire Novel</u>

Harper's Renegades

[Read after Four Tricks for best series context]

Omega Assassin

Dual Nature

Hidden Nature

Perfect Nature

-

<u>Hope Series</u>

Hidden Hope

Claiming Hope

Defending Hope

Obtaining Hope

-

Standalones

Nicolette - MC Feline Shifter Story

Lying Lainey - Dark Omegaverse

Books Not in Kindle Unlimited

<u>Elementi Series</u>

Discovering Synergy

Refining Earth

Liberating Water

Taming Fire

Rescuing Air

<u>Mercenary Queen Series</u>

Birthright

Dragon Queen

Forgotten Throne

The Final Battle